To Tracy,

Beth Solheim

Outwitted

Beth Solheim

Echelon Press

Publishing

OUTWITTED
A Sadie Witt Mystery
Book Two
An Echelon Press Book

First Echelon Press paperback printing / April 2011

Echelon Press
9055 G Thamesmeade Road
Laurel, MD 20723
www.echelonpress.com

ISBN: 978-159080-666-1
eBook: 978-159080-667-8

PRINTED IN THE UNITED STATES OF AMERICA
10 9 8 7 6 5 4 3 2 1

*For old friends who taught me to
believe in something more!*

My appreciation to my publisher, Karen Syed,
for her continued encouragement.

1

"You'd think I'd be used to the smell of embalming fluid by now." Sadie Witt fanned her fuchsia fingernails under her nose. She grimaced as the odor hit her again. "At least it hasn't affected my brain."

"I wouldn't be so sure." Sadie's sixty-four-year old twin sister raised her head and peered over the recipe magazine she had propped against Mr. Bakke's urn. The urn of ashes sat in the center of the kitchen table. "Remember the magazine article? It said the afflicted person would be the last to recognize the symptoms. Aren't you supposed to wear a mask when you use embalming fluid?" Jane sniffed the air. "That's one powerful stink. I thought Nan told you to rinse off when you finished embalming."

"I did. I toweled everything off. You know how fussy Nan is. The embalming cart glistened like a mirror." Sadie lifted the hem on her hot-pink crop top and took a deep breath. "I hope this smell doesn't ruin my new outfit. I plan to wear it tonight to the Fertile Turtle."

"You mean you dressed like a floozy for work? That's disgusting."

"I had my lab coat over it so Nan couldn't see it." Sadie raised the lid on Mr. Bakke's urn and peeked in. "Good morning Mr. Bakke."

"I'm not going to Senior's Night if you wear that outfit. When you bend over in your mini skirt, you'll clear the dance floor before the band knows what happened." Jane tucked her fists under her elbows. "Look at your hair. What color did Big Leon use? It looks like a flamingo exploded on your head."

"I'll have you know Big Leon played with colors for twenty minutes before he found the perfect shade to go with my outfit." Sadie picked at her heavily-moussed hair making sure the tapered ends stood erect. "Just because you dress like a cadaver doesn't mean I can't wear color." Jane had no taste whatsoever when it came to fashion. Her twin wore neutral colors to make her voluptuous five-foot-six frame appear smaller. It didn't. "I don't know why you bother to go shopping because all you ever buy is beige. Beige is not a color. It's a disease."

A twinge of optimism tapped on Sadie's brain. For too long she had endured the shroud of gloom trudging alongside Jane no matter where she went. But this week appeared different. Jane had finally regained some of the spunk she'd lost since Mr. Bakke's tragic death. Although Sadie would have preferred her sister's return to normalcy to lean more toward renewed energy than to sarcasm, Sadie welcomed the barbs once again effortlessly rolling off Jane's lips.

The fact that Jane considered going to the Fertile Turtle might constitute a miracle. It left Sadie speechless. Not a single crosser showing up at Cabin 14 for over a week might also be a miracle. Crosser free. Not a dead guest in residence. It still concerned Sadie that even after six months Jane refused to discuss the deceitful crosser who triggered Mr. Bakke's demise. Most recently departed who failed to cross over were gentle souls. But once in a while a downright nasty crosser made an appearance.

"I wonder if all funeral directors are as fussy as Nan. If I follow the rules and keep everything bacteria free, she thinks I'm doing a good job."

"Did you know the assistant's job would be so complicated?"

"It's not really complicated. After watching Mr. Bakke assist Nan all those years, I had a pretty clear idea. It's those darn regulations. They don't make me nervous, but Nan worries about a Health Department inspection, so she's forever scrutinizing my work. It drives me nuts."

"Maybe if you followed directions, she wouldn't check your work."

Sadie caught a glimpse of movement on the cabin's porch and strode over to the screen door. "Did you notice anything?"

"Did I notice what?" Jane placed a checkmark next to a recipe in the magazine.

Sadie put her hand over her eyes to shield the sun. Her gaze scanned from left to right before settling on the swaying porch swing. "I thought I saw a man on the porch."

Sadie joined Jane at the table. "Offering to assist Nan is the least I can do. It wasn't her fault she lost her helper. I was the murderer's target. Not Mr. Bakke."

"Are you sure he really wanted you dead?"

"Of course I'm sure. He wanted me dead so he could cross back over to the other side with me," Sadie explained. "He was too lazy to seek someone on the brink of death by himself, so he decided to take the easy way out. He set the trap to kill me. That worthless bugger intended to encroach on my light. Unfortunately, Mr. Bakke stepped in front of me."

"I know a horrible circumstance changed our lives forever, but it's not your fault you're a death coach. It must be a hateful job." Adding to Jane's already pinched expression, she continued, "It's not fair you have two jobs and I don't have any."

"Oh, not this again." Sadie released a weary sigh. "I don't have two jobs. Working as a funeral assistant is my real

7

job. Serving as a death coach isn't a job. It just happened. Don't tell me you don't have a job. You're co-owner of Witt's End Resort."

"Since we hired a manager, it doesn't seem like a job," Jane said. "I'd rather be busy like you. You're either dealing with the crossers or helping Nan at the mortuary. I sit here and twiddle my toes. Maybe you should find someone else to be a death coach."

"You know it's my duty to guide them. How else will they learn to cross over?"

"The fact they couldn't cross over shouldn't be your problem. Let them find their own way." Jane exhaled slowly as she ran her hand lovingly across the back of Mr. Bakke's chair. "It's nice not having any crossers this week. Thanks for spending time with me. It helped me relax."

"The crossers do take a lot of my time, don't they?"

"You're just noticing?" A smarter-than-my-twin revelation tweaked Jane's lips before it faded. "It would be easier if I could see them. You know how embarrassed I get when I sit on them." Jane waved her hand toward Belly LaGossa, the rotund canine snoozing on a braided rug. "Even our stupid dog can see them. It's not fair."

Sadie had to deal with the crossers and Jane lived the life of a normal mortal. That's what wasn't fair. Sadie lived as a mortal, but nowhere near normal. To observers, their twin status wasn't obvious, either. They looked nothing alike. Petite at five feet, if Sadie could get her hands on the man who deemed her a death coach, she'd stuff cheese in his nose. It had to be a man. What sane woman would saddle her with the responsibility of guiding the dead on their final journey?

Sadie caught another glimpse of movement on the porch and stepped back toward the screen door. "Did you notice anything?"

"Notice what?"

A tear rolled down Jane's cheek. Jane's bottom lip bounced in uneven tremors as Sadie put her arms around her sister. "It's not the crossers, is it? It's Mr. Bakke." Sadie pressed her mouth against Jane's temple. Air from her lips softly fluttered Jane's hair. "I know you miss him. I do too. I think about him every day."

"I do." Jane sobbed deeply. "I can't stand it without him."

Sadie rubbed her hand up and down Jane's arm. "If I could have prevented his death, I would have."

Jane dabbed at her eyes with her apron. "I'll always regret not telling him I loved him the day he died."

"He knew. Mr. Bakke knew how much you cared about him. He had a good life because of you."

Belly jerked his head up off the rug and stared at the door. He cocked an ear before drawing in a deep, inquisitive sniff.

"I'm not looking forward to any new crossers. I hope they're gone for good." Jane dabbed at her eyes again. "I hate dealing with their crap."

"For your information, it's not crap. It's important," Sadie argued. "You don't have to deal with the crossers. I'm the death coach. Not you."

"Why can't just one crosser enjoy a peaceful visit for a change?" Jane's voice rose as she finished the question. "They're always in turmoil."

"That's because they have unfinished business and aren't able to cross over. Death decisions aren't peaceful. They're stressful. Quit worrying about it."

"Then quit telling me about them."

"Then quit asking," Sadie snapped back.

Belly barked and nudged the door with his nose.

Jane glanced at the screen door. "What do you want, you silly thing? I just let you in ten minutes ago. Go back to sleep."

Sadie parted the curtain and peered out the window.

"What's so interesting?"

"A bare ass." Sadie crossed to the screen door and strained her gaze to see the right end of the porch.

"Someone in one of those nasty thong swimming suits?" Jane huffed in disgust. "They should be outlawed. I can't imagine how anyone can walk around with a string between their butt cheeks."

"Well this guy doesn't have one on. All I see is a bare ass." Sadie frowned and turned toward Jane. "Did you read the newspaper this morning?"

"Yes. Why?" Jane joined Sadie at the screen door.

"Was Jed Perry's name listed in the obituaries?"

"Not that I recall." Jane craned her head in the direction Sadie pointed. "Why would his name be listed?"

"I think Jed's about to join us."

"Good. I always liked Jed. Do you think he's looking to rent Mr. Bakke's cabin?" Jane pushed Sadie aside and grabbed the door latch.

"I doubt it. I think he's dead."

"No! Are you sure?" Jane pushed through the door. "Where is he?"

"I'm positive. He's standing three feet in front of you with his hospital gown flapping open. He's either dead, or he took a wrong turn in the hospital."

Jane shook her head slowly as Sadie's words sank in. "Do you realize what that means? Jed's parents never found a trace of his sister since her disappearance. Now you're telling me Jed is dead?"

Jed Perry's shoulders stiffened and he turned to face the

sisters. He hung on to the porch railing with one hand trying to keep a breeze from swirling his hospital gown up around his chest with his other hand.

He tugged at the fabric. His gaze darted from side to side as fear and confusion clouded his expression.

"What's going on?" Jed moved closer to Jane. "Why am I at Witt's End?"

"That's a shame." Jane retreated into the cabin. "Jed was such a nice man. Who'd have ever thought he'd end up in Cabin 14?"

"Jane?" A puzzled expression channeled Jed's brow. He turned to follow her.

"Jane can't hear you, Jed. She can't see you either." Sadie held the door open. "You'd better come in."

Jed looked down at his hospital gown. "What's going on? I'm supposed to be at the hospital. I'm scheduled for surgery." He grabbed at the back of his gown, clasped the edges together, and backed toward the railing.

"I think you should come in and sit down," Sadie held the door open. She gave a twiddle of her fingers to encourage him toward the entrance.

"I'm not going anywhere. I want to know what's going on." He patted his index finger over the bridge of his nose. "I'm dreaming. I'm having sinus surgery and I'm hallucinating, aren't I?" He nodded briskly at Sadie. "Aren't I?"

Sadie shook her head. Watching Jed sort through the terror and uncertainty left her unable to draw a breath. If she faltered, her overwhelming compassion for a friend and neighbor would rob her of the strength she banked on to deal with her new crosser.

"No, Jed. You're not hallucinating. You need to come with me. I've got something to tell you."

11

2

"They can't see you, Jed." Sadie watched Jed back up against the log siding and tug at the hem on his hospital gown. "Those guests are waving at me, not you." Sadie waited for him to realize stepping inside made more sense than sorting out his predicament with his particulars flapping in the breeze.

When she first became a death coach, Sadie's impatience flustered her crossers. Her abrupt attitude hampered the crosser's ability to understand why they ended up in Cabin 14 at the Witt's End Resort. After years of trying to zero in on one simple sentence to convince a crosser they no longer fell into the category of the living, she found the answer. There wasn't one.

Sadie understood her crossers cynical first impressions and endured their bouts of skepticism. However, she refused to tolerate their questions regarding her sanity. She already put up with the local mortals thinking her a bit off-kilter because she talked to imaginary friends. Sadie couldn't help it if she had to give instructions. She was their death coach. That's what death coaches do.

Belly waddled in behind Jed. Four black hairs protruding out of the tip of his stubby tail circled in staccato motion signaling his excitement. He grunted, flopped down, scratched at the hot-pink bandana around his neck, and rolled on his back waiting for Jed to acknowledge him. Slighted by Jed's lack of interest he pawed at the crosser's leg.

"What's going on?" Jed backed up against the door out of Belly's reach. "What's going on?"

"You sound like a parrot. Sit down and I'll tell you what's going on."

"I'm supposed to be in the hospital. Did they discharge me?"

"You could call it a discharge. You might call it a celestial discharge." Sadie smiled and pointed at the table. "I know this doesn't make sense, but if you're willing to listen, I'll try to explain."

Jed kept his gaze on Sadie and carefully skirted her. "What happened to your hair? It's usually not so colorful." As Jed pulled a chair away from the kitchen table, he waved his hand in front of Jane's face.

Sadie patted her gelled spikes. "There's nothing wrong with my hair. It matches my outfit." She lifted her shirt hem and held it up to her hair for a color comparison. "See?"

Belly propped his chin on Jed's knee and whined pitifully.

Jed circled his hand in front of Jane's face again. "How come your dog can see me but Jane can't?"

"He's not my dog. He belongs to our neighbor." Sadie paused, waiting for Jed's gaze to settle back on her.

Belly had wandered onto the Witt's End Resort property several years earlier and took up residence with the Witt sisters. Even though Belly bore his role as chief resort hound with an unflappable air, Sadie refused to claim ownership. No sense paying for a dog license.

Belly's heritage had everyone puzzled. He had long legs, a stubby nose, a rotund body covered in brown spots, and a cropped tail. The dog also had only one testicle.

"Jane can't see you because you're dead."

Jed released a heavy breath of resignation and slumped forward in his chair. "Now I know you're crazy."

Jed had worked as a handyman around Pinecone

Landing for years and years. His genteel manner and strong work ethic made residents seek his skills. No task proved too large, too difficult. Sadie held great respect for the six-foot-eight gentle giant. She knew cries of sorrow would ripple through the community when residents learned of his demise.

Sadie stared into eyes filled with apprehension. Her voice wavered. "Jane can't see you or hear you. Only other crossers, death coaches, or animals can see you. When you didn't cross over to the other side, you became a crosser."

Jed's mouth hung open as he stared at Sadie. "You've got to be kidding. How stupid do you think I am?" He dismissed her comment with a flick of his wrist. "If I'm dead, why…" He sat forward in his chair. "If I'm dead, why did I end up here? I've been in Cabin 14 a million times. I unclogged your drain. I sat at your table and ate pie hot out of the oven. I even said prayers over Jane's parakeet when we buried it. I wasn't dead then."

Jed's challenge echoed through the cabin. The same challenge every crosser offered, the defiance accompanying disbelief. "I know it doesn't make sense. That's why you need to listen. I'm a death coach and it's my job to help you."

"See, I told you it was a job," Jane chimed in. "You always say you don't have two jobs, but I just heard you tell Jed it's a job. Why don't you admit it?"

"Find something to do, Jane." Sadie set her jaw set firm with impatience. "Go watch TV or go down to the marina and check on the dock boys while I talk to Jed."

Witt's End Resort sat on the shore of Pinecone Lake in northern Minnesota. The year-round resort had doubled in size since the sisters assumed ownership thirty years earlier. It featured a motel, fourteen cabins, a thirty-slip marina, a live-bait shop, a gift shop, and a restaurant.

Harren Funeral Home sat at the edge of the resort

property. The Witt sisters had held a land lease on the mortuary and its five acres until Nan Harren purchased it outright a few months earlier. Nan and her eleven-year-old son, Aanders, occupied an apartment in the mortuary originally designed to house mortuary science students. Sadie loved Nan like a daughter. She cared for Aanders like the grandson she wished she had and relished the loving friendship.

Jed looked from Jane to Sadie and back to Jane. His eyebrows shot up in relieved recollection. "That anesthetic must have been a doosie. They warned me I might have weird dreams. Medication does strange things, you know, but I never thought they'd be this bad." A dry snicker caught in his throat as he forced a laugh. His fingers worked the hem on his gown.

Sadie pulled a chair from the table and sat next to Jed. She cupped her hand over his fist. "Is it possible you died during surgery?"

"No." Jed yanked his hand from hers. "People don't die from routine sinus surgery. Do they?"

"Something must have happened. Maybe you experienced complications."

"No. No complications. This is a bad dream. It's got to be a bad dream. What else can it be?"

Jed's shoulders jerked as a rap on the screen door startled him.

"Hi, Jed." Aanders flipped a carefree wave as he entered the cabin. He then nodded toward Mr. Bakke's urn. "Hi, Mr. Bakke."

"See? I'm not dead." A gasp of relief sputtered from Jed's lips. "Aanders can see me so I can't be dead." He hurried toward the door and stood in front of Aanders. "Tell her I'm not dead. Tell her you can see me."

"Oh, oh." Aanders grimaced and backed away from Jed's outstretched hand.

As Sadie approached, Jed held his arm up to ward her off.

"Aanders is a death coach, just like me. He can see the dead. If you'd give me a chance to explain, you'll understand."

"Stay away from me. You're crazy." Jed stumbled toward the screen door and pushed it open.

Aanders reached out to stop Jed, but the hospital gown slipped though his fingers.

"Let him go. He's got to accept this on his own terms." Sadie caught the door before it slammed against the frame.

Belly's head bobbed in rhythm with his panting while he watched Jed escape to the porch. He grunted, rose from the rug, and pawed at the screen. After receiving nothing but an irritated side glance from Sadie, he offered a muffled protest.

Jane nodded toward Sadie. "I take it Jed didn't like what he heard."

"He'll be back." Sadie pressed her finger tips into her neck muscles and kneaded them up and down.

"It must have been Jed's body Mom retrieved at the hospital," Aanders said. "She got a call a couple hours ago. She seemed really sad."

"I think everyone will be shocked. Jed isn't even forty-years-old yet, is he? You couldn't find a nicer guy." Jane poured a glass of milk and set it in front of Aanders. "Drink up. You're too thin." She slid a plate of Aanders' favorite lemon bars next to the glass before returning to the recliner.

"We need to let Jed sort it out. I'm sure he's even more confused knowing Jane can't see him but Aanders and I can. I'll explain when he comes back."

Aanders joined Jane in the sitting room and shouted

answers at the television screen like he used to do when Mr. Bakke visited Jane. *Jeopardy* had been their favorite game show. Jane tried to replace Mr. Bakke as a contestant, but failed miserably. Aanders held back on the easy questions so Jane's pile of pennies wouldn't become depleted too early in the game. He had tucked a few pennies in reserve down the side of the sofa cushion and replenished her stash when she wasn't looking.

A half-hour later, toenails clicking against the wooden planking signaled a canine happy dance as Belly pranced and greeted Jed's return with a slobbery bark.

Aanders winced and hugged his arms over his chest as an agonizing wail echoed from the porch. He glanced at Sadie before letting his gaze trail to the floor.

"That didn't take as long as I expected." Sadie patted Aanders on the shoulder. "He'll be okay. Give us a few minutes before you join us." She closed the door and stepped up to the porch swing. The weathered wood creaked as she sat next to Jed.

"Why me?" Jed sobbed and slumped heavily toward Sadie. "Why did this have to happen to me?"

Sadie took his hand and leaned into his shoulder to support his weight. She braced against the swing to keep from losing her balance. "I don't have an answer for you. I wish I did."

"I had so many things I wanted to do. So much I still needed to do for my parents. I can't believe this."

Through words barely audible, Sadie said, "Nobody ever does. Especially when they end up at Cabin 14."

Jed swiped at both eyes with the heels of his palms. "I wouldn't have believed you if I hadn't seen my body at the mortuary. I tried to talk to Nan but she ignored me." Sobs issued forth as Jed relived the experience. "When I touched her and she didn't feel it, I finally understood the truth."

"I'm so sorry, Jed. I'm as shocked as you are."

"I doubt it." His back went rigid. "Wait a minute. Are you dead, too?"

"No. I'm not circling the drain quite yet."

As Sadie opened her mouth to continue, Jed cried, "My folks. Who's going to take care of my folks? They'll be devastated. They're too old to go through this again."

"I know." Sadie leaned her head against the swing and rolled it back and forth in dismay. "Your poor parents. Losing two children is more than any parent should have to bear."

"Wait a minute. I'm not missing like my sister, am I?"

"Not if your body's in the mortuary."

A family of four, toting inflatable buoyancy tubes, hurried past the porch. "Hi, Miss Witt," one of the children shouted. "We're going for a pontoon ride."

Sadie waved back as the other child nudged his brother. "See. I told you she talks to imaginary friends. You didn't believe me, but now you saw for yourself."

"Aw, who cares," the child muttered, peeking at Sadie over the top of his tube.

"I'm sure your relatives are taking care of your parents, Jed. I'll ask Nan how they're doing when I see her. Right now, you've got other things to worry about."

"I need to be there for them."

"That's not possible. I know you mean well, but they wouldn't be able to see you even if you joined them."

Jed put his fist against his mouth and wept openly.

Sadie lifted his free hand and kissed it gently. Tears rolled off her cheeks.

Jed drew a few broken breaths. "How do you know all this crosser stuff? Did you become a death coach when you started working at the mortuary?"

"No, but it's a good question. I became a death coach long before I took the job. I have no idea why. It just happened." Sadie placed her foot on the porch floor to stop the swing from swaying. She held out her hand and motioned for Jed to follow. "Let's talk inside. People already think I'm crazy. Gossip has it I talk to imaginary friends. No need to kindle the fire."

"Is he back?" Jane looked up as Sadie pulled out a chair and sat at the kitchen table.

"He's back," Aanders said. "He's sitting in your chair."

"Did he figure out why he failed to go through the light?" Jane tucked strands of her gray bob behind her ears before tugging on the tips of her white lace collar.

"I didn't ask him, yet. He wanted to know how I became a death coach."

"Another death coach taught Sadie just like she's teaching me." Aanders sat forward with excitement rising in his voice. "I'm a death coach, too, but I've only been once since right before Mr. Bakke died."

"Is Jane a death coach?" Jed nodded toward Jane.

"Nah. Just me and Sadie, and we're here to help you figure out what held you back. You've got thirty days to figure it out and cross over to the other side." Aanders eyes widened with excitement. "While you're figuring it out, you've got to make a big decision."

"You can't be serious." Jed's eyes narrowed as he gazed at Aanders. "Are you dead, too?"

"Aanders isn't dead, but everything he told you is accurate. After you make your decision, you need to find someone on the brink of death so you can go back through the light. You're also going to be given the option to find something more, and I guarantee you will."

"Oh, please." Spittle sprayed from Jed's lips. "You can't

possibly think I've done something so dreadful it held me back. Sadie, you've known me all my life."

"It's not necessarily something you've done. It might be something you know that could help someone else, or it might be something you witnessed. There are lots of reasons. You've got to figure it out so we can work on it."

Sadie watched the same soul-searching creep over Jed's face as it did every other crosser forced to perform a quick sweep of their life. Most crossers stumbled and lingered over guilt. Sorting guilt from fact wasted precious time. It corroded the ability to make a sound decision and most often had nothing to do with the reason they did not cross over.

"Who made up these rules?" Jed pursed his lips in challenge before adding, "Show me where it says I've got thirty days or why I have to make a decision."

"They didn't give me a manual so I don't have anything to show you. I learned it from the man who trained me." Sadie nodded firmly at Jed. "You're going to have to believe me. This isn't a game."

Not only had Sadie not been given an instruction manual, but the assignment lasted a lifetime. She had to depend on past experiences to guide her crossers. Because each new crosser presented a different quandary, her mental wheelbarrow spilled over with information she needed to pass on to Aanders.

If only she could ignore them. She often wondered what penalty would befall her if she didn't help the crossers. A lightning strike? Being imprisoned in drab beige clothing for the rest of her life? She didn't want to find out. If she didn't guide the crossers through their death decisions in the allotted time, they risked slipping into oblivion. Their deaths would have been in vain. Sadie resented the responsibility.

"Believe you? I don't know what to believe. I'm here in a

hospital gown talking about crossing over to the other side and every time I look at you all I see is…," Jed searched for the right words, "a weird pink get-up you've got on and a worm tattooed on your stomach."

"That's not a worm. It's an asp." Sadie lifted her shirt. "See. It's Cleopatra's asp. What a grand movie. I loved it, didn't you?"

"Do you mean to tell me you showed Jed your tattoo?" Disgust oozed in Jane's tone. "What's wrong with you? Nobody wants to look at a gnarly old tattoo. You're sixty-four years old, for Pete sakes. Why don't you show some respect and quit dressing like a bimbo?"

"I know more about respect than I care to know. That's all Nan talks about at the mortuary. Respect this, respect that. She acts like my mother."

"At least she got you to quit calling them stiffs." Jane set two plates on the table and then a third one for Mr. Bakke.

"That's what they are, aren't they?"

"I think Nan prefers 'dearly departed.'" Jane rotated each dish until the biggest ivy leaf sat squarely in the bottom rim of the plate. She added flatware to each place setting. "Aanders? Would you like to join us?"

"Who's cooking?"

"I am." Jane nodded with enthusiasm. "I'm trying a new recipe."

"No thanks, I think I'll see what mom's fixing for supper."

Jed leaned closer to examine Sadie's tattoo. "It looks like a dried-up worm to me." He gestured toward Sadie's hair. He opened his mouth, but shook his head instead. "You're asking a lot of me, Sadie. It's bad enough I have to accept my death, but one thing I can tell you is I don't have any unresolved issues."

21

"You're a guest in Cabin 14," Aanders said.

"So?"

Jed's loud question startled Aanders. He straightened against the back of his chair. "Guests only end up in Cabin 14 if they have to take care of business. Listen to Sadie. She knows what she's taking about." Aanders pointed at Jed's feet. "If you don't have unresolved issues, why are you here in bare feet and a hospital gown? You don't even have underwear on."

Jed tugged at the gown's hem and glared at Aanders.

Sadie studied the crosser sitting in Jane's chair. Pleased at Jed's defiant glare, she said, "You're angry. That means reality's starting to sink in."

"Wait a minute," Jane shrieked. "Do you mean to tell me Jed is sitting in my chair with a bare ass?" She crossed to the kitchen sink.

"It's not polite to make a guest stand all day. Of course I let him sit there."

"In his bare ass?" Jane's voice elevated an octave higher than Sadie thought physically possible.

Jane turned toward the chair the Witt sisters had recognized as Jane's chair for the past forty years and waved the spray bottle. "Get out of my chair."

Jed stood and moved toward the door.

"What's the matter with you? That's no way to treat Jed."

"Is he out of my chair yet?"

"He's over by the door." Aanders retreated toward Jed.

A fine disinfectant mist spritzed from the bottle. Jane wadded up a paper towel and continued to chastise her sister. "A bare ass. I can't believe you'd let someone sit their bare ass down on my chair."

"That's not the first…"

"Aanders," Sadie interrupted, wagging a warning finger

at the young man.

"Don't let him sit down again until I get one of Mr. Bakke's old robes. He can wear it when he's in the cabin." Jane disappeared into her bedroom before returning with a brown plaid robe.

"You'd better put it on." Sadie unfolded the robe and handed it to Jed.

"Why? She can't see me anyway."

"Just do it. We'll never hear the end of it if you don't."

Jed slipped one arm through a sleeve and strained his other arm backward to maneuver into the garment. Stitches popped along the arm seam. "I didn't realize Mr. Bakke was such a runt." Gazing down at the twelve inch gap separating the front robe panels he struggled to get the fabric to meet in the middle. He looked up at Sadie. "This is ridiculous. I look like an idiot."

"Wow." Sadie stared at the lumbering doughboy standing in front of her. The robe's belt crossed over the center of Jed's chest under his armpits.

"Does it fit?" Jane glared at her sister while waiting for an answer.

As Jed sat down in a different chair, the robe raised up exposing his butt. He shifted back and forth before looking up and shrugging.

"It's perfect."

"How long do I have to wear this blasted thing?"

Sadie glanced sideways at Jane and watched her sister place the spray bottle back under the sink. She lowered her voice. "Not long. As soon as she leaves the room, I'll hide it. As long as the robe touches you, Jane can't see it. When you take it off, I'll tuck it out of sight until Aanders can hide it at the mortuary."

Jed loosened the ties while he watched Jane return to the

recliner where she picked up the remote.

"How come he's a death coach?" Jed nodded in Aanders' direction. "Isn't he too young?"

"Yes I am." Aanders shifted and glanced at Sadie. "At least I think I'm too young." His blond bangs hung low and twitched as he blinked. "I don't like being one either. It's too complicated. Sadie said I don't have a choice."

Eleven-year-old Aanders stared at Jed, slumped low in his chair, and stretched his long legs toward the table. Tall and lanky at five-foot seven, Aanders had inherited his mother's slim build and Scandinavian features. He bore no resemblance to his father's squat features.

"Does your mom know you're a death coach?"

"Nah. She doesn't know. She doesn't know Sadie's one either."

"What about your dad?"

"I haven't seen him in five years. I've talked to him a few times on the phone, but Mom doesn't like it when he calls."

"Are you talking about your dad?" Jane looked toward Aanders.

"Yeah. Jed wanted to know if Dad knows I'm a death coach."

Sadie watched as Jed glanced from Jane to Aanders. He appeared to focus more on his surroundings and she sensed his disbelieving fog begin to lift.

Jed leaned forward. "I owe you an apology, Sadie. When people said your pod didn't have any peas, I believed them. Now it makes sense. It's not imaginary friends you talk to, is it?"

"No more imaginary than you." Sadie smiled and tapped at her earring, setting the silver sailboats in motion.

"So what's this unresolved issue I'm supposed to deal with?"

"That's what we have to figure out. I'll help you." Aanders pulled his chair closer to the table and propped his chin on his fists.

"I'm not going to listen to a kid. I want Sadie to help me."

"Remember when the Fossum family died in a car accident about a half a year ago?" When Jed nodded his recollection, Sadie continued, "Then you must also remember it wasn't an accident. They were murdered."

"How can I forget? The whole family died."

"Who do you think convinced me to investigate? Aanders did. He insisted it wasn't an accident."

Jane pressed the mute button on the remote. "Are you telling Jed how Aanders helped solve the murder?"

"Well now I don't have to, do I? You just did." Sadie sighed in exasperation. "I'm trying to explain that Aanders has more insight than Jed realizes."

"I thought Deputy Friborg solved the murder," Jed said.

"Everyone does." Sadie gestured a hand toward Aanders. "One of the family members who died in the accident became a crosser and told Aanders about the murder. Aanders insisted I check it out."

"How did you get Deputy Friborg to believe you're a death coach?"

"I never told him."

"Then how did you tell him about the murders?"

"That doesn't matter. After you rest, we need to figure out what held you back. I have a good inkling, but want you to think about it first. Maybe your idea will match mine."

"Rest? I don't want to rest."

"You're strong now, but during your thirty days your strength will diminish. You need to be mindful. There's still so much I haven't told you. You not only have to resolve your issue, but you have to find a way back through the tunnel of light. Before you cross over, though, you have to make your declaration."

Jed shook his head and grumbled under his breath. He looked at Aanders and then back at Sadie. "I don't have a clue what you're talking about. Quit pussy-footing. Lay it out so I know what I'm dealing with."

"Maybe Jed was held back to solve his sister's disappearance." Jane thumbed through the television channels as she looked at her sister.

"I thought you had errands to run," Sadie retorted, her icy glare sending a warning. "I thought you wanted to stop by the bakery? You said you craved powdered-sugared donuts."

"And miss this? Are you kidding?"

"My sister? What does Celeste have to do with this? She disappeared over fifteen years ago."

"Bingo. Disappeared is the key. Do you think maybe you were held back to solve her disappearance? Have you thought about her since you got here?" Sadie waited for Jed's reply.

"Thought about her? There isn't a day I haven't thought about her since she went missing. The last time I saw her I remember her black hair swinging around her shoulders as she turned to leave. She always had a spark in her eyes." Jed paused and stared out the window. "Come to think of it, Celeste never said good-bye. Instead she'd grin and say, 'Later', like she couldn't wait for the future."

A tingle crept up Sadie's neck as reckoning washed over Jed's face. It exhilarated Sadie when clarity dawned for a crosser. Jed had cleared the first hurdle.

"Maybe you're her future. Maybe you can figure out what happened. You've got thirty days Jed. Use it wisely."

"I don't believe this. What makes you think I can solve her disappearance in thirty days when they couldn't solve the case in fifteen years?"

3

"What are you looking at?" Jane poured a glass of lemonade for her sister.

"A whale with toothpick legs. He just got out of his car."

"You mean Kimmer? What's he doing here?" Jane joined Sadie at the window. "Look at him. He's talking to our guests like he owns the place."

Judge Franzen Kimmer placed a heavy foot on the porch step.

"Pretend we're not here." Sadie held a finger to her lips.

Jane retreated to her bedroom and eased the latch quietly into place.

Kimmer rapped on the door. He leaned his bulk against the railing, ran his finger between his neck and shirt collar, and crossed the wood planking to knock for the second time. "Answer the door, you old biddy." He fanned his face with his straw hat before setting it on the railing.

Jane poked her lips through her slivered bedroom door opening. "Is he gone yet?"

Kimmer fidgeted with his suspenders lifting them off his shoulders. The unseasonably-warm mid-June weather delighted the tourists, but proved to be hellish for the judge who was nothing short of rotund.

Fed up with Kimmer's frequent harassment, Sadie had no intention of answering the door. Let him suffer. The past two times he'd stopped by to pressure her into selling Cabin 12, she'd hidden in one of the other cabins until he left. No such luck this time.

Kimmer pressed his nose against the screen. He cupped

a hand over his eye to shield the glare. "If you think I can't see your scrawny body, you're mistaken."

"Go away. You're wasting your time."

"Now, Sadie, is that any way to talk?"

"Go away, Kimmer." Sadie opened the door and headed for the porch swing. "You're not welcome here."

"I'm a judge. That means I'm welcome wherever I go." Kimmer dabbed at his face with an engraved handkerchief. "That lemonade looks mighty good."

"It is." Sadie took a long sip. "Nice and cool."

"I want my parent's cabin back!" Kimmer's lips trembled as he leaned closer to the swing.

"How many times do I have to tell you it won't happen?" Sadie tapped her foot on the porch floor to keep the swing in motion. She took another sip and gazed out over the lake.

The thought of Judge Kimmer and Oinketta, his greedy sister, regaining ownership to Cabin 12 made Sadie's scalp slither with imaginary vermin.

"That cabin rightfully belongs to us and you know it," Kimmer shouted.

"Your parents sold the cabin to us fifteen years ago. We've got the deed to prove it."

"I know, but they should have consulted with us first." Kimmer dabbed his handkerchief around the back of his neck.

Belly pushed through the screen door and ambled over to Kimmer. He sniffed the judge's shoes and an angry rumble burbled in his throat.

"Get your mongrel away from me. He's slobbering all over my leg."

"He's not my dog."

"Then who does he belong to?" Kimmer pushed Belly away with the tip of his shoe.

"The neighbor." Sadie watched as Belly circled Kimmer's leg and left a string of drool on the judge's shoe.

Sadie reached toward the porch floor and snapped her fingers. Belly sidled over and plopped down under the swing. He rolled over, let out a disgruntled sigh, and chewed on the corner of the leopard-patterned neckerchief stuck to his lip.

"Good-bye, Kimmer." Sadie twiddled her fingers at him. "You're wasting your time. We're not selling Cabin 12. The cabin sat empty for years after your folks moved away. Why didn't you or Oinketta do something about it then?"

"I never realized it meant so much." Kimmer shook out his hankie, looking for a dry spot. "Don't call her Oinketta. My sister's name is Etta."

"Your mother offered the cabin to us because it sat next door to the resort. It was her idea to turn it into a rental cabin."

"It rightfully belongs to me!"

The rage in Kimmer's voice cut through the humidity. Sadie winced. "If we hadn't bought it, it would be in shambles."

"No it wouldn't," Kimmer shouted. "It will be if you don't sell it. It's been empty since Mr. Bakke died. If you're the business woman you claim to be, you'd sell it and be done with it."

Kimmer clearly suffered from the heat. He had fallen into a pattern of shifting from foot to foot, fanning his face with his hat, readjusting his suspenders. The angrier he became, the faster the dance of discomfort. If he dressed like a tourist instead of trying to impress everyone with his expensive wardrobe, he'd feel a whole lot better.

A grin graced Sadie's face. She hid it by holding the glass against her bottom lip. The image of Kimmer in plaid shorts with toothpick legs protruding below the fabric moved through her mind in freeze-frame sequence. She had seen him in shorts only once. Kimmer's girth was the subject of jokes. It had been for decades. Apparently he didn't care.

"Is he gone yet?" Jane parted the curtains and whispered through the kitchen window.

"No I'm not gone yet. I'm not leaving, either. I'm here to talk some sense into the two of you."

"It's too hot to listen." Sadie walked over to the railing as she again twiddled good-bye at the obnoxious intruder.

Kimmer cocked his head and looked Sadie up and down. "How can you suffer from the heat? You're almost naked."

"You like it?" Sadie turned in a complete circle.

"I didn't say I liked it. What kind of animal gave its life to make those shorts? It looks like a diseased alley cat."

Sadie looked down and ran her hand over her hip. "It does not. It's leopard and it cost way too much. It's not real, though."

As Kimmer dabbed his brow, he glanced at Sadie from under a hankie flap. "Is skin hanging around your knees, or did your bloomers let go?"

"You're a fine one to criticize." Sadie nodded toward the shore. "Be glad the lake's not an ocean or you'd run the risk of being harpooned."

Kimmer opened his mouth to counter, but Jane butted in. "Would you like some lemonade?"

"No, he wouldn't." Sadie shot an irritated glare at her sister.

"I'd prefer an ice-cold gin and tonic." Kimmer smirked at Sadie. "At least Jane's got manners. She knows a drink is the only remedy for this miserable weather."

Belly ambled to the porch step and let out a bark. Kimmer turned in the direction of Belly's interest. "Oh good grief," he uttered, watching Nan and Deputy Lon Friborg cross the lawn between the mortuary and the resort.

"Kimmer." Deputy Friborg nodded sharply at the judge.

"The judge is leaving," Sadie said.

"No I'm not." Judge Kimmer tipped his hat toward Nan. "It's been a long time, Nan. I saw your name in the paper. I see you purchased the land the mortuary sits on."

Nan smiled. "That's right. It took a while to clear the title, but my attorney found a way to do it. The transaction got bogged down because someone apparently didn't want it to happen."

"Where'd you get the money?"

"That's none of your damn business." Lon put his arm around Nan's shoulder and pulled her close.

"Why? Because you had something to do with it? I noticed you've been sniffing around Nan more than usual."

Nan crossed her arms over her chest and stared out over the lake.

"Like I said, it's none of your business." Lon watched the women retreat into the cabin.

"Everything in this town is my business. If you want a promotion to detective, you'd better convince the Witt sisters to sell Cabin 12."

"Like I already told you, Cabin 12 isn't for sale. It won't happen." Sadie pushed the screen door open with her elbow and handed Lon a glass of lemonade.

"You'll regret it, Sadie. I'm going to make your life worse than hell. I'm calling in reinforcements. If you think I'm relentless now, just wait."

"I'm not worried. We survived your harassment before and we'll survive it again."

The Witt sisters watched as Kimmer crossed the driveway and kicked at Belly. "That man gives me the creeps. Look at this. I've got goose bumps and it's ninety degrees."

31

Outwitted

The tail lights from Kimmer's Cadillac Escalade blinked while he exited between the massive stone pillars gracing the resort entrance. Sadie resented Kimmer plucking at her strings of restraint. Even Belly sensed her distress. He had lowered his head and growled in warning as he watched every move Kimmer made.

Sadie shouted directions through the screen door to two resort guests who sought her assistance. She pointed twice in the direction she wanted them to go before she joined Nan and Lon at the kitchen table.

She stared at Nan and let out a resigned sigh. "It's not fair. All you have to do is shower and run a comb through your hair and you look beautiful. No matter how hard I try, I'll never look as good as you."

Nan grinned back at Sadie. "No matter how hard I try, I'll never look like you, either."

"Thank goodness," Jane mumbled, placing six ice cubes in Belly's water dish. She ran her hand across the dog's back. "If you need more, let me know."

"I don't understand why Kimmer's so insistent on Cabin 12. He'd have no privacy whatsoever." Nan shook her head in confusion. "There are plenty of other cabins for sale."

"We offered him Cabin 1 on the opposite end of the resort a few years ago, but he turned us down," Jane said. "That cabin had its own dock and lots of privacy. Kimmer refused to look at it. I get the feeling trouble's brewing."

4

"That's not good." Sadie stared out at the marina.

"What?" Jane drew a card from the top of the deck.

Sadie strained to see through the mesh screen. "I thought I saw a child on the dock, but I don't see her now."

Jane followed Sadie's gaze. "I don't see anyone."

"It must have been my imagination. The dock boys are there and they don't seem alarmed." Creases of apprehension formed around Sadie's eyes as she glanced back toward the dock.

Jane elbowed her sister. "Look. Lon's going into the mortuary again. It's Monday. He's got another yellow rose."

"That's eight Mondays in a row. He's getting serious." Sadie stared across the lawn toward the mortuary.

"I sure hope so. Nan needs someone to take care of her."

"Take care of her? Nan can take care of herself. She has no intention of getting into another relationship. She's still reeling from her marriage to Aanders' father." Sadie fanned her cards out in front of her. "Gin."

Jane fisted her cards and slammed them down on the table. "You're cheating again. You can't win six games in a row."

"I won because I'm a superior player."

"Bull," Jane said. "You're cheating." Jane lifted the lid on Mr. Bakke's urn, leaned toward it, and whispered, "Sadie's a dirty cheater."

Sadie separated a clump of hair with her fingers, coaxing the tapered gelled tufts to stand erect. Jutting her chin forward, she checked both sides of her reflection in the mirror above the bookcase. She liked the color much better this time. It took some convincing to get Big Leon to change the previous dye job, but he finally gave in. She patted her black, verging on blue, spikes.

Sadie still felt disappointed over the previous evening at the Fertile Turtle. It hadn't proved as advantageous as she had hoped. She spent money on a new outfit, but no one paid attention. She hadn't felt that sexy in a long time. Instead of admiring her outfit, everyone obsessed with her flamingo-tinted hair. It didn't help, either, that Jed had joined them and she spent the entire evening answering his questions. No one wanted to dance with a senior who talked to a vacant chair. A few Fertile Turtle patrons offered to pitch in for a train ticket to Locoville. She wasn't deaf. She'd heard them whisper they'd drive her to the station. No charge.

"Maybe Nan's luck with men is finally changing," Jane said.

"I think I'll check one of those internet dating sites." Sadie pointed at her computer. "If it doesn't work with Lon, I might be able to find her a man."

Jane's lips contorted into a scowl of disbelief. "You're the last person I'd depend on to pick a man. Your taste in men is atrocious."

"Says who?"

"Says me," Jane challenged. "How could you go out with stinky Roger Townsend? Especially after he dated no-charge Marge."

"For the same reason she did," Sadie said. "Because he owned the meat market. I'm not stupid, you know. Where do you think all the free meat in our freezer came from?"

"That's disgusting." Jane stared scornfully at her sister before reshuffling and dealing the cards face down on the table. "At least Nan has someone courting her now. Lon's loved her since they went to high school. Aanders seems to like him, too." Jane drew a card from the deck. "Do you remember the day Nan announced she'd married Clay? I've never seen Lon so devastated."

"I was, too. I can't imagine what possessed her to marry Lon's no-good cousin."

"I'm glad Nan's free. It gives her a chance to rebuild her life."

"Where is Clay now?" Jed closed the door to the inner room and joined the sisters at the kitchen table.

"Aanders told me Clay's living near Minneapolis."

"Why would I care where Clay lives?" Jane smirked at her sister. "I could care less."

"I wasn't talking to you. I answered Jed's question. He just joined us and asked about Clay."

"Jed better not have his bare butt in my chair."

"He's not in your chair. He's sitting in the chair under the clock."

"Judge Kimmer's a real piece of garbage, isn't he?" Jed stared at Sadie. "I overheard him pressuring you this morning. How long has that been going on?"

"He's been after us for years. He's obsessed with Cabin 12." Sadie picked an envelope off the table and fanned her face. "The heat is getting worse. I wonder if the humidity will brew up a storm."

"I hope you don't give in. Kimmer made my mother jump through hoops when she tried to have my sister declared dead."

"I believe it. It took months to subdivide our property so we could clear the title for Nan. I'll bet Kimmer caused the delay. He must have gotten wind Nan wanted to buy it."

"Sadie. Come here quick." The three turned toward the screen door as Aanders frantically motioned for Sadie to join him on the porch step.

Sadie, Jed, and Jane hurried to the door.

Aanders pointed at a small red-haired girl. "She keeps following me. Make her stop."

Sadie gasped. "Oh, dear. It's Sally Tyler."

"Where?" Jane strained to find the object of their concern.

"Right there." Sadie pointed toward the edge of the walkway.

"I can't see her."

"Right there. Follow my finger. She's petting Belly."

"Oh, no," Jane said. "I don't see her. Please don't tell me Sally's a crosser."

Sadie hurried over to Sally and crouched down next to her.

"I'm looking for my mom. She told me to wait in the car but it took too long." Sally put both arms around Belly's neck as he licked her face.

Sadie looked up at Jane.

Jane shook her head. "I can't see her. Is she there with you?"

"She's right next to me."

"Oh, no. I can't believe it. What happened?"

Jed knelt next to Sadie. "Sally? Where did your mother park her car?"

"At the Turtle. She went in to get some beer. She said she'd be right back but she never came out. A squirrel jumped on the car. Mom doesn't like her new car to get dirty so I chased it in the woods."

Jed scooped Sally off the ground and walked back to the cabin.

Belly grunted as he climbed the steps and followed Jed. The four black hairs on his tail flagged back and forth in excitement.

"Look at those bruises." Jed placed Sally on the sofa. He ran his hand over her translucent skin. "I'm Jed, and this is Sadie."

"I know. She's the crazy lady. Mom told me about her."

"She did, did she?" Sadie braced her hands on her hips.

Sally touched Jed's hospital gown. "Why are you in your jammies?"

"Do you have gauze so I can clean her scrapes?" Jed turned Sally's hand over to examine it for more cuts.

"I'll get it." Aanders opened a kitchen drawer. He flipped the lid on the first-aid kit and handed it to Jed.

Because each new crosser brought a unique circumstance, Sadie realized Aanders had so much more to learn. His eagerness pleased her, but their lessons would go on for years.

"Sally's not in pain. When crossers arrive at Cabin 14, their life pain has ended." Sadie gestured toward Jed. "When Jed came to me after surgery, he wasn't in pain."

Jed touched his face. He ran his fingers back and forth over the bridge of his nose. "You're right. I never thought about it, but I don't feel anything."

Jed gently ran his hand down Sally's arm. "She's only a child. We've got to do something. What about a glass of water?"

"She doesn't need water, either. Crossers don't need nourishment. The only thing they need is rest."

A week without crossers prior to Jed joining her had left Sadie bewildered. Had the powers-that-be demoted her? Was it because Aanders was now ready to take on his own crossers? In her forty-plus years as a death coach, she couldn't remember a single week without a crosser. She hoped this wasn't the respite before the flood gates broke loose.

"It can't hurt to show we care, can it?" Jed dabbed at Sally's scrapes with a tissue before applying a small bandage to her knee. He snapped the first-aid kit shut. "There you go, Miss Sally. That should take care of it. How old are you?"

"Five. Don't you have any puppy bandages?"

"I didn't see any, but I think the brown one will work."

Sally jumped down off the sofa. "I need to find Mom. She's going to be mad if I don't find her."

"How's Sally doing?" Concern rimmed Jane's eyes. "Did you find out what happened to her?"

"I don't think she knows. She's more concerned about finding her mother," Sadie said.

"How come you have a BA?" Sally pointed at Jed.

"A what?" Jed's lips pursed in bewilderment while he stared back at Sally.

Sally giggled and whispered, "You know. A BA."

"What's a BA?"

Sally tugged at Aanders' hand.

He looked down at her before yanking his hand away. She leaned into his long leg and gazed up at him. He pushed her away. "Go sit by Sadie."

Sally sidled around Jed as she peeked at him from the corners of her eyes.

"I think a BA is a bare ass," Aanders said. "That's what the kids in school call it."

"A bare ass?" Jane turned toward her sister and pointed her index finger. "He better not be sitting in my chair." She bent down at the sink and drew open the cupboard door. It rebounded against the adjoining door and slammed back, pinching her hand. "Where is he?" She aimed the disinfectant bottle at the table.

Jane's shoulder-length bob swung back and forth as she scrubbed in earnest. She tucked gray strands of hair behind each ear before straightening into an angry posture. "Why wasn't he wearing Mr. Bakke's robe?"

"Because it's too small. He looked like a scarecrow on a stake."

"How can you let him sit there bare-assed? It's not sanitary. Here, make him sit on this." Jane handed Sadie a towel.

"Where's Sally?" Sadie looked around. She scurried to the screen door and spotted Sally walking toward the beach. "Get her before she gets away."

"I don't want to. She's a pest," Aanders whined. "She followed me everywhere. She wouldn't leave me alone."

"Fate placed her in your hands because you're a death coach."

"I don't want to be a death coach. I hate it. I want to be normal."

"I know you do, but you've got to make the best of it," Sadie said. "Sally sought you out because she needs your guidance."

"How can a kid have unfinished business? That doesn't make sense." Aanders turned his back on Sadie and stared out the window toward the mortuary.

Sadie put her arm around his waist. "Don't worry. You don't have to keep your crossers at the mortuary. I'll keep Sally here in the inner room with Jed. Now go get her."

"Where's Aanders going? What's happening?" Jane peered over Sadie's shoulder.

"To get Sally. She's down by the lake."

"Aren't you keeping an eye on her? She's too young to wander around."

"I turned my head for a second and she disappeared."

"I'd do a better job if I was a death coach." Jane flipped her hair in defiance.

"Has Sally's family lived in the area long?" Jed's gaze followed Aanders' progress toward the shore. "I think I might have met them."

"Her folks are Carmen and Pete Tyler. Their divorce was final a few months ago. Pete got the raw end of the deal," Sadie said.

"Boy did he ever," Jane confirmed, addressing her comment toward her private chair.

"Jed's not in your chair. He moved to the chair under the clock."

Jane followed Sadie's finger and directed her conversation toward the empty chair. "Sally's mom's a real scumbag. She took Pete to the cleaners. Carmen won sole custody of Sally after she filed trumped-up charges of abuse." Jane grabbed the towel off her chair and threw it toward the chair under the clock. "Sit on this," she ordered.

"Everybody knew Carmen falsified her claim." Jane tugged at the points on her collar, pulling them sharply into alignment. "She used Sally as a pawn. That woman riles me to no end."

"Me, too. When Pete petitioned the court to regain visitation rights last month, Judge Kimmer would have nothing to do with it. You know Kimmer. If there's a pretty woman involved," Sadie paused, "well, use your imagination."

"Where's Pete now?" Jed looked at Sadie. "Doesn't he get to see Sally?"

"I heard he moved to Kansas to stay with his folks. Can you imagine losing the right to your daughter and then having to deal with her death?"

Sadie dared not look at her sister. The fiber weaving their sibling thoughts together might unravel. They knew Pete's pain would be too much to bear. "I admire Sally's father. He tried to make their marriage work, but monogamy isn't in Carmen's vocabulary."

The sisters looked toward the door as footsteps pounded across the porch, down the steps and then back up onto the porch. "Sadie," Aanders shouted breathlessly. "I can't find Sally. She was on the swing a minute ago, and now she's gone."

5

Attorney Reginald Carson glanced at Pam. It sickened him that this gorgeous nurse had no qualms about abducting infants, but thrilled him that her expertise put money in his pocket. Large quantities of money. "Are you sure you have all the information you need?" He closed the manila folder. Struggling to push aside his mounting irritation, he stood to face the couple.

"That's the third time you asked, Reggie. Settle down or you'll have a coronary." Pam Avery placed an open palm on the window and scanned the cityscape below. Streetlights winked in the distance. High above in a cloudless sky, tiny dots grew in intensity as planes prepared for approach to the Minneapolis-St. Paul International Airport.

Reginald's office occupied a portion of the posh twenty-third floor of the IDS Center in downtown Minneapolis. Industry giants frequented his elaborate office, depending on him to orchestrate the impossible. He had earned their trust. In fact, he had earned everything he owned. The hard way. Through determination and cunning.

Reginald crossed his office and pressed the dimmer switch into the full ON position. If he flooded the room with light, removing the ambience Pam had tried to stage, maybe he could get them to leave. He let out a sigh. Who was he kidding?

Unencumbered by his small stature, Reginald's aggressive mannerisms and the ability to close transactions in haste drew clients from all phases of the commercial realm. His skill had become a commodity. It also created enemies.

Legendary for his business acumen, Reginald had no need to promote his secondary activity of assisting the privileged in securing babies for adoption.

Wealthy couples turned to him to arrange additions to their families after failing to secure adoption through normal channels. Infinite funds became a prerequisite. So did desperation. If the couples met his criteria, he considered their case. Supplying an heir, who would in turn inherit their vast wealth and possibly become a future client, was the least he could do for these barren couples.

Pam watched the sea of headlights wind along the freeway as commuters inched their way across the horizon. Grasping her husband's hand when he approached to take in the view, Pam turned to Reginald. "What's your rush, Reggie? You're acting like you want to get rid of us. Afraid someone will think you're slumming?"

"We haven't failed yet, have we?" Dan Avery slipped his hand behind his wife's waist and pulled her close.

Reginald looked at Pam's empty glass before closing the door to the liquor cabinet. "I asked you not to call me Reggie. My name is Reginald. Please give me the courtesy of remembering." He tucked his tie neatly into his suit coat and faced the pair. The sooner they left, the sooner they'd complete the transaction and satisfy his quest.

"Why did you close the cabinet? I'm just beginning to feel the glow." Pam looked down at her empty glass. "I need courage. How else can I tackle your new assignment?" She signaled her disappointment with a pout.

Reginald paced. "This adoption is crucial. If it goes well, the prospective father will choose my firm to represent his next merger." Reginald didn't tell them the retainer alone put him into the financial realm to pay for an Aston Martin Roadster for his new wife. Maybe it would shut her up for a while.

"Don't forget when we bring the baby back, you and I are going to sit down and talk." Dan opened the liquor cabinet and reached for the brandy. "And it won't be about baseball. If it wasn't for me and Pam taking all the risk, your little adoption business wouldn't be so successful." Dan waved the brandy bottle. "I'll bet your partner in Pinecone Landing isn't hurting for money, either."

Reginald's breath caught in his gullet, forcing him to clear his throat.

"What's the matter, Reggie? Did you really think I didn't know about Franzen Kimmer?"

Retrieving a folder from the desk, Reginald hurried toward the door. "You and Pam are paid handsomely for your risk. If you don't like it, you can quit." He turned the knob and drew the door open. A hand reached past him and slammed the door.

Dan's hot breath billowed down over Reginald's face. "Like I said, Reggie, when we deliver the kid, we're going to talk. It's time for an increase." He ran his finger under Reggie's lapel. "Keeping the kid an extra two weeks wasn't in our original agreement. I'm not crazy about staying at Witt's End Resort to wait it out. This abduction is more risky than the last one."

"Yeah," Pam chimed in placing her finger on the dimmer switch. "Hospitals all over the state are on alert. Two abductions throw everyone into a panic. You're damn lucky your clients live in Tucson. Who knows? They might hear about it anyway."

"That's why I decided to keep the baby in Minnesota for an additional two weeks. I'll look like a proud new father when I board the plane. Even if newspapers all over the country feature the abduction, no one will recognize the baby." Reginald smoothed his lapel and stepped away from the door. "I've decided Pam's going to fly with me to Tucson to deliver the baby to the lucky couple. Pam's a nurse. She'll know what to do if anything goes wrong."

"It'll cost you." Pam spit the words at him as he finished his sentence. She pressed her thumb against the dimmer switch creating a darker, warm glow.

"No kidding," Reginald shouted. "Everything with you guys costs extra." The sweat beading under his shirt collar matched the clammy film on his hand. He slipped his hand into his pocket and wiped it against the lining. Drawing in a purging breath, he said, "After you secure the baby, I'll notify my clients the mother gave birth in Dallas and the release papers are finalized. First, we'll fly from Minneapolis to Dallas. Then we'll switch carriers before flying on to Tucson to meet the adoptive couple."

Dan greedily rubbed his fingers together.

Disgusted with Dan's increasing demand for cash, Reginald pushed the man's hand aside. "Don't worry. Pam will be paid for her efforts."

"We're not worried, Reggie. You've got as much to lose as we do. Maybe more."

Reginald peered at his watch. "Are you sure the nurse from the hospital wasn't suspicious?"

"In Pinecone Landing? I'm positive."

"Do you know for sure? From what you said, she asked a lot of questions."

"Don't get your gonads in the guillotine, Reggie. If Pam says she trusts her, she trusts her."

"She doesn't have a clue. As far as she's concerned, I'm a new friend with similar interests. After I met her at the conference, we communicated through email. Most of our conversations are about our jobs." Pam held her hand out and shrugged. "It's pure luck she works on the OB floor."

"They've become best of friends." Dan laughed into his glass as he took a sip. "She sent Pam some photos from work over the internet. I enlarged the portion showing her name badge and made one exactly like it. Pam bought an identical uniform, too. So accessing the OB floor at the hospital shouldn't be a problem."

"We know what we're doing, Reggie." Pam's words dripped with arrogance as she added, "We've got it mapped out through the final detail."

Pam's cocky attitude grated at Reginald. "Don't forget over-confidence can be your worst enemy. Remember, if you get caught you're on your own."

Dan swirled the ice in his glass. "That's not going to happen. But if it does, I hope you'll realize how stupid that sounds when you're locked up next to me in prison."

6

"Have you seen my Mom? I can't find her." Sally followed a five-year-old girl clad in a lime green sundress into Cabin 11. The screen door creaked and slammed behind them. "I looked everywhere. I need to find her. She might get worried if she can't find me."

Sally squatted next to the child and watched the girl's braid flop forward as she scooped up her doll and inserted a plastic baby bottle in its mouth. "What's in the bottle? Is it real milk? I wish I had a doll like that."

The girl's father slipped a straw into a cartoon-laden juice box and handed it to his daughter. "Mom ran over to the gift shop to get the book you wanted. I'll read it to you when she gets back."

Sally inched her knees closer to the girl and touched the doll's curly hair. As the girl placed the bottle on the floor, Sally picked it up. She shook it. White bubbles formed around the top of the bottle. "It's real." She giggled with glee. "Look. Real milk." Sally squeezed the bottle. When droplets failed to form on the nipple, she gave it another squeeze.

The girls glanced at the screen door when a muffled bark burbled and then erupted. Belly pranced in place, wagging in earnest while he stared at Sally.

"A puppy," the little girl shouted, dropping her doll on the floor. "Can I keep him?"

"Go on. Shoo." The girl's father motioned toward Belly with the back of his hand. "Go home you mutt."

"I want him," the child whined.

"His name is Belly." Sally looked at the girl. "He's

Sadie's dog. You can't have him."

Belly circled in front of the door before plopping down on his left haunch. He looked back over his shoulder through soulful eyes, whimpered, and turned his attention toward the lake.

Sally gathered the doll off the floor and cuddled her in her arms. She pressed her fingertips against the plastic eyelashes. "Hush little baby. Don't you cry," she whispered. "My daddy used to sing to me. He went away. Mom said he went away cuz he doesn't love me anymore."

A sharp cry jolted Sally from the recollection.

"My dolly! My dolly's gone."

Recoiling, Sally hugged the doll tighter.

"My dolly. I can't find her."

"She's here somewhere. You just had her a minute ago," her father responded. "Check under the chair."

The girl continued her frantic wail.

"Here she is. Take her." Sally held the doll by the left leg and pushed it toward the girl. She placed the doll in the girl's lap when the child flopped hysterically into the chair.

The girl gulped air for another round of wailing, but a shrill solo note is all that escaped as she felt the doll settle on her lap. She stared at the doll through tear-clumped lashes. She tapped it with her finger. The girl's gaze went from the doll to her father and back to the doll as she twisted a strand of hair around her finger.

"Can you come out and play?" Sally leaned her elbows on the wicker chair and propped her chin on her fists. "How come you won't talk? You're not very nice."

A thumping echoed from the far side of Cabin 12. Belly barked twice and the thumping began again.

The girl's father pushed through the screen door and walked over to the porch railing. "That infernal creature. He's doing it again." He leaned over the barrier and waved his hand at Belly. "Get out of there. It's bad enough you smell like rotten fish, but I shouldn't have to put up with your incessant scratching."

Belly ignored the reprimand. He continued to paw at the screen covering the narrow crawlspace access under Cabin 12.

Sally turned to face the sidewalk when the girl's mother approached Cabin 11, swinging a bright yellow bag imprinted with the Witt's End logo. When the child spotted her mother, she dropped her dolly and yanked the bag from her mother's grasp.

Sally looked up at the girl's father as he lifted his daughter onto his lap. "Can I sit with you, too? My dad used to read to me every night."

The young crosser leaned into the wicker chair and nestled her cheek against the man's warm arm as he read to his daughter. After turning the last page, he put the book down. "What is wrong with that blasted dog? He's getting on my nerves. He's been scratching on the screen for the past half hour."

"He did it yesterday, too." The girl's mother attempted to tuck stray strands of hair back into her daughter's braid. "I finally threw a piece of burger on the grass to see if it would stop him. It did for two seconds, but he went right back to scratching against the screen. I talked to the resort owner. She said every summer the dog's mission is to crawl under the cabin. They've had to replace the mesh several times."

"I feel like putting him in the Lexus and driving him to the opposite end of the lake. If I'm lucky, he won't find his way back." The girl's father lifted his daughter off his lap.

The screen door slammed behind Sally as she raced over to Cabin 12.

Outwitted

The girl's parents stared at the door. The mother peered through the window at the pine boughs. "It wasn't windy when I went to the gift shop."

"You have to go home. That man doesn't like you." Sally tugged on Belly's collar. "He's going to take you for a ride." She ran to the cabin's edge and peeked around the corner.

Belly pawed at the screen obstructing access to the crawlspace. He hooked his claws in the mesh and tugged.

"What's under there?" Sally knelt next to the dog and put one arm over his back. "I can't see. It's too dark."

Belly grunted as he sat down. He cocked his head back and forth when Sally looped her fingers through the mesh and pulled. "It won't come off."

"There you are," Sadie shouted, bolting toward Sally. "Don't move a muscle. I had a dickens of a time finding you. Where were you?"

"Visiting my new friend. I played with her dolly." Sally pointed at the screen. "Your dog wants to go under there."

"He's not my dog."

"But he lives with you. I saw him licking gravy off Jane's plate."

Sadie tugged at her red T-shirt. The knit top featured 'Easy Momma' spelled out in black glitter across her chest. "That's because Jane spoils him." Sadie winked at Sally. "Belly sleeps in Jane's bed. He's even got his own embroidered pillow."

"I used to have a dog. Mom kicked him out and made him sleep under the porch. He ran away." Sally pointed at Belly.
"He's digging again."

"I don't know what's gotten in to him. He's obsessed with getting the screen loose."

"I like your earrings, Sadie. My Mom has earrings, too."

"Would you like to wear one?"

"Really? You mean you'd let me?" Sally stood still while Sadie removed the tiny ring in her ear and replaced it with three red dangling baubles.

"You look snazzy."

Sally beamed as she tilted her head back and forth. She grabbed Sadie's outstretched hand. Together the fashion queens skipped back to Cabin 14, giggling as the beads tinkled a hollow tune.

"Look, Jed," Sally said, running up the steps and across the porch floor. She tapped on the baubles. "Do you like it?"

"You look gorgeous, Miss Sally."

"Do I? Do I look as good as Sadie?"

Jed grinned. "Better. Much better."

"I want to look just like Sadie when I grow up."

"Dear Lord," Jed mumbled, bending down and brushing dirt from Sally's knees. "You gave us a scare by wandering off. I don't want you disappearing again. Is that a deal?"

"Okay. Deal. I made a new friend, but she won't share. She wouldn't let me play with her doll."

Jed's brows sagged in empathy. "I'll bet you shared your dolls."

"I never had a doll."

"You never had a doll?" Sadie shifted her gaze toward Jed.

Sally kicked at a ridge in the flooring. "I got one last Christmas from Dad, but Mom took it to the pawn shop. She said she'd get it back. She never did."

"I'm sorry, Sally. I'll bet you loved your dolly." Pity filled Sadie.

"I did. My doll had long hair and a pretty white gown. She was a princess. Mom told Dad I lost it by accident."

A glare of contempt passed between the adults.

"Knowing your father, he didn't get upset," Sadie said.

"Dad told me there are no accidents." Sally stopped and looked up at Jed. "I never got to say good-bye to Dad. Mom said he left because he doesn't love me anymore."

"That's not true, Sally. Your dad loves you. I agree with him about there being no accidents. Everything happens for a reason." Jed lifted her off the ground and hugged her. "Your dad just had to go away for a while, that's all."

Sadie smiled softly. "I'll tell your dad how much you love him next time I see him."

Sally tried to wriggle free from Jed's grasp. "I want to go back to the cabin with Belly."

"What cabin?" Jed caught the back of Sally's shirt and pulled her back to his side.

"Cabin 12. Mr. Bakke's old cabin," Sadie explained. "I found Sally trying to help Belly take the screen off the crawlspace."

"Why?"

"I don't have a clue. It's probably cool under there. You know Belly always looks for a good place to nap."

"Did you ever check out what's under the cabin?"

"No. Too many spiders. Besides, what could be under there?"

7

Sadie clicked on an internet icon and waited for the site to connect. "Has it really been five years since you've seen your dad?"

"Yeah," Aanders said. "Sometimes it's hard to remember what he looks like unless I look at his picture."

"He doesn't call?"

"Once in a while, but he's usually drunk." Aanders skewed his lower lip. "At least that's what Mom says. She gets mad and won't let me talk to him."

"Is he still living near Minneapolis?" Sadie stared at Aanders over the top of the laptop screen.

"The last time he called, he lived there. Mom said he got a job driving a cement truck."

"At least he's working."

"Yeah." Aanders' body pulsed with each foot kick when his toe connected with the table's pedestal. "Can I go with you to the nursing home to get Jed?"

"Sure."

"Do you think he had any luck finding someone on the brink?"

"I hope so." Sadie raised her head to zero in on the bifocal portion of her lenses. She keyed letters into the prompt bar and waited for the information to appear.

"Jed didn't like it when I explained what he had to do to cross over." Aanders cast a puzzled look toward Sadie. "He told me he didn't want to hang around the dying or go through their light. How come he doesn't want to cross over?

"That's not uncommon. It'll make more sense when he

sees the tunnel form around someone near death. Most crossers think we're making this up until they experience it."

"Will you let me drive the shuttle when I'm old enough?"

"Of course," Sadie said. "What a good idea. Then you can gather the crossers." She nodded in approval. "Smart thinking, young man."

"I really like the new shuttle you bought." A wide grin beamed as Aanders continued, "Who'd have ever thought a hearse would make a good shuttle?"

"Jane sure didn't," Sadie said with a grimace. "She wouldn't talk to me for a week after I bought the used hearse from your mother." The battle that had ensued between the sisters still evoked chills. Sadie couldn't understand why Jane hadn't appreciated the interior revamping job the local car detailer had done on the hearse. In her opinion, it made a dandy resort shuttle.

"What's a French whore house?" Aanders continued to kick absentmindedly against the pedestal.

Sadie's head jerked so quickly to the left, her glasses slipped off the bridge of her nose. "Where did you hear that?"

"That's what Jane said the remodel job on the hearse looked like. Especially the purple interior."

"Pay no mind to Jane. She's got no taste at all." Sadie waved her hand in disgust.

"Take a peek at the screen. Sadie turned the laptop screen so Aanders could see it. She clicked on a drop-down bar and Jane's photo popped up. "I've decided it's time for Jane to start dating again. It's not Jane's best picture, but it'll have to do. It's already drawn some interest."

"Does Jane know about this?" Aanders leaned closer to read the text below the photo.

"Not yet. I don't want her to know, either. I've got it all arranged."

"Jane loved Mr. Bakke."

"I know she did. She'll always love Mr. Bakke, but Jane needs a man in her life, so I've baited the hook." Sadie grinned at Aanders and patted his hand. "I know what I'm doing."

"Mom said you have to wait a year after someone dies before you can date."

"A year?" Sadie laughed. "At our age, that's too long. Six months is more than enough." Sadie pointed at one of the five photos on the screen. "He looks like a good prospect. It says he's a regular churchgoer. Jane will eat it up."

Sadie nudged Aanders. "Quit daydreaming. What do you think about the man I selected?" Sadie tapped on one of the photos. "His name is Bernie Johnson."

"Are you doing this so Jane will quit driving you crazy?"

"Something like that."

"Mom told me Jane's getting on everyone's nerves. Lon agreed with her."

"Your mom's right. Jane doesn't have anything to do so she takes her frustration out by nitpicking everyone to pieces. She needs someone to fuss over."

"She's going to be mad. Really mad." Aanders exaggerated the words as he propped his elbows on the table and settled his fist against his cheek.

"What do you think of him?" Sadie tapped on the screen with a blue fingernail.

"He's old."

Sadie turned a disgusted glare in Aanders' direction. "He's supposed to be old." She ran her finger across the screen under his photo. "Not only does he go to church, but he likes to cook and clean."

Aanders jerked as Sadie shouted, "Whoo hoo. He's a winner. Can you imagine finding a man who likes to cook and is a neat freak, too? Jane will think she died and went to heaven."

"Mom says you meddle in Jane's business. She thinks it's going to bite you in the butt."

"I do not. Well maybe I do. Jane is so wishy-washy she can't make up her mind. So I made it up for her." Sadie tapped her temple. "I'm the one with the brains."

"Mom said Jane's the one with the brains."

Sadie's mouth fell open as she stared at Aanders. "I beg to differ. Who solved the Fossums' murder?"

"You did, but I helped. I'm the one who told you Tim could prove Paul Brinks murdered his dad."

"That's right. It took some doing, but we managed to solve the case." Sadie patted Aanders' hand. "I'm glad you believed Tim and insisted I listen to what he had to say."

Aanders looked at the computer screen. "Maybe Jane likes things the way they are. Maybe you should let her find her own man."

"And continue to watch her mope around all the time? Not on your life." Sadie hit the escape button. "I've arranged for him to check into Cabin 6 this weekend." Sadie closed the lid on the laptop. "I've booked a dinner reservation for them at Yerry's on the Bay. He wants to impress her. If Yerry's on the Bay doesn't impress her, nothing will."

"I know it's her favorite, but isn't it expensive?"

"So? I'm not paying for it."

"Jane's going to throw one of her snit fits and she'll do it right in front of Mr. Johnson. You'd better cancel before she finds out."

"It's too late. He's already on his way."

8

"Knock it off, Dan," Pam warned. She placed her arm on the back of the driver's seat and strained to look out the back window. Pam wiped her moist palms against her shirt. Dan's reckless attitude frayed her nerves into raw shreds. She watched the highway patrol disappear in the distance. "If you get a speeding ticket, they'll have record of us being in this county. He probably already ran our plates." She peered in the rearview mirror. "We're lucky nothing came of the speeding ticket you got last summer."

"Quit bitching. You always bitch when you're nervous." Dan hit the cruise control coast button several times allowing the car to slow down to the posted limit. "All you've done for the last hundred miles is criticize my driving."

Dan reached over and patted Pam's leg. "That patrol car went too fast to get a visual on our plates. Maybe he needed to take a piss." Dan slapped the steering wheel and laughed out loud. He reached over to tweak Pam under her chin. "Lighten up, woman. That's a joke."

Pam pushed his hand away. "Watch the road."

"You're acting like my mother. We've rehearsed our plan a million times. It ain't no different than the last one. We didn't get caught then, did we?"

Pam hated the memory of the last abduction. She hadn't expected to run into a former co-worker. She still worried the woman might reflect on their chance encounter and report it to the police. She hadn't summoned the courage to tell Dan about the near mishap. He didn't tolerate mistakes. The sooner their current task segued into history, the better. "I can't help it. You get so smug before we do a job, you become a different person."

"You worry about the same thing every time." Dan signaled to turn off the highway. "We're not going to get caught. Relax. When we pull up to the hospital, that's when you should get nervous."

Dan drove the rental car into the gas bay and climbed out of the vehicle. Bending back into the car, he reached across the driver's seat. "Give me some cash."

Waiting as Dan filled the tank, Pam whispered, "Why am I doing this?"

"You're doing it for the money," Dan snarled and dropped into the driver's seat. He grabbed Pam's wrist and yanked it toward him. "I told you there's nothing to worry about. Get a grip, Pam, or I'll do it myself."

Pulling her hand from his grasp, Pam rubbed her bruised flesh. "You couldn't do this without me and you know it. I'm the one who abducts the babies. I'm the one who earns the money. I'm the one who risks everything. Not you."

Dan took a deep breath. "You're right. You're right." He cupped Pam's face in his hand. "I apologize. You're the most important player on this team. Let's just chill. Everything's going to be all right."

Dan eased his way back onto the highway. He reached across the car and pulled his wife to his side. Placing a quick kiss against her temple, he said, "You're good at what you do, Babe. That's why you get away with it. With your Scandinavian features, you blend in like every other blond nurse in northern Minnesota."

"I'm lucky I fit in, but I'm afraid panic will get the best of me. I might screw up." Balling her hand into a fist Pam tapped her chest. "Last time my heart hammered so hard I almost passed out. I had to bite my lip to keep from screaming."

"You didn't. That's the point. You didn't. You pulled it off like a pro." He ran his hand along the back of her neck, kneading it gently.

She pushed his hand away. "You don't understand. I'm not sure I can go through with this anymore."

When she stood in Reggie's office, she exuded confidence and welcomed the challenge. Thinking back on it, it must have been the alcohol heightening her conviction. Since then, her courage had dwindled to a mere puff of air. The bolder Dan's bravado, the weaker her self-esteem.

"Then you really won't want to hear my new idea."

"What new idea?" Before Dan had a chance to take another breath, Pam repeated, "What new idea?"

"We can keep the money and cut out the middle man."

"You mean Reggie?"

"That's exactly who I mean." Dan pulled a sheet of paper from his shirt pocket and unfolded it. "Look what I've got. When I saw this on Reggie's desk, I noticed the name Franzen Kimmer. I remembered the name from when we visited Pinecone Landing last summer. Kimmer is a judge there. We're going to deal directly with him."

"We don't know the first thing…"

"It can't be that hard. He's already hooked up with Reggie. Imagine money beyond your dreams. Think about it Pam. We'll buy the house on Lake Minnetonka you've always wanted. I'll buy you cars and clothes and we'll travel all over the world."

Pam stared into the oncoming lane of traffic as she considered Dan's proposal.

"Reggie doesn't have a fancy office because he sits on his ass and shuffles papers all day. He's rich because of us. We take the risks. It's our hard work buying Reggie's toys."

Dan slapped the steering wheel. "It's not right he gets the biggest share when we do all the work."

"I do all the work," Pam said. "I do all the work." She leaned back against the headrest, closed her eyes, and drew a jagged breath. "Do you really think we could do it ourselves?"

"Absolutely, and you get all the credit for taking the risk."

The soothing hum of tires against the pavement eased Pam's stress while she pondered Dan's statement.

"Do you really think we can make enough to buy the house?"

"Of course. There's no limit. Consider what Reggie owns. Think about his car, his yacht, his mansion."

Pam threw her arms around Dan and kissed the side of his face repeatedly as he grasped the steering wheel with both hands.

She leaned forward and looked into Dan's eyes. "This is the last job we do for Reggie? After this we're on our own?" A hesitant smile betrayed her skepticism.

"Last one," Dan said. "He never appreciated us, anyway. You know what they say. Payback and friendly fire are one and the same."

"Then I'll do it."

Several miles passed while Pam stared at the road, contemplating her future.

"I found a couple more interesting names on the paper I took off Reggie's desk. They're attorneys in California. I looked them up on the internet." Dan's voice rose with excitement. "You should see all the attorneys on the West coast specializing in adoption. We can establish ourselves with some of them. Then when we snatch a kid, we can hop a plane and take care of business."

Pam pivoted to face Dan. "I'm good at setting things up. I have a flair for business. In fact, when I worked at the hospital, my director complimented me on my organization skills."

"There's the Pam I fell in love with," Dan said. "Why do you think I'm convinced we can do this? It's because you're good at what you do." He patted her leg and let his hand rest on her warm flesh.

Giddy with enthusiasm, Pam reveled in Dan's praise. She loved the rush she felt when he expressed his appreciation. Wait till her sister saw her new house on Lake Minnetonka. Pam always knew she had what it took to outdo her sister. Now she'd prove it.

"Remember you're the one who suggested we drive up to Pinecone Landing to check out the hospital." Dan placed his hand on her thigh and squeezed. "It was you who suggested getting a floor plan when you saw the new construction. I wouldn't have thought of anything so clever."

"You're also a genius to come up with those disguises. You know what I admire most about you? You're thorough."

Pam grinned, soaking up Dan's approval. Her elation abruptly evaporated as two marble pillars supporting the hospital portico glistened in the distance.

9

"Where have you been? Your soup's cold." Jane shook a metal whisk at Sadie as she walked through the cabin door. "You should have told me you'd be late."

"I didn't think I would be," Sadie said. "If Jed hadn't helped with the prep, I'd still be at the mortuary."

Jed followed Sadie through the door, grabbed a chair, and plunked down. "Hi Mr. Bakke." He tapped the urn, lifted the lid and shook the urn. Ash powder wafted through the air. Glancing sideways at Jane, he quickly brushed the powder off the table with the palm of his hand.

"Jed prepped his own body?" Jane's jaw hung in disbelief.

Sadie pulled a screw driver, a spiked dog collar, and a baggie containing a dead mouse from her purse and laid them on the table. "Darn. Where is it?" She rummaged further, retrieving a shiny tube of lipstick. She dabbed it on her upper lip. "What do you think?"

"I don't think Jed should embalm his own body. You probably broke some kind of mortuary code."

"It wasn't his body. Are you nuts? Do you really think there's a code saying you can't embalm your own body?" Sadie squinted at Jane in exasperation.

"What are you doing with a dead mouse in your purse?"

"I took it out of a trap in one of the cabins. You've never heard so much squealing in all your life."

"Poor thing."

"I'm not talking about the mouse. I'm talking about the guest in Cabin 2. I thought we'd have another customer for

Nan."

"Speaking of customers, did you see the newspaper this morning? I see they found Sally's body in the swamp behind the Fertile Turtle. The reporter quoted the sheriff as saying Sally must have wandered off looking for her mother. He said it appears she fell into the swamp when her foot became wedged between two fallen branches."

"I read the article." Sadie said. "At least they determined it wasn't foul play. The coroner shipped her body down to St. Paul for an autopsy and the funeral will be in Minneapolis where her grandmother lives."

"Poor Pete. First he lost custody of his daughter and now he has to deal with this." Jane released a sigh heavy with empathy.

Sadie crossed over to the mirror and pursed her lips. She dabbed at the excess lipstick before turning to Jane. "Don't you think this makes me look younger?"

"Younger? No. You know who you remind me of in that lipstick? You remind me of Hollywood. Remember her?"

"That's the same thing you said last time I bought new lipstick. I didn't like your comment then either. Hollywood's pasty makeup made her look like a cadaver with lipstick."

Jane smiled. "E-x-a-c-t-l-y. Now you know what I think about your lipstick." She turned the burner up under the soup kettle.

"For your information, I bought this color to go with my purple mini skirt."

"If you're wearing it to the Fertile Turtle tonight, I'm not going."

"Why? All the old ladies wear purple. It's what they're supposed to wear."

"Not when they bend over and don't have on underwear."

"I'm wearing underwear. I'm wearing a purple thong."

"Oh good Lord," Jed muttered, turning away from Sadie's exposed buttocks. "Why can't you dress like a respectable adult? Look how professional Jane looks."

"I'm not going to dress like Jane. I happen to like color."

"Who are you talking to? Is Jed here?" Jane put her hands on her hips and glowered at her chair. "He better not be sitting on my chair with his bare ass."

"How come Jane lets you sit on her chair with a bare butt, but I can't?" Jed tugged his hospital gown down around his hips.

"Because she hasn't added up the numbers yet," Sadie whispered, tapping her temple.

Turning her back on Sadie, Jane picked up a wooden spoon and slammed it into the stock pot. "I worked all day on this soup, and you can't even come home on time for supper."

"Somebody's cranky," Sadie said.

"I'm not cranky. I'm a nervous wreck." Jane shook the spoon at Sadie. "You made Aanders keep an eye on Sally while you helped Nan at the mortuary. She's a handful. Aanders darted around this cabin all afternoon, slamming doors and hollering while he tried to keep track of her." Jane sank into her chair. "I can't take much more of this."

"Where are they now?" Sadie watched Jed frown as he walked over to the window.

Jane groaned. "Why do you ask, you know I can't see her."

Sadie dipped a teaspoon into Jane's stock pot and took a sip. "What is this?"

"Oxtail soup." Jane placed two bowls on the table and a third bowl for Mr. Bakke.

Sadie had hoped Jane's grieving ritual would have diminished by now, but it hadn't. At least she'd quit putting food on Mr. Bakke's plate. Belly had gained nine pounds since Jane's best friend and love had passed.

Belly's toenails clicked against the wooden floor while he begged for a sample.

"You're not serving swinging sirloin again, are you? I'm tired of eating rear end."

Jed shifted in his chair and rubbed his eyes with two index fingers.

"Are you tired, Jed?" Sadie placed her hand on his shoulder.

"I must be. I'm seeing things." Jed leaned closer to the window.

"You're probably losing your stamina. That's not uncommon at this stage."

"I hope that's what it is." Jed craned his neck forward and gazed more intently through the window. "I don't believe it."

"What?"

"That looks like Clay going into Cabin 12."

"What? It can't be." Sadie joined Jed as he strode to the window. "Good grief, it is. What's he doing in Pinecone Landing?"

"What's going on?" Jane pulled the curtain aside and followed Sadie's gaze. "Is that Clay? Does Nan know he's back? If she doesn't, she's going to have a conniption."

Three raps against the screen door interrupted the trio's concentration.

"Sadie?" The resort manager's voice faltered. "Can I talk to you for a minute?"

Sadie waved him in. The manager blurted, "I made a mistake. A big mistake." He tiptoed quietly across the wooden flooring as if a silent approach would make him invisible. He joined them at the window.

"Are you sure it's Clay Harren?" Jane looked back toward Cabin 12. "I don't' remember Clay looking so heavy."

Eight disbelieving eyes watched Clay lift a second box out of his trunk and carry it into Cabin 12.

"I'm afraid so." The manager backed away from the window and cleared his throat. "I didn't realize it would be Clay who would occupy Cabin 12 when I signed the contract."

Jane removed her glasses and wiped them on her apron. She slid the bows back over her ears and leaned closer to the window. "What do you mean you didn't know it was Clay? He doesn't look tremendously different. How long has it been since you've seen him?"

"Clay didn't sign the contract."

Jed and the Witt sisters stared at the manager.

"Well?" Sadie's shrill remark caused the manager's elbows to jerk at his sides.

His Adam's apple rose slowly and sank. "Judge Kimmer signed the contract and paid for a year in advance. He said he wanted to rent it for a friend."

"A friend," Jane cried. "Since when is Clay a friend of Kimmer?"

Echoes of foreboding ping-ponged back and forth between the sisters.

"I'm sorry. I had no idea. If I'd have known, I wouldn't have signed the lease." A pallor of remorse dulled the manager's expression.

"Can't you cancel the lease?" Jed returned to the table. "Tell Kimmer someone else already rented it."

"Call Kimmer and tell him it's a mistake," Sadie said. "Tell him you already rented it to another party. We've got to get Clay out of there before Nan finds out."

Jane dropped into her chair. She rubbed her index

fingers against her temples. "I bet this is what Kimmer meant by bringing in reinforcements. He thinks we'll sell Cabin 12 just to get rid of Clay."

"Then he's mistaken." Sadie pointed at Jane. "You just sat on Jed."

Jane jumped out of her chair as the manager peered around Sadie and stared at the empty seat. He looked at Sadie and back at Jane.

Jane drew in a deep breath and set her jaw before noticing the manager's wide-eyed stare. She looked over the top of her glasses at her sister. "Somebody better be making their way toward the towel."

Puzzled, the manager inched toward the chair with the towel.

"Not you," Jane said. "You can sit over there."

Sadie paced the kitchen floor. "Go back to the lodge. Call Kimmer and tell him we're cancelling the lease."

"I already tried." The manager peered at the empty chair under the clock. "Judge Kimmer said he had a signed contract and we couldn't get out of it. He said he'd sue if we tried."

"That rat!" Sadie swallowed hard. The bitter taste of hatred stung her throat.

"How are you going to tell Nan?"

"Me?" Sadie shot Jane the evil eye. "Why do I always have to bear the bad news?"

"Because you're always in trouble."

The manager shifted his eyes from his lap to look at Sadie and dropped them back again.

Sadie gestured frantically. "This is going to devastate Lon. He loathes his cousin. It will end his romance with Nan." Sadie ran her hands through her spiked hair, dislodging an earring. She tried to catch it as it bounced off her shoulder. It skittered across the floor. She crossed the planking and bent to pick it up.

"Dear Lord," Jed said.

"Oh geez." The manager grimaced, looking even harder at the bony butt pointing at him. "You've got a tattoo?"

Sadie put her hand on her left cheek. "You mean this?" She pointed at the array of colors.

"What is it?" The manger grimaced again.

Sadie placed her hands on her hips. "It's Paul Bunyan."

"It is?" The manager wrinkled his nose. "Why would you put Paul Bunyan down there?"

"I needed a tattoo to cover my birthmark. I had to choose between two large tattoos and I didn't want Oinketta the Wonder Pig following me around forever." Sadie waited for the manager's reply as she watched Jed shake his head. "It's bad enough Oinketta's brother is trying to buy Cabin 12. I didn't need her on my ass, too."

Sadie appreciated her manager's capabilities when it came to running the resort. Anal to a fault, he'd make a good match for Jane if he wasn't thirty-five years too young. Sadly, his preference for cleanliness and minuscule details had squelched his sense of humor. Dipped it into the minus column.

"They make Oinketta tattoos?" The manager's upper lip skewed up to meet his nose as he stared at Sadie in disbelief.

Sadie had the urge to hand the manager a leaf of lettuce. He looked like a rabbit with his large front teeth exposed.

The manager jammed his hands into his pockets. "Speaking of Oinketta, she accompanied Kimmer when he signed the lease."

"Oinketta was here?" Sadie and Jane looked at one another.

"The cops took Oinketta's driver's license away," the manager said. "I heard Kimmer gives her a ride to town now and then. Maybe that's all it was."

"I doubt it." Foreboding darkened Sadie's expression. "She'd do anything to coattail her brother's authority. Every time she sees us she rubs in the fact he's a judge."

"I didn't know she'd lost her license," Jane said. "That must be why she drives down the highway on her riding mower."

"That's what happens when your car crashes through the church wall and ends up in the elevator shaft." The manager chuckled. "I'd have given a free month's rent to see how the firemen hoisted her car out of the pit."

Glancing at his watch, the manager reached for the door. "We've got guests coming in a few minutes. I'd better get back to the lodge."

"I just realized we're missing the obvious." Jed watched the manager cross the lawn. "I'm supposed to figure out what held me back. I think my unfinished business has something to do with Clay. If he's still drinking, maybe I'm supposed to scare him straight."

"That isn't possible." Sadie waved her hand in dismissal. "Nobody can scare Clay straight. You can't unpickle his brain."

"Don't' be so sure. I'm the one who has to figure it out. I'm the one who's dead."

Sadie didn't like Jed's wry challenge. Most crossers lingered in denial. Not Jed. He acknowledged his demise. He also cleverly avoided tackling his decision by making others his priority. First Sally. Now Clay. But not his sister. That conflicted with Jed's original insistence the sheriff keep Celeste's case open after it had been declared a cold case.

Sadie tapped a manicured fingernail on the table. "You've got one issue to solve and it's to find out what happened to Celeste." She grabbed his fist as he rose from the chair. "Sit down, Jed. You've skirted this issue long enough. You owe it to Celeste. Something happened to her and you need to figure it out."

Sadie opened the drawer on the sideboard, pulled out a pad of paper and a pen. She handed it to Jed. "Start writing."

"Start writing what?"

"Start with the year before her disappearance and make notes. Where did she work? Who did she date? Did anything odd happen you know about?"

"While you're writing, Jane and I have to figure out why Kimmer rented Cabin 12. That scares me."

10

"Did you really let Jed put his own makeup on after you embalmed him?"

"Sure. Why not?" Impatience etched Sadie's face as she watched her sister. "He knows he's dead."

Jane grasped the neck of her blouse and fanned it against the clinging heat. "That's a bit morbid, isn't it?" She pulled the rotating fan close to the kitchen table before pressing the on button.

"I let him select his own clothes, too. His folks brought a couple shirts when they met with Nan. He picked his favorite."

"What about pants?"

"We rarely put pants on the deceased," Sadie said. "No one realizes it because it's hidden below the casket's lower lid." The corner of Sadie's mouth twitched upward as she watched Jane mull her comment.

"You're kidding. That's disgusting. You better put pants on me. I'm not going to meet my maker naked from the waist down."

Jane glared at her sister, crossed her arms, and pressed her back into the chair rungs. The glare eased into compassion. "Did Jed see his folks when they came to the mortuary to view his body? I can't imagine seeing them and not being able to tell them he stood next to them."

"He saw them." A sigh of sorrow escaped as Sadie relived the scene. "There are events too private to be witnessed by bystanders. Jed's encounter with his parents was one of them. At first Jed sobbed in the background while his parents stood over his body. Then he stopped. It seemed he had flipped a fortification switch." Sadie had watched the gentle giant run the back of his fingers down his mother's cheek before he patted his father's shoulder. Pure devotion filled the room. Intrusion had not been Sadie's intent.

Tears spilled from Jane's eyes and settled on her apron while she listened to Sadie relive the experience.

"I wanted to shout out and tell Jed's mother how much he loved her. Then Jed touched my arm. 'She knows,' he said. 'She's always known.'"

The bond linking the twins constricted as the image overwhelmed them. An unbearable loss. An unbearable reality. An unbearable sorrow.

"That's the second child they've lost." Jane dabbed at her eyes with her apron. "Who's going to take care of them now?"

"Jed provided for them in his will."

"That sounds like Jed." Jane's shoulders sagged.

A loud clap of thunder broke. Jane spread her arms wide in front of the rotating fan. "I hope the rain brings relief."

Sadie paged through the mail Jane had placed on the bookshelf. "Did my Victoria's Secret catalog come today?"

"No. If it had, I would have dropped it in a trash barrel on my way back from the mailbox. You've got enough sexy underwear. Why can't you buy regular underwear like I do?"

"Because I refuse to wear my waistband up under my boobs like you do."

Jane's hand slid to her stomach. She frowned and pushed at the elastic with her thumb.

Sadie grabbed her purse. "I'm going to the nursing home to gather Jed and Sally. I'll be right back."

"I'm going with you." Jane slipped her fingers through the handles on a plastic bag and followed her sister onto the porch.

"You are?"

"Someone needs to wipe off the shuttle seats." She held up a spray bottle and a roll of paper towels.

Jane braced against the dash as Sadie started to pull away from the parking spot. "Wait," she shouted. "There's Aanders."

Sadie pushed the gear into park.

Aanders slipped into the back seat. "Thanks for waiting." He ran his fingers along the tufted purple fabric lining the door. "I'm sure glad you bought this hearse from Mom. It's really cool." He stretched his legs across the back seat and nestled into the soft fabric.

Sadie pulled out onto Witt's Lane.

"Don't encourage her," Jane grumbled. "It's ridiculous she thought this would make a resort shuttle. How would you like to wait for a shuttle at the airport and a hearse pulls up beside you? That would scare the bejesus out of anyone."

A huge grin crossed Aanders' face. "Who wouldn't want to ride in a hearse? It has the Witt's End Shuttle sign on the door, so people should understand." Observing Jane's wilting glare, he slunk back against the seat.

"Is your signal broken?" Sadie jerked at Jane's shrill voice piercing the air.

"No. Why?" Sadie tested the signal up and down.

"You didn't signal when you turned onto the road."

"Signaling is for tourists. I know where I'm going."

Jane unrolled two paper towels and tore them from the roll. "Did you see the new guest who checked in this morning? When he walks, he looks like a flamingo riding a bicycle. I've never seen such long, skinny legs."

"What's with you and flamingos? First you criticize my hair color, now you're criticizing a man's legs."

"You're the one who said I never use my imagination. So

I used it. That's exactly what he looks like minus the feathers." Jane jutted her chin in defiance.

"What cabin is he in?" Aanders cast a wary peek at Sadie.

"Cabin 6."

"Have you met him yet?" Sadie returned Aanders' anxious glance.

"Met him? Why would I? I don't meet all our guests. I suppose you think I'm not being a good host because I didn't meet him." Jane squeezed the spray trigger and a scented mist settled over the paper towel cupped in her hand. She handed the wad to Aanders. "Wipe off the fabric on the back seat."

"You seem to know a lot about his legs, so I thought you met him," Sadie said.

"Oh pish posh." A strand of hair escaped from behind Jane's ear as she spritzed another layer of paper towels. "Now where did Jed sit this morning?"

"He always sits in the same spot in back. Aanders just cleaned it. Now I can hang a sign on the side of the van declaring the shuttle is 'pecker-track free'."

"Sadie! Shame on you. Aanders shouldn't have to listen to your vulgar comments."

Aanders tried to stifle a snicker before tucking his chin against his chest.

"I told you to quit encouraging Sadie." Jane contorted her body to stare at Aanders over the front seat. She clenched her fists behind her elbows as she crossed her arms. "I fibbed."

"You what?" Sadie looked at her sister.

"I said I fibbed."

"A little lie now and then doesn't hurt. What did you lie about?"

"It wasn't a lie. Just a fib."

"Okay. What did you fib about?" Sadie set her jaw in anticipation. She guessed Jane had tossed her favorite catalog in the trash after all. Jane had been overly accommodating all morning. Syrupy and clingy. She had even changed Sadie's bed and washed her sheets. One for the history book.

"I met the flamingo man."

Aanders' head swiveled from Jane to Sadie.

Apprehension wafted overhead as Sadie stared at Jane. As Jane sank lower into the passenger seat, Sadie coaxed, "And?"

"And nothing." Jane tightened her elbows against her fists.

"Then why mention it? You've met other guests before."

There it was. Jane's evasive posture. Ignore the question and all will be well. Sadie had put up with this annoying habit for the past six months since Mr. Bakke's death.

Jane stared out the window as tree after tree after tree disappeared behind them. Her gaze wandered to the rearview mirror. "Quit looking at Aanders. Keep your eyes on the road."

"I wonder if Jed had any luck today," Aanders said. "He told me about a man at the nursing home who wasn't doing well."

"Jed hasn't concentrated enough on his declaration. He's not ready to go yet." Relieved Aanders had changed the subject, Sadie added, "It's my fault because I haven't been firm enough with him. I'm going to insist Jed discuss Celeste tonight at our session. I still think his sister is the reason he failed to cross over."

Jane shifted back and forth in her seat before blurting, "Well if you must know, I'm going for a boat ride after supper."

"I didn't need to know." Sadie shot a confused look

toward Jane.

"What do you mean you didn't need to know? You forced it out of me."

Sadie observed Jane over the top of her lime and pink polka-dot rimmed glasses.

"Are you going with Aanders?"

"With Aanders?" Jane let out an aggravated sigh. "Not with Aanders. With Bernie Johnson, the guest from Cabin 6."

Aanders sat back in his seat. His foot beat nervously against the door.

"That's nice," Sadie said, talking into the mirror.

"No it's not. I feel terrible. I should've never agreed to go."

"That's ridiculous." Sadie pulled up under the nursing home portico and stopped in front of the 'No-Parking sign'. "You've got to start dating sooner or later."

"It's not a date. It's a boat ride. You wouldn't call it a date if I went for a ride with Aanders, would you?"

"No. I'd call it an Amber Alert. There's no way Aanders will ever go with you in the boat again."

"Well I didn't mean to tip it over. Are you ever going to let me forget?"

As Jed and Sally climbed into the shuttle, a nurse waved at Aanders and shouted through the open hearse window, "I saw your dad at the grocery store. I bet you're glad he's back."

Aanders waved back at the woman before looking toward Sadie.

Sadie swiveled in the driver's seat. "Did you know your dad had returned to Pinecone Landing?"

Aanders nodded.

"Does your mom know?"

Aanders shrugged.

"Do you want to talk about it?"

"No"

Jed reached across the seat and patted Aanders' leg. "What did your dad say? Did he tell you why he's back?"

Aanders stared through the window.

Jed tapped Aanders on the arm. "I'm talking to you. I'd appreciate an answer."

A tear rolled down Aanders' cheek followed by a second. "He didn't recognize me."

Jane turned to peer over the seat at the tearful child. "I'm sorry, Aanders. How long has it been since your dad saw you?"

"Five years. I sent him my school picture each year. I don't understand why he didn't recognize me." He swiped at his damp cheek with the back of his hand.

"Did you go to his cabin?" Sadie looked at him through the review mirror.

"No. I ran an errand for my mom and when I walked by Cabin 12 I saw him on the porch. At first I couldn't believe it was him. When I waved and hollered, he looked at me and kept folding the money Kimmer had given him. Then he went in the cabin."

Sadie looked in the rearview mirror and uttered, "Kimmer? Do you mean Kimmer and Clay were on the porch? Together?"

"Yup. I saw Kimmer hand him some money."

"Are you sure?"

"Of course I'm sure. I saw it."

"Do you know if your Mom is aware Clay's back in town?"

"I doubt it. If she knew, we'd have heard about it. She's not going to like that you rented to Dad."

"Don't worry," Sadie said. "I'll think of a way to tell her."

11

"Thanks for filling in, Sadie. One of our clerks called in sick this morning." The resort manager pressed a button on the two-way radio and announced four new guests had arrived and needed an escort to their cabins. A courtesy cart pulled up in front of the lodge. The manager lifted the guests' bags onto the luggage carrier before helping them onto the cart.

"Whenever you need me, just holler." Sadie watched the cart head for Cabin 4 as the manager rounded up a group of binocular-toting bird watchers and led them down the paved path and into the woods.

"Welcome to Witt's End," Sadie said, as a man approached the reception desk and pulled out his billfold.

The man looked at Sadie then swept his gaze around the room. He turned back to the desk, his scrutinizing stare settled on Sadie's tattoo.

"I'm Sadie. Can I help you?"

"I'd like to register."

Sadie pulled the computer keyboard to the edge of the counter. "Name?"

"Do you work here?"

"Yes. I'm Sadie Witt and I own the place." Sadie grinned broadly at the man. She patted her chartreuse gelled spikes and gave one of her asp earrings a tug.

"Wow. You're not what I expected. Who's pictured on the brochure?" He pointed at an acrylic stand next to the cash register.

"That's my sister. I used to be on the brochure, but our

78

manager suggested I take my picture off. He thought it would look more professional." Sadie pulled her glasses down and looked at the man over the rims. "He's a fuddy-duddy. He thinks he knows all there is to know about marketing."

The man smiled and handed Sadie his confirmation. "Avery. Dan, Pam, and Chelsie," he said.

After reading the confirmation number, Sadie entered the Avery's information into the computer and pulled a key for Cabin 9 from the locator board. "Congratulations on the birth of your daughter. When your wife called and said you might not be able to make it because of her due date, we felt bad."

"We're lucky. Pam delivered early, so the timing worked for us."

Sadie stretched to look past Dan. "Can I see her?"

"Chelsie's in the car with Pam. She's sleeping." He lifted the brochure from the stand and fanned it open. "Looks like you've got a lot going on."

Sadie pointed out some of the resort's featured items. "Let us know if you need anything. Did I mention the marina has several rentals available?"

"We probably won't do much on the lake. We've waited a long time for Chelsie and want to spend time with her before we go back to work."

"If you change your mind, I'll watch her for you. I love babies. We also have staff available to baby-sit."

Dan Avery glanced at the wrinkled tattoo peeking out from beneath Sadie's chartreuse tank top. "Thanks for the offer, but I don't think we'll need a sitter."

"Do you want to pay with a credit card?"

"You don't mind if I pay in cash, do you?"

"Not at all. What the IRS doesn't know won't hurt them."

Dan's eyes twinkled in agreement as a grin parted his

lips. He slid his change back in his billfold. "By the way, nice tattoo."

The three o'clock ice-cream cone rush dwindled to a handful of patrons who lingered on the deck under striped umbrellas. Sadie wove her way among her guests. She stopped and listened to exaggerated tales of fishing escapades uttered by members of a group who had booked five cabins for a family reunion. The throng clustered on the lakeside deck. Their children ran helter-skelter through the maze of adults while toddlers clutched at available knees and traipsed through a forest of legs. Shrieks of glee echoed over the bay.

After tweaking a few cheeks on her way through the crowd, Sadie waited until Dan and Pam Avery settled comfortably onto deck chairs. "Quite a hullabaloo, isn't it?"

Shaded by a heavy pine eave, Dan scanned the crowd. "Looks like a huge gathering. They seem to know each other."

"It's a family reunion. You're one of the few couples not related to them." Sadie stuck her hand out. "You must be Pam."

"You must be Sadie. My husband told me about you," Pam said, releasing Sadie's hand.

"We've actually met quite a few of the reunion crowd." Dan tossed a colorful beach ball back to a child who had kicked it against his deck chair.

"I think you have the only sleeping child in the whole resort," Sadie said.

Pam smiled down at the pink bundle in her arms. "I had trouble getting Chelsie back to sleep. The noise doesn't seem to bother her now, so I'm going to enjoy the view while she's sleeping."

"I won't ask to peek at her, then. How old is she?"

"She's seven days old," Dan replied.

A small hand tugged at Sadie. "Can we go out in the boat?"

Sadie pulled Sally into her hip and patted her head. "Later," she whispered.

Pam looked up. "Pardon me?"

Sadie's eyes grew wide as she saw Sally lift the blanket off the baby's face.

Pam looked down at Chelsie and drew a sharp breath. She quickly pulled the blanket back over the child's face. She looked at her husband. "Don't move the blanket, Dan. I don't want her to wake up."

"I didn't."

"Yes you did, you uncovered the baby's face."

Dan looked toward Chelsie. "No, I didn't."

Pam looked down at Chelsie's again exposed head. She quickly covered it. She looked sideways at Dan. "I didn't realize the breeze had such strength."

"It creeps up when you're least expecting it." Sadie reined in Sally's outstretched hand. "It's a lake phenomenon."

"We're going to need directions to the courthouse," Dan said. "We've got an appointment with Judge Kimmer."

Sadie's brows shot up. "Kimmer? You know Judge Kimmer?"

"Not yet. We're looking forward to meeting him. He's an acquaintance of a friend of ours."

After giving directions, Sadie waved farewell and headed toward the marina.

Dan waved back. As soon as Sadie disappeared around the corner, he said, "You idiot. You've got to be more careful."

"Me?" Pam looked around and lowered her voice. "Whose stupid idea made us sit out here in the first place?

Yours. How was I supposed to know the wind would flip the blanket?"

"Be more careful next time."

"There's not going to be a next time. I'm staying in the cabin from now on. If that weird woman suspects anything, we're in trouble."

"Don't be an imbecile. We're too close to hitting it big. People don't go on vacation to sit in their cabins. If we don't blend in, she'll get suspicious."

Pam held the baby close and stood up. "What did Sadie have on her belly? It made me cringe."

"I don't know. It looked like a worm. I suppose because she owns a fishing resort, she put a worm on her belly." Dan tapped Chelsie's blanket. "Sadie offered to baby-sit."

"You're kidding. Can you imagine waking up to an old woman with a spiked hairdo? Talk about damaging a child for life. Whatever color that was, they should throw away the bottle."

Dan leaned back in his chair. "We actually lucked out. Sadie took a liking to us. She might be able to give us information about Judge Kimmer. We need an edge if this is going to work."

12

Jed pulled out Jane's chair and sat at the kitchen table. He tapped the urn. "Hi Mr. Bakke."

Sadie and Aanders joined him and both offered similar words of greeting to their departed friend.

"I still think I didn't cross over because it's my responsibility to scare Clay straight," Jed said. "If he can't see me, I might have an impact on him by making him think he's crazy. Maybe it will get him to quit drinking. In fact, I'm positive it's why I was held back."

"Nonsense. Clay has nothing to do with you being held back." Sadie pointed toward the drawer. "Get your list out. Let's see what you wrote about Celeste."

The screen door banged against the frame. "See you later," Jane shouted.

Sadie, Aanders, and Jed watched Jane try to keep up with Bernie Johnson's incredibly long strides as they walked toward the marina.

Jed unfolded two sheets of paper. "I wasn't sure what you wanted, so I wrote what I remembered. Celeste moved here to live with my folks after her divorce. She took a job with Franzen Kimmer as his secretary."

"I remember," Sadie said. "We all wondered why she'd take a job in a one-man office after she'd worked in a corporation."

"Your sister worked for Kimmer?" Aanders leaned closer to the table.

"She took a job in Kimmer's law office because his other secretary left. Celeste welcomed the change. He offered a good salary and an up-front bonus and Celeste liked the idea of a one-boss-one-support-staff office. In other words, no more ass-kissing to compete for a job. She also said Kimmer hired her because of her experience. Of course, it took place before Kimmer became a judge."

"Her looks didn't hurt, either." Sadie put a check mark next to the first line on Jed's list.

"Probably not. Celeste was a stunning woman."

"Then what?"

Jed wrapped his feet around the chair legs and leaned on the table. "Celeste worked for him for about three months. Then something happened. She became withdrawn. Sometimes tearful, sometimes anxious, but she wouldn't talk about it."

"You have no idea what caused it?" Aanders leaned forward waiting for Jed's answer.

"Nope. Something scared her. She said she couldn't tell me because she didn't want me involved."

"You told the sheriff about this?" Sadie pulled Mr. Bakke's urn close and rotated it back and forth.

"I did. Because I'm related, they wouldn't give me much information. I dated the secretary at the police station a couple years after Celeste disappeared and she let me see the reports. It looks like the police did a thorough job of checking everything they could. When they talked to Kimmer about it, he said he hadn't noticed anything other than Celeste had been high strung before her disappearance. He told them she had been doing a great job."

"Think about those weeks leading up to her disappearance again. Are you sure you don't have any idea what frightened Celeste?" Sadie continued to jiggle the urn.

"Nope. She said the less I knew the better. After a few more weeks of my trying to pry information, she called late one night and said she had something to show me. She didn't want Mom and Dad to know I arranged to meet her."

Aanders sat forward in his chair. "What did she show you?"

"I don't know. She never showed up."

Sadie clearly remembered Celeste's disappearance. The majority of town folk had volunteered to search the rural areas surrounding Pinecone Landing. Then fifteen years slipped away. In spite of Jed's efforts, the crime team's search dwindled to nothingness, resurrected only by a few sporadic sightings of the missing woman. The local newspaper featured a small front-page article the day 'Cold Case' had been stamped on her folder. The folder and evidence box ended up tucked away on a shelf in the courthouse basement.

"I know you'll disagree, but I have to give Kimmer credit for offering a reward," Jed said.

"Actually I do agree," Sadie replied. "One-hundred-thousand dollars is quite a reward."

"Kimmer really came through for my folks. He held off hiring a new secretary because he felt sure she'd come back. They appreciated the gesture. They still sing his praises."

"I never thought I'd hear Kimmer and praise in the same sentence."

"At the time he seemed genuine. He figured Celeste had run off with someone she fell in love with. Kimmer thought it might be a guy my folks wouldn't approve of." Jed shook his head. "Her disappearance devastated my folks. Mom never got her spark back."

"Kimmer doesn't have a kind bone in his body. I'll bet he covered for the man she ran off with," Sadie said.

An hour of digging into the recesses of Jed's brain passed before the cabin door banged shut behind Jane. "What a nice man." She drew in a satisfied breath. "I'm so glad I agreed to go."

"What's he like." Sadie pulled a chair out for her sister and patted the seat.

"A perfect gentleman. We went to his cabin for iced tea instead of a boat ride. You should see how neat he is. There wasn't one thing out of place. Can you believe he likes to clean?" Jane's eyes sparkled.

"So he's a keeper?"

"As far as I know, he's only here for the weekend."

Sadie persisted. "You'd be willing to see him again?"

Cocking her head to one side, Jane tugged at her collar points. "I think so."

"Good. Because Aanders and I got his name off a seniors' dating site and invited him for the weekend."

"I didn't invite him." Aanders held his palms up and stepped back. "Sadie did. Her idea, not mine."

"You what?" Jane's words grated like chalk on a blackboard. "You what?"

"You heard me. I selected him as your date."

"How could you? Are you out of your mind?"

Sally closed the inner room door and clacked across the floor in Sadie's orange platform shoes. "Mom said everyone knows Sadie's crazy."

Jane paced in front of the kitchen table. "No wonder he knew so much about me. What did you tell him?" Before Sadie answered, Jane added, "Now I'll never be able to face him."

"That's ridiculous. If you like him, what's wrong with seeing him again?"

"He'll think I'm not capable of finding my own dates."

"He already knows. I explained it when I posted your photo on the website." Sadie grimaced as Jane let out another shriek. "You don't think men will come here without knowing what you look like, do you? You could be Oinketta the Wonder Pig for all they know."

Jane planted her fists firmly on her hips. The veins in her neck pulsed. Her lips barely moved as she growled, "What photo did you use?"

Aanders hugged his arms across his chest and slid lower in his chair. Jed tried to do the same, but his butt cheeks stuck to the chair.

"The picture of you on the porch swing." Sadie pointed to a photo on the bookshelf.

"Sadie Witt. I'm never going to speak to you again."

"Why? Bernie agreed to meet you, didn't he? He must have found something intriguing in your photo."

"Tell Jane I like her picture," Jed said. "Tell her she looks prim and proper."

"Jed said to tell you he liked your photo. He thinks you look sexy."

Jed let out a gasp. "That's not what I said."

"At least he didn't cancel like the other man did." Aanders looked at Jane.

Jane's head swiveled so fast she tilted sideways. "You mean someone cancelled a date with me? Why?"

"Actually, I cancelled your date," Sadie said. "For one reason, he barely spoke English. Do you remember last week when you answered the phone and you couldn't understand what the caller wanted?"

"You mean the Chinese man?"

"That's the one. Every time he responded to my emails, all he talked about was sex."

"Sadie. Not in front of Aanders."

"I know all about sex. My friends told me." Aanders blushed and lowered his chin to his chest.

"You made it sound like you had another reason to

cancel." Jane shot a curious glance at her sister. "Are you going to tell me?"

"He sounded too frisky for you. From what I understood, he kept talking about what he wanted to do with his toes. It was either his toes or a hose."

A hearty laugh escaped from Jed before he covered his mouth with his fist.

"What?" Aanders and Jane posed the question at the same time.

"It had to do with fishing." Sadie rose and opened the fridge. "Ice tea anyone?"

"He fishes with his toes?" Aanders directed his question toward Jed.

Jed nodded at Sadie. "You're the one who brought it up. I'm not going to explain Kama Sutra to these two."

"It doesn't matter. What matters is Jane's interested in Bernie Johnson."

A commercial blared from the television as Sally dropped the remote and wandered over to the window. Pressing her nose against the screen, she said, "Bernie Johnson is that man's dad."

"What?" Sadie crossed the floor and stood behind Sally. "What man?"

"That man over there." Sally pointed to a man unloading his fishing gear from a pontoon.

Jed lifted Sally off the floor after he joined Sadie at the window. "Did Mr. Johnson's family come with him?"

"I don't think so." Sadie frowned. "No I'm sure they didn't. Why would he bring them on a weekend date? It's a one bedroom cabin."

"He called him Dad when he got on the pontoon," Sally said.

Jed kissed Sally's forehead. "I think you misunderstood.

It must have sounded like Dad, but I'm sure it wasn't."

"What are you looking at," Jane joined Sadie at the window.

"That man on the pontoon," Sadie explained, pointing at the man.

"What about him?"

"Sally said he's Mr. Johnson's son."

Jane stepped closer to the window and stared at the man. "No he isn't. Mr. Johnson told me he didn't have any children."

"Yes he does," Sally said. "They talked about fishing. Then he shouted, 'Bye, Dad'."

13

"This would be Sadie," Sadie said, answering the phone. She jotted down directions to the retrieval site and handed the note to Nan.

"I've asked you to say Harren Funeral Home when you answer the phone, not 'this would be Sadie'."

"I forgot." Sadie pointed toward the embalming room. "I've finished with the other body, so I'll go with you."

"Oh no you won't." Nan used her body to barricade the door. "You're not going anywhere looking like... like you look."

Sadie grimaced. Nan drew a deep breath to repeat her favorite lecture for the umpteenth time. Sadie knew it by heart. If Nan would set aside her bias and appreciate a senior citizen's unique traits, it would be a tad easier to work for her. Just because the profession demanded protocol, didn't mean she couldn't tweak it now and then.

Nan jingled the hearse keys. "Go change your clothes. Wear the black outfit I bought you. If you're not ready in ten minutes, I'm leaving without you."

"What's wrong with this outfit? It's new. I got it yesterday."

Nan calmly gave Sadie the once over. Her shoulders settled as she sighed, a calming sigh perfected by those in her profession. Cupping her hands in front of her chest, she blinked twice. She tilted her head to one side. "You're wearing an orange shirt and zebra leggings. You're supposed to be in black." She pointed at Sadie's hair. Her mouth opened, but nothing came out.

Sadie patted her gelled spikes. "What's wrong with it? Big Leon said everyone's wearing their hair like this."

"You've got orange glitter falling out of your hair. It's clinging to your lenses."

Sadie squinted trying to look at the inside of her glasses. "The loose stuff will fall off before we get there."

"Then there'll be glitter all over the front seat of the hearse."

Sadie never dreamed anyone could one-up Jane when it came to cleanliness. Nan could. Sadie was convinced they both came into the world toting vacuum cleaners, dust rags, spritz bottles and a strong desire to rid the world of bacteria. She'd better ditch the glitter before they left on the retrieval. If she didn't, she'd get the evil eye. Nan's evil eye was a lot worse than Jane's piercing glare.

Black clothes and depression mirrored one another. At least Sadie believed her theory held merit. Lime. Orange. Purple. Red. That's what people should wear. She'd never met anyone with a healthy disposition who wore black. Well maybe one. The more she looked at Nan, the more Sadie realized her boss looked darn spiffy in her black suit. Sadie had to give Nan credit for maintaining a positive nature.

When an earlier retrieval call came in, Nan had changed from a pair of blue shorts and a T-shirt into her black suit. Her right leg peeked through a sexy slit in her midi-length skirt. Sadie watched her lift her blond bob from her neck, gather it in her hand, and slip a band around it. Blond curls sprung loose. The humidity raised havoc with Nan's wavy hair and she managed it by securing it at the nape of her neck. If Nan would only make an appointment with Big Leon. He could do wonders.

"There you are," Jane announced as she walked through the funeral home door. Bernie Johnson ducked to avoid the top of the door frame as he followed Jane over the threshold.

"You must be Bernie." Nan drew her gaze up and extended a hand.

"Nice facility," Bernie said, looking around the lobby. "A lot cheerier than most."

"Busy place." Lon followed Bernie in and closed the door behind him.

A yelp pierced the air as Belly protested in pain. "Sorry fella." Lon patted Belly on the back after he straightened the zebra bandana. "I didn't know you were behind me." He walked over to Nan and kissed her cheek. "What's going on?"

"We're getting ready to go on a retrieval."

Lon leaned close to Nan. "You're letting Sadie go dressed like that?"

Jane beamed up at Bernie. "I'm giving Bernie the grand tour. This is our last stop."

"I've been in lots of funeral homes, but not any connected to a resort." Bernie chuckled and patted Jane's hand. "Kind of like the last resort."

Jane screeched with laughter. "Stop it. I'm getting a sore side from laughing so much."

Sadie squinted a one-eye, brow-lowering, you're too obvious squint.

"Nan? Did Sadie tell you I met Bernie through an internet dating site? It's a website for seniors."

"Sadie didn't tell me, but Aanders did. I'm glad you stopped by. I wanted to tell you about the fund Mr. Bakke established for Bakke Manor. I added to the balance this morning and we've got enough money to break ground this summer."

Jane clasped her hands in front of her chest. "I can't believe it. Mr. Bakke would be so proud. It was his life dream to establish a home for the mentally challenged."

"You're going to get calls from Social Services," Lon said. "They've already gotten wind of it. Our dispatcher took a few calls from outlying agencies this morning."

"We've needed this for a long time. Thanks to Mr. Bakke, Pinecone Landing will benefit from his dream." Nan put an arm around Jane and pulled her close.

"Thanks to you, too, Nan. You've worked hard to make sure it happened. I'm sure Mr. Bakke's smiling down on you."

"Mr. Bakke was my friend." Jane looked up at Bernie. "He believed our mentally challenged would be better served in a mainstream setting than in an institution."

"I agree," Bernie said. "We've got several similar homes in Minneapolis."

Jane grabbed Bernie's hand and led him through the viewing rooms, explaining as she went. They disappeared down the stairs to the prep area.

"Wow," Lon whispered. "Jane's smitten. I never thought she'd experience romance again."

"She's gone goofy." Sadie waved her hand in irritation. "It's only been a day and a half since she met him, but she's already bossing him around. I hope he doesn't regret responding to her singles ad."

"At least she's got something go do." Lon's voice dropped as Jane reentered the lobby.

"Well?" Jane walked toward Sadie.

"Well what?"

"Did you tell her yet?"

Sadie's back stiffened. The surge of confidence Jane had gained from Bernie's constant attentions blared like a trumpet announcing a contest. The blame game had begun and Sadie had to make a move.

"I thought you'd like to tell her," Sadie said.

"Me? Why me?"

"Tell who what?" Nan lowered a hip onto the desk and sat next to Lon. A gaze of concern locked on Jane.

"Clay is living in Cabin 12."

"What?" Nan shot to her feet.

"Our manager rented Cabin 12 to Clay by mistake." Jane tugged at her collar points. "You tell her, Sadie."

"You can't be serious." Lon stood and stepped toward Sadie. "What is she talking about? Clay hasn't been around for years."

Sadie patted the air with her palms. "Just relax. I'll explain."

Nan's ashen tone against her black suit concerned Sadie. "You need to sit down."

Lon led Nan to the lobby sofa, turned her around, and backed her onto the cushion. "Is he really living at the resort? Why would you rent to him? Are you out of your mind?" The words tumbled from his lips in one angry stream.

After listening to Sadie's explanation, Nan said, "You've got to get him out of there. I don't want Aanders anywhere near his father."

"We can't. We already checked. Kimmer signed the lease and threatened to sue if we try to cancel."

"Kimmer? What's Kimmer got to do with it?" Lon stared at Sadie.

"Kimmer approached our manager and rented Cabin 12. He paid a year in advance. He told him he rented it for a friend. A year lease is rare and we need the money. Our manager had no idea Kimmer rented it for Clay."

Nan grabbed Lon's arm. "Isn't there anything you can do to break the lease?"

"I doubt it. I'm sure Kimmer would sue if Sadie tried to void the lease. I'll bet Kimmer thinks you'll sell the cabin if Clay is living there."

"Over my rotting, shriveled, stinking body," Sadie said.

Nan paced in front of the sofa. "Kimmer used Clay in the past to do his dirty deeds. He bartered for booze. Remember when Clay got caught breaking into Kimmer's folks' cabin after Sadie bought it? I never did understand why Kimmer bailed him out. Then Clay left town. I'll bet Kimmer had a hand in Clay's hasty departure." Nan stabbed the air with her index finger. "They acted like the episode was a drunken mistake, but I didn't believe it."

"I didn't either," Lon said. "Sadie dropped the charges so we never found out what Clay was up to."

"We didn't need more aggravation. Tourist season was at the summer peak and I wanted to forget the whole thing," Sadie replied.

"Me too," Nan agreed. She turned toward Lon. "I'm so sorry. I had no idea Clay had moved back. This is devastating."

"It's not your fault." Lon took Nan's hand. "We just need to figure out what Kimmer's up to."

"How will I tell Aanders?" Lines of concern rimmed Nan's forehead.

"He already knows. He caught a glimpse of Clay and tried to approach him." Taking a bracing breath, Sadie added, "Clay didn't recognize him."

"Oh, no." Lon put his arm around Nan as she moaned in anguish. "I can't imagine how Aanders felt."

"You better talk to your cousin, Lon. See if he'll tell you why he came back," Jane said.

"That's exactly what I'm going to do. Nan's getting her life back together and I'm not going to let him ruin it. I don't like this. I don't like it one bit."

14

Pam set the baby bottle on the Adirondack chair as she took in the breathtaking view. A flock of Grosbeaks circled overhead before landing to vie for the limited number of morsels scattered under a tree. What began as sociable jabber rose to a frenzied pitch. Pam smiled. If everything went right, she and Dan would own their own lake home and she'd experience this same slice of heaven every day for the rest of her life.

"Damn it, Pam," Dan mumbled under his breath. He dropped into the wooden chair next to her. "I told you to keep the baby in the cabin."

Pam shifted the pink bundle in her arms and looked back toward the shore.

"Did you hear me? Take her inside." Dan held a beer bottle out toward Pam. "Do you want this or not? I don't have all day."

"You suggested we made sure everyone saw the baby. You said we needed to blend in."

"I changed my mind. That ditzy broad has been snooping around. What if the wind blows the blanket again?" He turned sharply to the right at the sound of footsteps crunching gravel. "Oh shit. Here she comes. Now hurry up and take the baby inside."

Pam straightened in her chair and grabbed the beer bottle. How an old woman could wear a hideous outfit in public amazed her. Talk about a warped hot-pink fashion sense. She still couldn't believe this outlandish creature owned the resort, or how her disgusting dog tagged along behind her.

Dan stood and met Sadie as she stepped up onto the porch. Sally jerked her hand free from Sadie's grasp and ran over to the baby.

Between tongue-hanging pants and slobbery snorts, Belly lumbered up the steps, sat in front of Pam's chair, and nudged the pink bundle with his nose.

"Would you call your dog?" Pam grimaced and leaned away from Belly's head. "He's getting drool all over the blanket."

Sadie tugged at Belly's collar. "He's just curious. Everybody loves babies. Even dogs." Sadie reached toward the pink blanket "Can I take a peek?"

"Maybe later. She's sleeping and I don't want to wake her," Pam said.

"She must be a good baby. I haven't heard a peep out of her." Sadie sat in the wooden chair next to Pam.

"She is. We're blessed."

The blanket's edge flipped sideways, exposing a bald head. Pam quickly tucked the fabric back into place. She shot Dan a look of alarm.

Belly's jowls rose, releasing a puff of air as he let loose a muffled bark. Pam recoiled and wagged her wrist to motion him away. "Does your dog always follow you?"

"He's not my dog."

Pam didn't want to engage Sadie in conversation, but felt the words tumbling from her lips. "Whose dog is he?"

"He belongs to the neighbor." Sadie reknotted the hot-pink bandanna around Belly's neck. "He thinks he belongs to us, but he doesn't. I don't have the heart to tell him he's homeless."

Pam's forehead furrowed deeper as she raised her eyes and looked at Dan over the top of her sunglasses.

"Can I hold her?" Sally lifted the blanket again.

Dan's expression tightened as he glared at Pam. He licked his finger and held it up. "There must be a draft. You should take her in and put her in the crib. She might catch a cold."

"It's those wind currents off the lake." Sadie hurried to grab Sally's outstretched hand. "We'll stop back when the baby's awake."

"I want to hold her," Sally cried. "I want to hold her."

Pam watched Sadie hurry down the steps. "That means you, too." She gave Belly a shove with her foot. His bulk shifted, but he refused to budge.

Sadie crouched down and put her hands on Sally's shoulders. "I've told you before people can't hear you. They can't see you, either."

Sally held out her hands. She turned them over. "I can see me." She held her hands up. "See?"

"I know it's hard to understand, but the baby's mom can't see you."

"Yes she can," Sally argued. She ran back up the steps. "You can see me, can't you?" She held her hand under Pam's nose.

Sadie clomped back up the porch steps and grabbed Sally's arm with one hand and looped her fingers under Belly's collar with the other. "See you later," she sang out.

As Sadie rounded the cabin's corner with two stubborn customers in tow, Dan said, "That's one wacko broad. She keeps talking to herself."

"You think I didn't notice? She did the same thing last time she came nosing around."

"Do you think she's mental?"

"Mental?" Pam shook her head in disgust. "You think everybody who doesn't act like you is mental. Sadie's eccentric. Not mental."

"She's mental like your Aunt Perkie. For all we know Sadie's a clepto, just like Perkie. She'll probably walk off with Chelsie and get us in trouble." Dan dropped into the chair next to Pam. "That's why I don't want you bringing the doll out here anymore. You're taking a risk."

"No I'm not. You're right about people needing to see us with a baby. If they don't, what will they think when we show up with a live one?" Pam tapped a finger sharply on the arm of Dan's chair. "You'd better start trusting my judgment. Remember, if it wasn't for me, this job wouldn't take place."

Dan took a deep swig from his beer bottle. "Don't get too cocky. One little mistake is all it takes."

"Don't worry. I know what I'm doing." She leaned her head back against the chair. Since Dan returned from town an hour ago, he'd done nothing but gripe. It wasn't like him to start drinking so early. If his tension rubbed off on her, she'd be a basket case. She needed to concentrate on her plan and keep the self-doubt at bay.

Pam gestured toward Dan with the beer bottle. "Why the worry? You weren't this concerned yesterday."

Dan drained his bottle. "I need another beer." As he returned to the porch, he leaned on the railing. "Guess who I talked to today."

"Reggie?"

"I talked to him, too, but that's not who I meant. Reggie's having one of his usual nervous breakdowns. He screamed so loud I had to hold the phone away from my ear. His clients are getting antsy."

"Did you tell him we need to complete our reservation after we get the kid? We don't want people getting suspicious."

Pam had been more enthused about the abduction after

Dan told her they'd cut out the middle man, but Dan had been too blasé. If they realized a house on Lake Minnetonka, she wasn't going to let Dan's careless arrogance get in the way.

"I told him, but he didn't like it. What Reggie doesn't know is I went to the courthouse and introduced myself to Kimmer."

"Does Kimmer realize Reggie's the connection between the two of you?"

"He does now. When I told him Reggie seemed stingy and kept most of the profit, it didn't take much to convince Kimmer we should cut out the middle man. He liked the idea so much he said he'd provide all the work we can handle."

"How do you know you can trust him?"

"He's a judge. I trust him." A smug grin crossed Dan's lips. "I'll either be his best friend or his worst enemy. He's got too much to lose to cross me."

Pam watched Dan peel at the bottle's label with his fingernail. He wadded the scraps into a ball, placed it on his thumb, and shot it across the porch with his forefinger. The need to take charge overwhelmed her. Their good plan appeared viable only if carried out properly. Dan's careless attitude could ruin their future. She knew she could keep Dan under her thumb without him ever realizing it. She'd establish her own channel with Kimmer. On her terms.

Dan propped his feet on the railing. "Kimmer has an excavation job for me. First I have to hook up with a guy named Clay in Cabin 12. It has something to do excavation."

"In Pinecone Landing?

"It's right here at the resort."

15

"What the hell?" Clay stepped back. "What the hell?" He ran his fingers down the right-hand side of the screen door. "Who took my door knob?" He squinched his eyes into thin slits as he bent down and peered through the darkness. Balancing with his hands braced against his knees, he caught a glimpse of light reflecting off the knob on the left-hand side of the door. "What the hell?"

Clay looked from one side of the door to the other. He shrugged. As he opened the door, the clock's digital display flipped to 2:00 AM. He plopped down on the sofa and kicked off his sandals. Paper crinkled under his rear end. He raised his left cheek and tugged on the thick paper. It didn't budge. Rising, he removed the paper and threw it on the floor.

"What the hell?" He bent and retrieved the bundle of paper. Unfolding the top sheet, he held it closer to the lamp. "Hospital?" He smoothed the sheets against his lap and ran his hand over the blueprint. "What's this doing in my cabin?"

Clay traced his finger along the red line meandering from the hospital's front entrance to the bank of elevators. Paging deeper through the stack, he found a second sheet with more red lines. He followed the route until it ended with a large circled X in the obstetrics wing. He shifted his gaze from the top of the sheet to the bottom. "What the hell?"

He refolded the bundle and tossed it onto an adjacent chair. "I don't want to build no hospital. Whose big idea is this?"

Clay made his way across the cabin floor to the fridge. As he drew the refrigerator door open, his hip bumped against the counter knocking a pink blanket to the floor. His hand groped along an empty shelf. "What happened to my beer?"

He rearranged the condiment bottles trying to find his beverage of choice. "Geez Louise," he mumbled as he discovered one lone beer bottle. After twisting the cap, he took a deep swig and leaned his hand on the counter.

His hand settled on a tiny face. He jerked back and slammed the fridge door. A loaf of bread sitting on top the fridge tottered before plopping onto the baby, causing both to fall to the floor.

"Oh no." He bent over to look at the baby. He patted it on the head. "Am I supposed to be babysitting?" He took another swig and picked the doll off the floor. "Nobody ever tells me anything."

"Look toward our cabin. Did you see anything?" Dan held perfectly still.

"What?" Pam swam up behind Dan and put her arms around him. The entire evening had gone too fast. She hadn't felt this relaxed in months. She loved it when Dan catered to her every need. When Dan selected Yerry's on the Bay to celebrate their anniversary, Pam had been thrilled. Until she saw the prices. Dan didn't waver and insisted they order the best wine on the menu. He hadn't been this attentive since the summer he tried to convince her infant abduction could be their key to wealth. And now this late-night swim. What a slice of heaven.

"There it is again," Dan whispered.

"What?" Pam peered around Dan's arm as warm lake water rippled over her shoulders. Treading water, she rubbed against his body.

"A light just flicked on and off in our cabin."

"You must be seeing things," Pam said.

"There. Look." Dan pointed as a shadow crossed the window.

"Are you sure that's our cabin?"

"Of course I'm sure." Dan pushed Pam away.

"Who do you think it is?" Pam's heart rate rose as Dan drew a deep breath and propelled toward shore.

She stroked frantically trying to keep up with Dan. "Wait," she burbled, swallowing a gulp of lake water. "Wait."

When Dan touched bottom, his legs struggled against the weight of the water as he ran toward shore. He turned back and reached out to Pam. "The gun. Where's the gun?"

"In the nightstand. Right where you told me." Pam fought the rising bile in her throat.

"Shit," Dan muttered.

"You told me to put it there."

"Quit whining and shut up. Let me think." Dan patted his temples with his index fingers. "Come on. Follow me."

They edged behind Cabin 14 before crossing to Cabin 9. A bark erupted from Cabin 14. Dan dodged behind a Norway pine and grabbed Pam, pulling her in behind the tree. "Don't get so far behind. Someone will see you."

Struggling to pull precious air into her lungs, Pam said, "Then don't go so fast."

Peeking around the pine, Dan signaled to the left with a point of his finger. "Are you ready?" He bolted across the second clearing and stopped at the corner of Cabin 9 to wait for Pam. He held a finger up in silence as Pam rounded the corner. "Stay here."

Dan crept up onto the porch and leaned against the logs just as the screen door flung open and a man stepped out.

The man looked up at the number on top of the door. "Nine?" He groaned. "No wonder. This isn't Cabin 12." As the man stepped forward, Dan's fist connected with his jaw.

"Who is he?" Pam bent over the fallen body. She fanned her hand in front of her nose and straightened. "He reeks."

Dan rolled the man sideways and dug for his billfold. He ran his finger over the name beneath the plastic window. "It's Clay Harren."

"Isn't he the guy Kimmer wants you to hook up with?"

"Yeah," Dan said, folding the billfold and shoving it back in Clay's pocket.

"Now what?"

"Let's get him inside." Dan shook Clay and patted his face. "You stink."

They pushed Clay into a sitting position. "Come on. Wake up." Dan pinched the skin on Clay's forearm.

"Ow," Clay mumbled. His hand went to his jaw. "What the hell?" He slapped at Dan's hand. "What are you doing?"

"You took a tumble. We're trying to help you."

Clay looked from Dan to Pam. "That's nice." He gazed at Dan's legs. "Where's your clothes?"

"Inside." Dan ran his hand over his chest. "We went for a midnight swim."

Clay leaned on Dan as they went into the cabin. "I broke your baby." Clay pointed at the doll on the sofa.

Pam scooped the doll up and grabbed the blanket off the floor.

"I'm sorry. I didn't mean to break her. You never told me I had to babysit." Clay dropped into the log chair. "One minute she was there," Clay pointed toward the kitchen, "and the next minute she was on the floor. You're still going to pay me for babysitting, aren't you? I'm broke."

Dan motioned toward the bedroom with his chin. "Don't worry about the baby. She's fine. Pam's putting her to bed." His gaze followed Pam as she walked into the bedroom and shut the door.

"Do you have any more beer? I drank the last one."

Dan looked at the empty beer bottle on the coffee table.

When Pam returned, Dan motioned toward the screen door. "Our friend is thirsty. Check the trunk. I picked up another case this afternoon."

Pam's head wagged back and forth in disgust as she let the door slam behind her.

"I understand we have a mutual friend." Dan pulled a shirt over his head.

"Oh yeah? Who?"

"Judge Franzen Kimmer."

"You know Kimmer?" Clay's jaw clicked as he yawned. He rested his head against the chair's cushion and wriggled into a snug position.

The screen door slammed again, as Pam returned with the case of beer. Her flip-flops slapped against her heels as she crossed the cabin floor. She hoisted the case onto the kitchen counter.

"We sure do." Dan smiled with enthusiasm. "I'm doing some work for the judge. I need to hire help. Would you be interested?"

"I didn't know Kimmer had decided to build a hospital. I'm not sure I want to work so hard."

Dan frowned at Pam. "A hospital?"

"Yeah. I saw the blueprints. It looks like too much work."

Pam's eyes sparked panic as she saw a corner of the blueprints sticking out from the chair cushion.

"Oh, the blueprints. That's for a job in Minneapolis," Dan said. "I need your help on something else."

"Does it pay good? It better, cuz I'm short on cash."

"It does. It's an excavation job and you won't have to leave the resort."

16

"Here Belly," Sally said, picking a crisp French fry off the floor in Cabin 12. She sniffed it and held it out toward the dog. "It's got vitamins. It's good for you."

Belly swallowed the dusty fry without bothering to savor the flavor. He nosed under a T-shirt and came up with two more dried morsels.

Sally stepped over yesterday's newspaper and jumped up onto the sofa. She grabbed the remote control. "What do you want to watch?" She placed the doll she had taken from the neighbor's cabin next to her on the cushion and covered it with a damp towel. "Pew!" She grimaced and grabbed the towel. She threw it on the floor. "That stinks."

Belly pawed at the towel before flopping down and rolling on it.

"Do you want to watch cartoons?" She clicked through the channels. Her foot beat in rhythm with the music as a bright blue character ran back and forth across the screen. When a commercial interrupted the antics, she walked the doll across the length of the sofa, across Belly's back, and then dropped the rubber dolly on the floor.

Belly licked at the inside of a glass he had discovered until it lodged under the sofa.

Sally squatted. She fingered the edge of a heavy iron ring that peeked out from under a wrinkle in a braided rug.

Belly sat down next to her, cocked his head, and watched her delicate fingers pry at the ring.

"I can't lift it. It's stuck."

When Sally walked away, Belly dug at the ring with his

claws, gouging the wood.

"Here, I found something," Sally said. She returned with a table knife and pushed Belly aside. Kneeling, she inserted the thin end of the knife under the ring. A grunt escaped as she twisted it back and forth. The knife snapped in half.

She looked up at Belly. "Oh, oh. Now you did it. I'll get another one." She climbed back up on the kitchen chair and pushed the utensils around in the drawer. Returning to Belly's side, she leaned her shoulder against the dog's bulk and pried at the ring. This time the knife bent in half. She sighed heavily. "Piece of crap."

Belly whined and pawed at the ring.

A third trip to the utensil drawer proved beneficial when Sally returned with a bulky, stainless steel soup ladle. Metal creaked in protest as the ring budged. Moving closer to the ring, her foot caught in the rug and she tripped forward.

"A secret door?" She looked at Belly and repeated through a whisper, "Look, it's a secret door." She brushed the crumpled rug to one side. She ran her finger along the slit outlining the door. Inserting the ladle handle between the wood slats, she pried, struggling to lift her weight. The trap door inched a fraction before settling. Sally moved off the door and pried again. The door rose. She grabbed the edge and lifted it.

"It's dark." Sally nudged Belly with her shoulder. "Do you want to go down there?"

Belly's nostrils flew into overdrive as he sniffed in rapid succession. He whined and danced in place, looking from Sally to the black hole and back to Sally.

Sally's gaze rose to a black flashlight perched high on a shelf over the fridge. She tried to push Belly aside. "I need a flashlight. I can't see down there. Can you?" She lowered her head into the hole. "It smells."

Her head swiveled sharply toward the front door. She let go of the trap door and it slammed shut. "Sadie's calling me. We'd better hide."

Sadie's voice grew louder and then faded in intensity. Sally put her finger to her lips. "We have to go. We'll come back tomorrow."

17

"Are you sure you don't want to go to the Fertile Turtle tonight?" Jane watched Sadie remove the lid on a makeup bottle.

"I'm too busy." Sadie dabbed at the recently deceased Dave Robert's forehead with a makeup sponge. She stood back to assess her work. "There. What do you think?"

Jane and Bernie Johnson crowded closer.

"Looks good." Bernie ran his hands under Burt's suit lapel. "Nice suit. Too nice for a burial."

Bernie gestured toward Sadie. "Speaking of nice clothes, I like your suit. Now you look like a funeral director's assistant."

"I look like an old lady," Sadie shot back. "Nan bought this for me. I hate it. Hate it, hate it hate it."

"That's exactly what Mom said you'd say." Aanders stare moved from the black suit jacket up to Sadie's moussed hair.

"You should wear the suit to the Fertile Turtle." Jane looked up at Bernie through an infatuated haze. "Men like women in respectable clothes, don't they Bernie?"

"Baloney. If I go dancing, I'm wearing my new outfit." Sadie smoothed the silk pillow under Dave's head. "How do you expect me to get a man if I dress like you? I like looking sexy. I can't help it if I'm God's gift to man."

As Bernie and Jane walked back across the lawn toward Cabin 14, Sadie dabbed at the deceased man's makeup one last time. She pointed to a floor-standing floral arrangement and asked Aanders to move it closer to the casket. He complied. After following Sadie's instructions, Aanders placed a basket containing sympathy cards next to the podium.

The front lobby door swung wide and Clay Harren barreled across the floor.

"Nan. Nan," Clay hollered lunging toward a visitation room. He threw open the double doors. One of the doors bounced off the door stop and rebounded back hitting his sandal. Clay's gaze rotated wildly from corner to corner. "Nan? I can't find you. Where are you?" He faltered as he made his way toward the casket.

Clay's hip bumped against the casket knocking a floral swag to the floor. "Nan? Is that you?" He looked down at the body on display.

Sadie shrieked. "Clay! Get away from there." She grabbed his elbow and attempted to direct him away from the casket.

Clay wrenched his arm from her grasp and turned back to the body. He patted the man's face. "Boy am I glad it's not Nan. When did old Dave die, anyway? Nobody ever tells me anything." He turned toward Sadie. "That is Dave, isn't it? He looks peaked."

Sadie signaled to Aanders. She looped her arm through Clay's arm and turned him toward the door.

Aanders followed Sadie's example and grabbed Clay's other arm. As they marched him between the row of chairs, Clay tried to shrug out of the young man's grasp. "Who the hell are you?"

Anguished emotion engulfed Sadie as she glanced at Aanders. Clay had literally sucked the air from her. "Come on, Clay," Sadie said in a hushed tone. "Let's go." When he didn't move, she tugged on his arm. "Come on. We're going back to your cabin."

"Oh please, Sadie, let me stay. I need to talk to Nan. I

need some money. Can I borrow some money?" He smoothed his hair and ran his hands over his shirt to force out the wrinkles. "I'm broke."

"Broke? I thought Kimmer gave you some money."

"He did. But it's gone." Glancing down, Clay noticed his shirt tail hung loose. Trying to regain his balance after stumbling forward, he unzipped and began to tuck the shirt tail into his pants.

"Oh good grief." Repulsed by the ludicrous scene, Sadie averted her gaze.

"You don't have any underwear on," Aanders whispered.

"I don't?" Clay grabbed his waist band and held it out. "You're right. What happened to it?"

"Come on, Clay. Move it or you know what I'll do."

"Oh damn, Sadie. Don't call the cops. Last time they kept me for two days and it cost me four hundred bucks. The food tasted like shit. You know I don't have money." Clay whimpered as Sadie led him out the door.

"That happened five years ago. I'm surprised you remembered." Sadie led him across the mortuary porch and down the steps. "You've got to get out of here before Nan sees you."

A patrol car pulled into the mortuary parking lot as Sadie led Clay across the lawn.

"What's the problem, Sadie?" Lon started to open the car door.

"It's nothing. I've got it under control."

Lon removed his cap and ran his hands through his black hair. "That's not what it looks like." Static burst from the speaker on his shoulder. He pushed the call button. "I'll be there in thirty minutes."

"You called the cops?" Clay let out a low growl. "You traitor. I thought you were my friend."

"I thought you told me you quit drinking," Lon said, glaring at his cousin.

"I lied. I heard you were boinking Nan so I started drinking again. I couldn't help it."

The mortuary door closed and Sadie noticed Aanders behind the glass. He swiped at his cheek with the back of his hand.

"Nan told me she hired you to take care of the graves. If I ever hear you've caused her grief, you'll answer to me." Lon stood so close to Clay the toes of his black shoes touched Clay's sandals.

"Yes sir, pussy boy." Clay gestured with a salute that came nowhere near his forehead. "I see a uniform finally gave you balls."

"It has nothing to do with my uniform. When Nan told me she offered you a job, I was against it. The only reason she did is to keep an eye on you. She doesn't want you bothering Aanders."

"He's my kid. He needs me."

"If he needs you so bad, where were you the past five years?"

"Here and there. Mostly there." Clay shoved his hands in his pockets. "Can I borrow some money?"

"Get out of here, Clay. Stay away from Aanders." Lon headed back toward his squad car.

"No can do."

Lon stopped and turned to face Clay. "One thing hasn't changed. You're still a loser."

"When I finish an excavation job, I'll be rich. Then we'll see who she prefers." A challenging smirk parted Clay's lips.

Trembling, Lon stepped back toward Clay. "You stay away from Nan. Do you hear me? You're not going to come between us again, no matter what I have to do."

18

Aanders cast a shadow over Sally as he hovered over the wicker chair and pointed his finger at her. "Now sit there and don't move. I'm going back to the mortuary to get my DVD so I can hook it up to Sadie's television."

"Okay." Sally kicked off her sandals and resituated her legs in Jane's rocker. "Are we going to watch a movie?"

"Yup. You better behave. If you don't, I'll tell Sadie."

"I'll be good."

As Aanders closed the screen door behind him, Sally ran to the door. "I want to watch the Chipmunk movie."

"I'm not going to watch your stupid movie again," Aanders shouted from the end of the paved path. "We're going to watch what I pick this time."

Sally pressed her nose against the screen watching Aanders jog across the mortuary lawn. Standing in place, she hopped from one foot to another trying to maintain her balance before hopping back across the kitchen floor.

She opened the refrigerator door. "Do you want to eat?"

Belly trotted over to her. The four hairs protruding from the end of his tail waved in unison as he sniffed the shelves and danced the butt-wagging rumba.

Sally tugged a yellow China plate off the refrigerator shelf and placed it on the floor. She pushed Belly away.

The dog's tongue smacked against the roof of his mouth while he attempted to spit out a piece of plastic wrap he had pulled off the top of the gravy-drenched pot roast. Sally put her fists on her hips and her nose two inches from Belly's snout. "You don't got no manners. Mom would make you stand in the corner until it got dark if she knew what you did."

Drool dripped onto the floor as Belly whined and pawed at the plate.

Sally broke off a piece of beef and held it out. Belly gulped it down. "Did you like it?" She broke off another chunk and continued feeding the dog until the beef disappeared and Belly slicked the plate clean. Swiping with disgust at the appreciative licks Belly bestowed across her nose, Sally yanked on a kitchen chair and pulled it over to the cupboard. She climbed up and placed the tongue-washed plate neatly on top a stack of matching plates.

Sally followed Belly to the door. She sighed and leaned her cheek against the frame. As Belly nudged her hand, she said, "I'm tired of waiting. Aanders must have forgot."

A family of five hurried past Cabin 14. Clothed in swimming suits and toting beach towels, two of the children ran ahead shouting instructions for the rest to hurry.

"Can I come, too?" Sally ran after the children. "Wait for me. I'm going with you." Catching up to them, she noticed a man coming out of Cabin 12.

Belly saw the man, too, and detoured over to Clay's cabin.

"Get out of here you stupid mutt," Clay shouted as Belly lumbered up the steps.

Belly plopped down at Clay's feet and rolled over.

"I said get out of here. Don't piss on my shoes again." Clay stepped over Belly LaGossa and grumbled profanities at the dog. When Belly didn't budge, Clay picked his shoes off the porch and threw them into the cabin.

Sally joined Belly and watched Clay drive out of the parking lot, hit a curb, back up, and drive over one of Jane's prized Hydrangea bushes before turning out onto the highway.

Sally sat on the top step leaning into Belly's bulk. The warmth of his fur felt comforting against her arm. If only her mother would let her sit like this. Her dad used to let her cuddle, but her mother always seemed too busy. Her mom had to work and didn't have time for nonsense. Maybe her mother would change her mind the next time she saw her.

Sally put her arm over Belly's back and pulled him closer. "I sure miss my dad." She tucked her face into Belly's orange bandana. "When do you think he'll come back?"

She looked back toward Cabin 14. With elbows propped against her knees and her chin on her fists, her gaze darted from Cabin 14 to Clay's door and back to Cabin 14. "Aanders must have forgot."

Inside Cabin 12, Sally looked up at the flashlight perched on the shelf above the fridge. She grunted and tugged at the chair. A high-pitched scrape pierced the summer air as she dragged the chair across the wooden planking.

The stainless steel soup ladle lay on the rug where she had left it the day before. Pushing the braided rug into a wad behind the trap door, Sally coaxed the ring out of its hole. She tugged at the rusted iron. "Get off. You're too heavy," she said, pushing against Belly's right side. His skin shifted, but he didn't move. She pushed again.

The wood creaked as she forced her foot into the opening and hefted with all the strength she could summon. The door wavered on its hinges and fell open with a thud.

Belly retreated at the frightening sound. After sniffing valiantly to check for danger, he moseyed over to Sally whose head and shoulders had disappeared into the black hole.

Reaching for the flashlight, Sally said, "You can go first if you want." She struggled with the flashlight button as the dog nudged her arm with his nose.

Belly stretched his neck into the crawlspace opening. He rocked back and forth trying to gather courage to dive into the darkness. After a few more hesitant jerks, he took the plunge. Landing with a grunt, he circled back and put his paws up through the opening before disappearing under the floorboards.

"Wait for me," Sally ordered. She waved the flashlight beam across the dirt floor. "You better wait. If you don't, I'm not coming down there." She dropped into the opening. Belly let out a muffled bark. Straining to see into the distance, Sally noticed a shaft of light radiate through the mesh air vent, casting a weak glow under the cabin.

"Where are you?" Sally turned her head in the direction of Belly's panting.

Dirt flew up between Belly's rear legs as he scrambled to rearrange the loose soil.

When Sally passed the flashlight's beam in his direction, a haze of grit wafted toward her. "Quit that. I can't see." Two rapid sneezes followed her command.

She propped the flashlight on a broken concrete block next to where Belly clawed at the soil. "Quit that." She pushed him sideways. As the silt settled, Sally crouched down next to Belly. A dark object protruded from the soil. She brushed at it. "It must be a secret treasure." She brushed at it again with the palm of her hand before tugging at the corner of the object. "I can't get it. It's stuck."

Belly whined and raked his claw across the top of Sally's hand.

"Quit that," she hollered. Her hand flew to her mouth. "We have to be quiet. Pirates might come back. Mom said they steal kids."

Sally duck-walked in a crouch across the dirt floor. She

reached for the flashlight. "Wait here. I need to get something." Fanning the flashlight's ray across floor, she made her way back to the trap door opening.

Dirt sprayed out from between Belly's back legs as his front legs assaulted the lump in the ground.

"Here, I found this." Sally held up a white plastic measuring cup before setting the flashlight on the ground. Leaning toward the dark lump, she scooped away the dirt Belly had dislodged.

As her eyes readjusted to the darkness, she sat down and dragged her bare heel back and forth, widening the span of loose dirt with each swipe. Clack. Clack. The clicking sound repeated with each pass of her heel. She held her foot in mid air. "That must be the treasure."

Belly stuck his nose on one of the items and snorted.

Sally leaned closer and drew in a sharp breath while staring at what she had uncovered. She brushed at the dirt until an ashen item rolled off to one side. "It's an old pirate."

Tattered fabric flecked with mouse droppings clung to the skeleton's frame. Leg bones skewed at an unthinkable angle. Sally raised the flashlight and held the beam on the skeleton's head before pulling Belly close. "He's dead. See these bones? That means he's dead."

Unseen vermin clinked tins together in the far corner of the crawlspace in their haste to flee the disruption. Sally dropped the flashlight and scampered back.

Belly lumbered toward the corner barking in protest. He nudged the wooden beam with his nose as a mouse disappeared between two floor boards. Upset and ready to protect his find, Belly returned to the mound and dug frantically at the skeleton. Pelvic bones jutted through a hole in the fabric.

"Quit that!" Dust swirled around Sally's face. She fanned

the air, adding to the volume of dust she inhaled before pulling her shirt up around her nose and blinking away the scratchy residue.

Sally brushed at the silt covering the skeleton's hair and lifted the tangle away from the skull. A shiny object glistened in the flashlight's beam. She reached for it. Following the length of chain with her fingers, she tugged to free it. It caught on a button. As she loosened the button, the fabric shifted and an object slid down inside the garment and plunked against the dirt floor.

Sally sat back admiring the necklace while Belly sniffed with fervor. The detective's snout blew puffs of dust into the air. The young crosser held the silver charm and watched it cast a dancing glimmer across a floor beam as it mirrored the flashlight's ray.

Belly's jaw snapped at the light as it arched across the wood.

Sally coaxed gray silt off the tattered fabric and pushed the bottom of the shirt up against the skeleton's rib cage. A neatly-woven wad of straw, the former home of a family of voles, lay nestled in the rib cage. A small brown notebook splayed open against two rib bones.

"Sally? Sally?"

Wide eyes stared into the light coming through the mesh air vent at the far side of the crawl space. "It's Aanders," Sally whispered.

Belly whined. As he opened his mouth to bark, Sally nudged him.

"We have to be quiet. Aanders will tattle and I won't get to watch the movie." She held her finger to her lip and pulled Belly close. Her body bobbed in rhythm with Belly's heavy panting. When he protested with a whine, she pressed her finger against his snout.

Aanders' voice faded as he walked toward the beach. "Sally?"

Sally grunted as she grabbed Belly's rear legs and hoisted him through the trapdoor opening. "Wait a minute." She flipped the flashlight on and duck-walked back under the floor boards.

Belly rotated his head in curiosity listening to the faint sound emanating from the black hole.

Poking her head up through the hole, Sally held up a fist full of treasure. She raised the flap on her pocket and tucked the treasure inside.

Belly pranced in place while Sally swung one leg up and pulled herself out of the hole. The trap door slammed shut with a thud as Sally ran to the screen door. Waiting for Belly to follow, she held her finger up with one final warning. "Don't tell no one about the treasure."

Belly lumbered across the floor behind Sally, but stopped near the door. He sniffed Clay's shoes, raised his leg, and peed on them.

19

"Do you want to join us, Sadie?" Bernie Johnson picked up a wooden spoon and dipped it in the kettle Jane had moved to a back burner. "We're taking the pontoon out." He dipped the spoon back in for a second sample of chili.

"I'll go," Sally shouted, running up to Bernie.

"You're not going anywhere," Sadie said. "You're staying here so I can keep an eye on you."

"On me? Why would you need to keep an eye on me?" Bernie's curious expression deepened the furrows on his leathered face.

Jane's gaze darted from Sadie to Bernie. "She doesn't. She misunderstood you. Sadie doesn't have time to join us, so it'll just be the two of us."

"That's even better." Bernie lifted Jane's hand and held it to his lips.

"I want to go." Sally dropped down onto the floor as the door closed behind Bernie. She slammed her fists against the floor in protest.

"You're going with me to the hospital this afternoon." Jed reached for Sally.

"I don't want to. It's boring. I want to go fishing with Jane and Bernie. Maybe we'll see his kids again."

"Bernie doesn't have children," Sadie said. "I don't know what you think you heard, but Bernie doesn't have children. He checked the no children box on the dating website questionnaire. He also told Jane he didn't have kids."

"But he does." Sally broke free of Jed's hold. She ran toward the inner room and slammed the door. She shouted,

"I'm going to tell Jane you have a BA on her chair again."

"I wish I had her energy," Sadie said "I'm tempted to put Belly's leash on her. Every time I turn around, she's gone."

Sadie stood in front of the mirror and turned her head from side to side. "I don't like this new hair gel as much as the other one."

"You mean it's not supposed to look like mange?" Jed bit back a smile.

"It's not supposed to look all glumpy. It sticks together in big wads instead of fanning out like it's supposed to."

"What color is it?"

"Puce."

"Puke?"

"Puce," Sadie corrected. "It's a kind of bluish red with a hint of raspberry. Big Leon insisted it's supposed to be captivating and romantic."

"Really?"

Sadie walked over to the screen door and waved at Jane and Bernie as they boarded the pontoon. She held the door open for Aanders to enter the cabin.

Aanders sniffed the air. "Chili?" He lifted the lid off the kettle and drew in a deep breath. "Who made it?"

"Jane."

"Did you taste it yet?"

Sadie pulled out a chair and sat next to Jed. "No, but Bernie did and he's still alive."

"Did she make up a recipe or follow the book?" Aanders' doubting eyes stared at Sadie.

"She followed the recipe. Bernie bought her a new cookbook yesterday when they went to town."

"Thank goodness." Aanders reached for the wooden spoon. He eased the hot mixture off the spoon with his teeth and closed his eyes. "That's really good."

"You should tell Jane. She still feels bad about her latest fiasco." Sadie followed Aanders' lead and dipped a second spoon into the chili.

"That wasn't Jane's fault. Sally put the cinnamon on the hamburgers," Jed said. "She tried to help. You know how she loves to imitate Jane."

"Bernie doesn't know what happened. It wouldn't hurt to compliment Jane in front of Bernie."

"Oh, oh."

"What?" Sadie turned toward Aanders. When he didn't reply, she repeated, "What?"

"I wasn't going to tell you, but yesterday, before Sally put cinnamon on the hamburgers, I caught her with Jane's spice jars spread all over the table. She said she wanted to play cooker lady."

"She loves to pretend. As long as you put them back before Jane saw the mess, it's okay."

Aanders turned his back to Sadie.

"Spit it out, Aanders. What else happened?"

"The lid was off Mr. Bakke's urn."

"Oh, oh," Jed and Sadie uttered. Sadie hurried across the floor and peeked out the window toward the marina. Wooden rings slid across the curtain rod with ease as she pulled the panels tight.

Sadie lifted the urn's lid and set it on the table. Three noses moved in unison followed by three sets of hunched shoulders while they leaned closer and peered in.

Sadie whispered, "Mr. Bakke? You okay in there?"

They focused on the jar's interior.

"Oh, oh." Once again in unison.

"It smells like the leaf junk Mom's got in bowls in our apartment," Aanders said.

"Yikes. The last time I visited with Mr. Bakke, the urn

was less than a quarter full. Look at it now." Sadie tipped the jar and a poof of clove essence filled the air.

"Are the spices mostly on top?" Jed leaned closer.

Sadie dabbed a finger into the jar and held it under her nose. "Smells like it. Hopefully she just dumped spices in and didn't shake it up. Maybe I can scoop them off and Jane will never know the difference."

"What is that?" Jed pointed into the jar's cavity.

Sadie squinted. "Looks like chunks of pepper corn."

"No, I mean there." Jed jabbed his finger toward the right edge of the interior.

Sadie put her face over the jar and reached in. She retrieved a green leaf coated with multi-colored powder and held it between two fingers. "I think it's a bay leaf."

"I'm sorry, Mr. Bakke," Sadie said with a sigh. "I hope you're not upset. Sally meant no harm."

Sadie handed a spoon to Jed. "Let's do what we can, but be careful not to scoop out any gray ash."

As Sadie wiped down the table, removing the last trace of spice, a horn tooted in the distance. Sadie shielded her eyes and focused on the marina. Jane and Bernie waved vigorously as they stepped off the pontoon.

Before Jed replaced the urn's lid, he glanced in one more time. He squinted. "I still see something. My hand is too big. See if you can fish it out."

Sadie slipped her slender hand in and gently felt around. "I don't feel anything."

"It's over by the edge."

She dabbed her fingers over the ashes until her fingernail struck an object. She edged it over to the center with her little finger. Lifting it from the urn, she tapped it gently against the rim to dislodge the ashes. "It's a bone. I don't think it belongs to Mr. Bakke. It doesn't look like it went through the crematory. It's too white."

20

Jed took a deep breath and let out an irritated sigh. "I'm not going to change my mind no matter what you say. I'm going back through the light. I want to find Celeste so she can tell me what happened."

"There's no guarantee you'll find her," Sadie said. "She may have gone to the parallel world."

"She didn't come to your cabin as a crosser, did she?"

"I know where you're going with this." Sadie shook her head in disapproval. "You want to believe Celeste didn't go to the parallel world so you can justify going back through the light."

"So?" Jed crossed his arms over his chest.

"It's not like you to back down from a challenge. I've known you all your life. You've always done what's right."

"What's your point?"

"You're a care-giver, Jed. Celeste doesn't need your help anymore. Those in the parallel world do. Two options are open to you. Either go back through the tunnel of light and take your chance, or opt for the parallel world where you can do some good."

When Jed didn't meet her gaze, Sadie raised her voice. "I still believe you were held back to solve Celeste's disappearance. What if you go back through the light and never find her. You'll never know what happened. Can you live with that? Maybe if you concentrate on solving her disappearance before you go, you'll realize it's not necessary to go back through the light."

"I told you, I'm not going to the parallel world. Who

decided to name it the parallel world, anyway? It spooks me. It's like I'm going to take off in a shape ship with a bunch of aliens and end up on another planet."

Aanders leaned into the table. "If you go, you can help kids who are scared. Some don't have their moms with them."

"That's not what I've chosen to do. It's my decision and mine alone. I'm willing to take my chances."

Exasperation filled Sadie. Stubborn crossers stirred the kettle of challenge, yet Sadie understood Jed's argument. His need to make sense of Celeste's disappearance weighed heavy. Jed had worked tirelessly to find clues to Celeste's disappearance and had watched sorrow take a toll on his parents. Now, they grieved the loss of two children.

Sighing deeply, Sadie said, "That's right. It's your decision, but it's my job to help you make the best declaration you can make. I believe going to the parallel world is by far a better choice. You'll gain nothing by finding Celeste after the fact. Trust me. You've got to solve her disappearance before you leave or you'll regret it."

21

"Don't look at him. It will only encourage him," Judge Kimmer whispered to his sister.

"Who?" Etta looked back over her shoulder.

"I said don't look. It's Clay Harren. He's standing by Cabin 12." Kimmer kept his head bowed, but peered out under the brim of his straw hat.

"When did Clay get back? I thought his ex-wife told him he couldn't come back." Etta cast her line into the bay and stared at the ripples surrounding the bobber. "She should get the cops to run him out of town again."

When Clay waved in his direction, Kimmer kept his head down. He picked at the tangle in his reel and let out a stream of expletives that made murky water drinkable in comparison. Satisfied after a test cast, he clicked the locking mechanism into place. "Clay booked the cabin for a whole year."

"Now I know Sadie's lost her mind. I've been telling people for years, but they ignore me," Etta said. "A sane Sadie would never let Clay set foot on her property."

He peeked toward Cabin 12. "Maybe she didn't know about it."

"I can't believe it. That old witch sticks her nose in everything. I think she's got a radar implant in her brain."

Kimmer braced as the boat slid against the dock. The dock boy threw him a rope and Kimmer pulled tight until the craft settled against the mooring. "Fill it up, son."

"Okay, Judge." A Cheshire grin lit the dock boy's face as he unscrewed the gas cap. "Do you want some bait, too?"

"Is it the same price as last time?" Kimmer grabbed a dock post, placed his foot on a boat seat, wheezed, and stepped up onto the wooden planking. As his foot left the seat, the boat rocked wildly. Etta let out a scream and grasped the side of the boat.

The dock boy glanced back toward Cabin 14. "Same price as last time." He dipped a small mesh net into the live-bait tank and scooped a net of wriggling minnows. "Does this look like enough?"

"Plenty." Kimmer dabbed his handkerchief over his forehead. "Damn hot today, isn't it?" He raised his chin to peer above two men bent over the bait tank and looked toward Clay's cabin. Clay no longer stood near Cabin 12.

"I'll be right back," Kimmer shouted, waving in Etta's direction. He climbed the four wooden steps leading to the paved path, glanced at Sadie's cabin before veering off toward Cabin 12. He circled to the back side of the cabin, making sure Sadie's radar wouldn't detect his presence. Hearing no sounds coming from Clay's cabin, he opened the screen door.

"Good grief." Kimmer grimaced at the putrid odor permeating the humid air. He dabbed at the back of his neck with his handkerchief. His mother had always taken such pride in making this cabin a fun place for their family to visit. How could his mother have been so stupid to fall for Sadie's devious ways and sell her their family cabin? His mother would spin in her casket if she saw this rat's nest. A smile seized the corner of his mouth. Maybe you got what you deserved, Mommy dear.

He kicked at the clothing strewn across the floor; the toe of his shoe clinked against a beer bottle, causing it to skitter across the floor. "What a pigsty."

Kimmer peeked around the corner. The trap door lay

wide open against a clump of braided rug. He looked back toward the screen door. As he stepped closer to the rectangular opening, the trap door slammed shut. His hand flew to his chest. He swung around. "Who's there?" The words caught in his throat. Swallowing to keep caustic acid from rising higher, he repeated, "Who's there?"

Belly pawed at the screen door, his jowls fluffed and a muffled bark erupted from his lips.

Scurrying across the floor, Kimmer's foot caught in an arc of bunched rug. He looked back at the trap door and then at the dog. It must be the heat. Dehydration had caused him to hallucinate in the past. That must be the case. He needed water. He needed fresh air.

Sitting on the porch step, Kimmer drew in long, deep breaths. He placed his palm against his chest. He counted the rapids beats. "One. Two. Three."

Belly's puce neckerchief flapped wildly as he danced in place at Kimmer's side.

"Damn," Kimmer mumbled and pushed Belly away. "You're getting slime all over me."

The dog plopped down, placed his snout in Kimmer's crotch and snorted.

Kimmer groaned, "Now look what you did." He removed his handkerchief from his pocket and dabbed at his zipper. Placing his meaty palm on the railing, he pulled until he rose to a standing position.

The dock boy waved at Kimmer and shouted, "Your boat's ready."

Kimmer waved back in acknowledgement. Standing at an angle to the steps, he eased down one step at a time until he placed his triple E boat shoes on the ground.

Etta squinted against the sun, watching Kimmer approach the dock. She stared at his crotch. "What did you do? Piss in your pants?" As Kimmer placed one foot in the boat she ranted, "Be more careful this time. Last time you darn near capsized the boat."

"Oh yeah? If I recall, you came close to triggering a tsunami when you got in. In case you haven't noticed, you're no Tinker Bell either."

Kimmer looked toward Sadie's cabin. Seeing no sign of the despicable, meddling lunatic, he reached in his live well and pulled out a six-pack of beer. He set it on the dock. "Take it before Sadie sees it."

The dock boy also looked toward Cabin 14 before nonchalantly walking over to the cans. He inserted his fingers through the plastic loops, glanced over his shoulder one more time, and leaned over the dock. He eased the cans into the water and watched as they settled to the bottom. "Thanks again, Judge. It's a pleasure doing business."

A sharp sigh erupted behind Kimmer. The judge flinched as Etta's eyes bore into him. "Hurry up. I don't have all day. Where did you go? Did you go up to the lodge?"

Kimmer untied the mooring rope. Just what he needed. More aggravation. He had wanted to tell Clay to stay away from him when they frequented the same public areas, but Clay wasn't in his cabin. He couldn't risk having Sadie see them. It had been Etta who insisted they fish in Sadie's bay. He did his sister a favor and all she'd done the whole time was harp. He had no choice but to keep tabs on Etta. She had recently moved back to town after the death of her husband. She'd been married to the only person Kimmer ever confided in and he needed to know if their secret had slipped out on his brother-in-law's death bed.

"What's taking so long?" Etta reeled in her line and glared at Kimmer. "I'm sick of sitting here. I haven't had a single nibble."

"Pipe down. I'm going as fast as I can." Kimmer turned the key and the motor sputtered before spinning over. He eased the boat toward the end of the dock.

"Hey Kimmer. Where you going?" Clay Harren stood at the end of the dock.

Kimmer shielded his eyes from the sun and looked in the direction of the voice. "What are you doing?" Judge Kimmer peered through tiny slits, trying to focus against the glare.

"What does it look like I'm doing? I'm squirt peeing the Star Spangled Banner." Clay swayed as he turned to look at Kimmer. "Want to join me?"

"Put that back in your pants right now," Kimmer uttered with a gasp, steeling against the revolting sight.

"I'm not done, yet."

Etta bellowed, "What's he doing?"

"I'm taking a leak," Clay said.

"He's what?" Etta's screech escalated into a choking spasm as she turned to stare in Clay's direction.

"Oh hi, Oinketta," Clay shouted and waved with his free hand. "I didn't know you liked to fish." Clay wavered as he zipped his pants. "Catch any?"

Etta stood and the boat rocked wildly. "What did you call me?" Her caterwaul echoed over the lake.

"Oinketta. That's your name, isn't it? That's what Sadie calls you."

Etta's fleshy nose bobbed as her nostrils flared. In words distinctively detached from one another, she said, "My name is Etta. Not Oinketta."

Clay pointed at Etta. "Oh, I get it." He rolled his head back on his shoulders and let out a belly laugh.

"You get what, you sorry sack of shit." Etta stepped forward.

"Sit down before you tip us over." Kimmer grabbed the

sides of the boat. When Clay came closer, Kimmer growled, "Get out of here, Clay."

Clay dabbed at the tears in his eyes before leaning on a mooring post. "You have to admit Sadie's one honest broad. She calls them like she sees them."

"Clay!" Judge Kimmer motioned frantically for Clay to move away from the boat.

Clay's grin turned dark and his head sank back on his shoulders. "I don't like my cabin. I want another one."

"There's nothing wrong with your cabin." Kimmer glanced at Etta out of the corner of his eye.

"I want a nicer one. One with a lock. Somebody's been messing with my stuff. There are broken knives all over the floor."

"How would you ever know? It's probably because you stepped on them."

"I don't eat on the floor."

"You could have fooled me. I stopped to see you and it looked like a tornado went through there."

"That's exactly what I mean. Somebody's been in there. There's dolls and toys and junk all over the place." Clay's elbow slipped off the mooring post.

"In your cabin?"

"Yeah. Right by the big hole in the floor."

Kimmer glanced sideways at his sister again.

Clay's eyebrows met in the middle as he frowned. "I came home the other night and there was a big hole in my floor."

Kimmer ignored Etta's pout of impatience. He remembered Etta's husband complaining how one morning she woke up in a pissy mood and it had lasted for twenty years. Now he had to put up with it.

A young couple strolled nearby on the beach. The man

nodded in Kimmer's direction.

"Hey, Dan," Clay shouted. "Come on over and talk with us."

"Not now," Kimmer whispered, looking toward Cabin 14.

"Why not?" Clay looked from Dan to Kimmer. It'll just take a minute."

"We can't right now," Dan said. "We've got to get the baby back to the cabin. Maybe later."

Wiping his brow with his damp handkerchief, Kimmer started the motor.

Clay looked toward Kimmer. "Did you know Dan hired me to do an excavation job? I'm going to meet with him tomorrow to find out exactly what it is."

22

"What's Belly got in his pocket?" Sally crouched down and looked under the dog.

Jed and Sadie stared at the young crosser.

"Right there." Sally pointed at Belly's lone testicle.

Jed let out a laugh.

"It's empty," Sadie said. "Some dogs have big pockets but don't keep anything in them."

"Why?"

"It's too hard to reach."

Sally clomped across the floor in a pair of Sadie's black and white polka-dot heels. A large smear of purple lipstick adorned her lips.

Sadie parted the curtain as a motor quieted and a pontoon glided silently toward the dock. A Great Dane puppy bounded off the pontoon. Sadie watched his massive paws splash along the water's edge while he nipped at pencil waves teasing the shore.

"Since when do dogs have pockets?" Jane looked up from her magazine. "Do I need to know what you're talking about?"

"Not really."

"Did Jed have any luck at the hospital today? Has he found anyone on the brink?" Jane dog-eared a page corner before closing the recipe magazine.

Jed hooked his feet through the support rungs on the chair.

"When I walked through ICU at the hospital, I heard the doctor recommend life support be pulled from a patient. It sounded like they'd wait until his family arrived. Possibly tomorrow."

"Is he the man Lon hoped to question?" Sadie watched Belly plop down on the braided rug before rolling on his back.

"I think so. I saw Lon leaving the nurses' station when I arrived."

"What are you talking about? Question who?"

"I was responding to Jed's question. He told me about a patient who isn't expected to make it."

"That's a shame. Is it anybody we know?"

"Not unless you've been hanging around the guys running the meth lab that blew up."

Sally leaned against Jed's leg. "Are you going dancing with Bernie and Jane?"

Jed lifted her up onto his lap. "I don't think so. I think you and I will stay home and rest up for tomorrow."

"I don't want to go back to the hospital. It's no fun."

Jed removed a napkin from the holder and dabbed at Sally's lips. When she tried to turn away, he said, "Hold still. You want to look beautiful like Sadie, don't you?"

She pursed her lips and let him dab at the smears.

Sadie turned toward her sister. "Did you enjoy your pontoon ride with Bernie? You've been spending a lot of time with him."

A delighted grin spread over Jane's face. She tucked her hands in her apron pockets and shrugged her shoulders toward her ears. "He's absolutely wonderful. I never thought I'd feel like this again. He listens when I talk about Mr. Bakke and encourages me to tell him everything. There's no jealousy whatsoever. He even talks to Mr. Bakke's ashes, bless his soul."

Sadie patted her sister's hand. "I can tell you've been

around Bernie. You sound just like him. I'm happy for you, but you need to be realistic. Just because he added a week to his stay doesn't mean he's going to be around forever."

"I wouldn't be so sure." Jane grinned.

"Don't tell me he's thinking about moving up from Minneapolis?" A chill ran down Sadie's arm causing goose flesh to prickle along the surface. Vulnerability and Jane went hand in hand. Jumping heart first into another relationship could produce devastating consequences.

"He's hinted at it." Jane plopped down into her chair. "Can you imagine anyone thinking enough about me to relocate?" She fluffed both sides of her bob as a kittenish grin formed. "Bernie thinks I'm sexy."

"My mom is sexy," Sally said. "That's what her friend tells her when my dad's not home. I sure miss my dad."

Jed brushed his lips across Sally's forehead "I know you do. I'm sure he misses you too."

"By the way," Jane said, "you think you pulled a fast one on me, but you didn't. Nan asked me to help her at the mortuary and guess what I found. Mr. Bakke's robe. Right where you hid it."

"I didn't hide it, Aanders did."

"Baloney. I know you hid it. How many times do I have to tell you I don't want Jed sitting on our chairs with a bare ass?"

Sally giggled. "He always sits with a BA."

"Hello, Mr. Bakke." Aanders entered the cabin and patted the urn. He took a chair next to Jed. "Did you hear thunder last night, Sadie?"

"That was thunder? I thought Jane and Belly had another one of their snore fests. I thought my bed would levitate there was so much racket going on."

"It was thunder," Sally gushed, wide eyed, as she

glanced from Aanders to Sadie. "The spooky kind. I crawled into bed with Sadie in case she got scared."

"You did?"

"Yup. I put my arm around you so you wouldn't cry."

"Thank you, Sally." Sadie raised Sally's chin with her index finger. "Did you by any chance put Clay's billfold on my pillow last night?"

"Clay's billfold?" Jane scrunched her face in bewilderment. "What are you talking about? Why would I have Clay's billfold?"

"I was talking to Sally, not you. I woke up with Clay's billfold next to my nose this morning."

"What? How could that be?"

Sally stubbed the toe of her sandal against Jed's leg.

"Sally. Answer Sadie. Did you put Clay's billfold on her pillow?" Jed placed his nose against Sally's ear. "What did I tell you about taking people's property without permission?"

"Actually, I'm relieved Sally put it there. I thought I had too much to drink at the Fertile Turtle. Clay was there and kept pestering me to buy him a drink. You know, his usual mooch fest."

"What does the Fertile Turtle have to do with Clay's billfold? I don't have a clue what you're talking about." Jane huffed in frustration and tossed her dishtowel on the counter.

"It appears Sally visited Clay during the night and took his billfold. She left it on my pillow. I'm relieved because I thought I'd brought Clay home with me."

"Dreamer," Jane said, through a sly grin. "Who'd pay you for you-know-what?"

"Lots of guys. Just because you're…"

"That's enough, ladies," Jed warned. "Little ears are wide open."

Sadie retreated to her chair, set her jaw, and stared at

Jane.

"Just because I'm what?" Jane's look of irritation mirrored Sadie's.

"Tut. Tut. Tut," Sadie said. "Little ears."

"I suppose you went through his billfold like a nosey Nellie." Jane's head wagged in a know-it-all accusation

"You bet I did. It was on my pillow, wasn't it?"

Jane sat forward. "Did he have anything interesting in it, like money?"

"None. Not a stinking dollar bill."

"Nothing? How about a driver's license? How about photos?"

Sadie glanced at Aanders. "Just a couple pieces of paper. I saw a business card from Dan Avery and a list."

"A list of what?"

"The paper was so crumpled I had a hard time reading it. I saw three things on the list. If I read it right, one of the items was a short-handled shovel."

"A short-handled shovel? How do you stoop over and dig with one of those?" Jane's nose tweaked with confusion. "That's how you get a bad back. What else did you see?"

"Plastic bags and a crow bar."

"Lon mentioned Dan Avery hired Clay to do a job," Sadie said. "Maybe the list is tools for the job."

Aanders glanced toward the mortuary as a door slammed in the distance. "There's Mom. I think she's looking for me. I better go."

Jed shook his head. "It's like Grand Central in here. All the years I've known you, Sadie, I never realized your life to be so interesting. You've got people coming and going all the time. If people only understood what you deal with, they'd never call you crazy again. I'm going to miss you." Jed set Sally on the floor and she ran toward the inner room.

"I'm going to miss you too," Sadie said.

"I think I'll hang around the intensive care unit tomorrow in case the guy dies. I've decided to go back through the light and I'm taking Sally with me."

"I wish you'd rethink your options."

"No. I've made my declaration. Maybe it's you who needs to open up to another possibility."

"Like what?"

"Like when Sally's father comes back to Pinecone Landing, you'll find a way to tell him she's loved and taken care of. He needs to know. I believe deep in your heart you know I'll do a good job."

"I don't doubt it for a minute. With your compassion, why can't you go to the parallel world and create a better life for the crossers?"

"Because I don't want to. I want to find Celeste. I'm willing to take the chance she already crossed over."

"Then you better remember whoever steps into the tunnel of light first, determines the final destination."

"I know. You already told me."

"If Sally steps into the light before you do," Sadie explained, "she determines where you go. If she has no preconceived declaration, and you know that's exactly what she's got, you'll both end up nowhere."

"Then I'll lead the way. It's time to find Celeste and take care of Sally."

Aanders placed his nose against the screen door. He signaled to Sadie and whispered, "Mom's purse is missing. Will you check in the inner room and see if Sally took it."

As Jed and Sadie both crossed the floor to the inner room, Sadie said, "What does it look like?"

"Black leather."

"Sally? Have you seen a black purse anywhere?"

"No." Sally hopped up on to her bed and crossed her hands over her lap.

"Then what do you call that?" Jed pointed to a black leather purse tipped on its side on the floor.

"A purse."

Sadie lifted the purse off the floor. "We need to get this back to Nan."

"Noooo," Sally wailed. "I want it."

"It's not yours. It's not nice to take people's things without asking. You don't want to make Nan feel bad, do you?"

Sally evaded Jed's question and reached for the purse.

"Here it is, Aanders." Sadie handed it to him.

"I want to get my stuff out." Sally's tears began to flow.

"What stuff?" Sadie pulled the purse back as Aanders stretched a hand to grab it.

"Just stuff." Sally lowered her head.

"What stuff?" Sadie lifted the leather flap. "Show me."

"That." Sally pointed to a wadded tissue. "That's mine."

"What is it?"

"Nothing." Sally took the wad from Sadie's hand.

"Oh no you don't." Sadie followed Sally into the kitchen. "Show us what you've got."

Sally placed the tissue on the kitchen table and unrolled it.

"Is that a bone?" Jed leaned toward the wadded tissue.

Aanders picked it up and rolled it over in his hand. "It looks like a bone. It must be from a chicken or something."

Jed took the bone and examined it. He looked down at Sally. "Where did you get this?"

"I got two of them. The other one's in Mr. Bakke's jar."

"Where did you get them?" Jed glanced at Sadie.

"I can't tell you. It's a secret."

23

Dan Avery stretched his frame across the front seat, unlocked the passenger door, and swung it open for Pam.

"What do you think? Can you pick out my features?" Pam held the floral arrangement in front of her face. Fern leaves and baby's breath tickled her cheeks as she peered through the bouquet. "I need to be sure it's thick enough so no one can identify me."

Removing the arrangement from his wife's hands, Dan leaned between the seats and placed the vase on the floor behind the passenger seat. "I couldn't see your face at all. You did good, Babe. It's much better than those scraggly flowers you bought last time."

Dan patted Pam's leg as he pulled into traffic. "Relax. Everything's going to be all right." He placed his hand on her shoulder and worked his long fingers into her lower neck. "Your muscles are like concrete. Loosen up. When we mapped everything out this morning, you seemed okay with it."

"I am okay with it, but it doesn't mean I can relax," Pam grumbled, pushing Dan's hand off her shoulder. "You know how hard it is for me to relax." She pulled away as he reached for her hand. "Stop it. I'm so edgy my skin's on fire. I hate it when I lose control." She pressed her fist into her stomach to quash the burn, as the acidic knot tightened.

Dan slapped the steering wheel. "Listen, Pam. If you can't pull this off, tell me right now. You weren't this nervous last time."

Staring straight ahead as they neared the hospital parking

lot, Pam jerked at the impact of Dan smacking the steering wheel for the second time.

"Damn it, Pam. Make up your mind." Pulling into one of the first available parking spaces, Dan took a deep breath. "Listen. I'm sorry. I'm wound up, too. You need to remember this is our last job using a middle man. After this, we're going to cut Reggie out and run our own show." He ran his hand the length of her thigh. "We'll be rich, Babe. We can get the house you always wanted. We'll start a family."

A small grin formed as Pam turned toward Dan. "Promise?"

"Like I told you, we're smart enough to do this on our own."

"When we have kids, we're going to quit this business," Pam said. "If we get caught, we'll lose everything."

"Then let's get this over with. The only way we'll rake in the bucks is to cut Reggie out." He grasped her clenched fist and squeezed it. "Trust me, Babe. I know what I'm doing."

Dan surveyed the parking lot before he backed out of the parking space and relocated closer to the hospital's front entrance. He pushed the lever into park and reached for the flowers.

Pam removed a plastic clip from her hair. Thick blond hair cascaded over her shoulders. She bent over and fluffed it into a mass, swirled it around her face, and made no attempt to smooth it back into place.

Holding the floral arrangement close to her shoulder, she kept her gaze on the sidewalk. The thudding inside her chest intensified. A cluster of hospital employees exited the building, a nurse commented on the fragrant purple petunias lining the portico's flower beds. Pam aimed for the glass doors. She gripped the gym bag tighter as several more pairs of shoes passed beneath the green fronds in the floral arrangement.

Dressed in jeans and a gray polo shirt, Dan waited until Pam entered the building before getting out of the car.

The pneumatic opener slid the glass doors to one side. Pam followed two uniform-clad employees into the building. She clenched her fist against her stomach. Scanning the area for security cameras they had located on their practice run, Pam held the arrangement in front of the roving eye while she approached the bank of elevators. Elevator three swooshed open.

Bypassing the admissions desk, Dan purchased a newspaper in the gift shop before sitting directly under the wall mounted security camera. He checked his watch, took a reinforcing breath, and rested his elbows on the wooden armrests. He opened the newspaper. Peering above the headline, he fixed his gaze on the elevator. The countdown had begun.

Stepping off the elevator onto the Obstetrics unit, Pam held the arrangement in front of her face. Her knuckles formed a white ridge around the gym bag's handle. Laughter erupted from the nursing station as a nurse relived a tale of a soon-to-be-forgotten blind date. With eyes cast downward, Pam passed the crowd at the desk and turned left toward the women's restroom. Her foot rammed against a thick rubber wheel. She peered down at the obstruction. A stainless-steel food cart stood next to the restroom door.

A fearful breath escaped Pam as a hand landed on her shoulder. "Are you all right? Those wheels can raise havoc with toes. Especially when you're wearing sandals."

Stepping around the cart, Pam responded without looking toward the voice. "No problem. I'm fine." She shut the restroom door and leaned against it. Her legs buckled. Gasping for air, she slid down the door until the coolness of the gray institutional tile permeated her shorts. She placed the base of her palms against her forehead.

"Get a grip," she whispered. Pulling her knees to her chest she repeatedly tapped her forehead against her knees. "Get up. You can do this."

Glancing at her watch, she realized Dan would panic if she didn't hurry. She opened the gym bag and removed a nursing uniform.

One week earlier, and in hopes of obtaining information, Pam had emailed the nurse from Pinecone Landing whom she had befriended at a conference. The woman had unwittingly obliged. Confident her uniform matched the scrubs worn by the OB nurses, and relieved her new friend wasn't on duty, Pam drew in a deep breath in preparation for the rigors ahead.

Removing her casual clothing, she folded the articles and placed them on the floor. She dug a comb, a yellow nametag, a stethoscope, a rubber binder, and a pair of white tennis shoes out of her bag. Her hands trembled as she looped the laces into a bow.

She secured her hair with the binder. Turning the faucet handle, she cupped her hand to gather water and patted her bangs until they lay flat against the top of her head. She ran the comb along her scalp repeatedly until the shorter hair melded with the longer strands. She sprayed them with hairspray. Wiping a tissue over her lips to remove her lipstick, she checked her image to make sure the woman leaving the bathroom did not resemble the woman who had entered.

Mentally listing the steps Dan had laid out for her, Pam unzipped a pouch and pulled a white receiving blanket from the opening. She also removed a denim draw-string bag. She shook open the blanket and tucked it into the main cavity of the empty gym bag smoothing it against the bottom. Picking her clothing off the floor, Pam placed the items in the denim bag.

She tugged on a pair of Latex gloves. One final item to check and she'd be ready to go. She pulled a small wad of gauze from a zippered bag. Checking the moisture content, she prayed she wouldn't have to use it.

Pam cracked the door open and fixed her gaze on the hall. She slowly inched the door wider and scanned the corridor. A mother, heavy with child, walked hand in hand with her partner, pushing an IV drip pole with her free hand. The expectant mother shuffled in discomfort. The young man beside her rubbed her back, attempting to ease the pressure on her lower spine.

Pam quickly shut the door and flipped the locking mechanism as a jubilant gathering emerged from one of the patient's rooms. She leaned against the door. She clutched her stomach. The gnawing pain had intensified since they had pulled into the hospital's parking lot. As voices faded, she edged the door open and peeked down the hall. Relatives and two nurses surrounded proud parents of newborn twins as they prepared to take their infants home.

"Perfect," Pam mouthed. The distraction suited her needs. She put the gym bag over her shoulder and adjusted the strap's length so her hand rested within the bag's opening. She looked both ways. Everyone in the hall concentrated on the throng surrounding the newborn twins. She grabbed the flowers and held them in front of her face.

The Obstetric unit contained private maternity suites featuring a bedroom, a bathroom with a shower, a toilet, and a sink. A rollaway bed and a fake-leather recliner sat next to each mother's bed for partners who wished to experience every moment of their new infant's life.

Passing the first door, Pam slowed to observe the

occupants. She noticed an infant lying in a clear plastic bassinet. The pink bundle stirred and the newborn squeaked in protest announcing she needed attention. A long leg slid from beneath the bed covers as a young woman pressed the mute button on the remote control and lowered her foot to the floor.

Pam moved on. A tan privacy curtain hanging from a metal track mounted to the ceiling obscured the occupants in the second room. Their voices filtered through the barrier. Laughter and two pair of shoes firmly situated on the tile beneath the privacy curtain urged Pam to hurry down the corridor.

As Pam neared the end of the hall, she met the strolling couple pushing the IV pole. Their pace had slowed. An expression of impatience added to the woman's already obvious discomfort as she waved limply.

Pam's doubts swelled to paralyzing proportions. Tension sucked the air from her lungs. She willed her feet to cross over to the next hall.

Loving words offered to a newborn filtered from one of the rooms as Pam rounded the corner. She watched the mother secure the tabs on a tiny diaper before running her finger over the child's forehead.

"My lazy boy. You couldn't even stay awake long enough to finish nursing." The mother rewrapped the infant in a blue blanket. Lifting a tiny soiled diaper from the bed, she wrapped the vinyl securely with its own tabs before dropping it into the wastebasket. She placed the infant back in the bassinet. Kissing his forehead, she said, "Mommy will be right back. I'm going to take a shower." She pulled a clean nightgown from her suitcase before walking into the bathroom.

Pam strolled a few feet past the patient's room. She

looked back to see if anyone else stood in the corridor. Shifting the flowers to her other hand, she approached the doorway.

Sally ran down the hall to catch up with Pam. "Wait for me," she shouted. "Jed might come, too, but he's still upstairs." She followed Pam over to the baby's bed. Standing on her tiptoes, she reached into the bassinette and ran her finger across the blue knit cap cradling the infant's head. "I'm Sally. Were you just borned?" She strained to reach further into the bassinet.

A lock snapped into place from inside the bathroom. A stream of water sputtered to life. As shower curtain rings slid along a metal rod, Pam set the bouquet on the rolling stand and placed the gym bag on the edge. She drew the security curtain. With trembling fingers, she lifted the small plastic baggie out of the bag, opened the sliding lock, and checked the chloroform-laced gauze. She placed it on the bed.

"What's in the bag?" Sally fingered the baggie.

Tucking the blue blanket snugly around the newborn, Pam slid her hands under him. The child remained deep in slumber. She pulled the denim bag out of the duffle bag and replaced it with the bundled infant. She situated the white receiving blanket around the baby. She paused. Confident the intrusion hadn't agitated him, she placed the gym bag over one shoulder and the denim bag over the other before picking the chloroform baggie off the bed. Clutching the gauze in her hand, she slipped it into the duffle bag and let it rest next to the infant's head.

Turning an ear toward the door, she slowly slid the privacy curtain to one side. Water still spewed from the shower.

She hugged the floral arrangement close as two nurses followed her to the elevator. One of the nurses rattled loose change as she talked about what she intended to purchase from the vending machine. Pam pushed the ground floor button. Several visitors followed the nurses into the elevator, causing the doors to retreat into the open position. As the doors finally closed, a beeping sound went off at the nurse's station.

"What's dinging?" A young boy looked up at his mother. "Do you hear it?"

"It's probably a patient ringing for a nurse," the boy's mother responded.

"We've had trouble with alarms going off in the birthing center this morning," the change-jingling nurse said. She smiled at the boy. "They installed a new system and they're working through the problems."

"Or it could be you know who," the second nurse commented. "I spent half the morning running errands for that demanding woman. Just because she's the wife of our mayor doesn't mean she has the right to treat me like a servant. Thank goodness her doctor signed her release."

Pam's heart beat with such intensity, she imagined everyone could hear the roar pulsing through her ears. Holding the wadded gauze steady next to the baby's head, she felt the elevator slow and settle to a stop. Open. Open. Open. The words raced repeatedly through her mind. She waited for the doors to part and set her free. Standing at the back of the elevator, she fought the urge to crumble into a heap as the rest of the occupants emptied the cavity. She stepped out into the hall. Twenty more yards and she'd be out the front door and on her way to a glorious future.

"Where are you going?" Sally followed Pam out of the elevator.

When Pam exited the elevator, Dan drew a ragged breath. He folded his newspaper. He strode across the aisle to a magazine rack and paged through the first issue within reach. He kept his head lowered and his gaze on Pam.

Pam placed the floral arrangement on an end table next to the chair where Dan had been seated and carefully slid the duffle bag under the chair. She turned and walked toward the restroom. As she pushed on the heavy door, she heard three loud beeps over the intercom. She listened for the announcement.

Dan returned to his chair. He removed the duffle bag from behind his legs. Slipping the strap over his shoulder, he slid his hand into the bag and located the gauze next to the infant's head. He glanced nonchalantly around the room. As he peered at the others in the lobby, a voice announced, "Amber Alert. Newborn baby boy. Amber Alert. Newborn baby boy. Blue blanket. Black hair." While the third repetition blared over the speaker, Dan walked past the sliding doors and exited the building. Assuming a normal pace, he kept his eyes focused on the ground until he reached his vehicle.

Pam released the rubber binder holding her hair and shook her head to encourage the thick mass to frame her face. Removing her street clothes from the denim bag, she scrambled into her shorts and shirt and jammed the uniform, stethoscope, and tennis shoes into the denim bag. To finish the transformation, she dug in her pocket and retrieved a tube of lipstick.

Sliding the lock, Pam opened the door a fraction and listened to the murmur in the hall. Hearing the words 'Amber' and 'alert' from staff scurrying past the restroom, she crossed the aisle and walked over to the gift shop. She selected a 'Get Well' card from a kiosk centered in the shop. Pam approached the counter, pulled a five-dollar bill from her pocket, and paid for her purchase. As the clerk placed the card in a bag, Pam bristled as the Amber alert again broadcast over the loud speaker.

"I bet it's a drill," the clerk said. "It's like the security director has a new toy. He's been conducting drills ever since they installed the new system. I can't imagine anyone losing a baby, can you?"

Pam's eyes burned while the woman droned on and on. She blinked away the irritating dryness, watching the woman's lips flap. She listened, but nothing registered. The clerk bagged the card and placed it on the counter.

Thanking the clerk and tucking the change into her pocket, she left the counter.

"Miss. Miss," the woman called. "Don't forget your card."

Dan eased out of his parking space as Pam approached the vehicle. He tucked his pistol under the car seat. Stopping long enough for Pam to get into the car, Dan signaled and began his departure. The couple listened to sirens growing in intensity. Dan pulled away from the stop sign, sighed with relief, and smiled as several patrol cars converged on the area and screeched to a standstill near the front entrance. Home free. Their middle-man would soon be a memory.

24

"I have to go on a retrieval," Nan said. "It's up in the next county, so I won't be back for a few hours. Will you stay in the office in case the family arrives?"

"Sure. I'll go through those invoices. I'll pay the ones you marked." Sadie pulled the rolling chair out from under the desk as she lifted the phone's receiver. "This would be Sadie."

Nan grimaced and waited for Sadie to end the conversation. "I told you not to answer the phone using your name. How are people going to know if they reached the right number?" An exasperated sigh took forever to escape Nan's lips before she started in again. "Before you sit down, I want you to go home and change into your black suit."

"I hate wearing black. Black isn't my color. It's depressing."

"No it isn't," Nan argued. "It makes you look professional. Now go change your clothes." Nan smoothed the lapels on her suit jacket and picked at a piece of lint. Checking her watch, she said, "I'm late. I should have left twenty minutes ago."

Three minutes after the hearse exited the mortuary's loading bay Clay entered the office, tugged on a guest chair and dropped into it. "Where's Nan going in such a hurry?"

Startled at the sound, Sadie's fingers slipped off the keyboard.

"That's the first time I've seen a hearse burn rubber. Isn't there a law against it? There should be." Clay tipped the pen holder over as he propped one foot on the desk.

"She's going to meet Johnny Depp. She brought the hearse in case he wants to have sex."

Clay's head sank back on his shoulders as he stared at Sadie. "Really? The pirate guy?"

"Would I lie?" Sadie pulled the keyboard closer and hit the backspace key. She corrected the entry before clicking an icon to accept the data.

Jerking again when Clay's weight brushed the back of her chair, she said, "Quit sneaking up on me. Jane does it all the time and it drives me nuts. What are you doing here, anyway?"

"I'm looking for Aanders. I want to go fishing. How come you're wearing black?"

"They had a sale at 'Funeral Homes R Us'."

"Really? You never wear black."

"Nan made me wear it. I don't know why she insisted I wear a suit considering who's coming."

"Who?"

"The yahoo whose brother died in the bike accident."

Sadie stood and side-stepped Clay. He had invaded her territory. Pilfered the air from her private space. Clay attracted trouble the way her black suit attracted dog hair and she didn't want him anywhere near her.

"Aanders can't go fishing. He's too busy. Besides, you know Nan doesn't want you around when she's gone."

"That's why I'm here. What she doesn't know won't hurt."

"Bull. You can wave your pipedream good-bye. She'd skin me alive if I let you take him fishing."

"What the hell happened to your hair?" Clay leaned forward as his gaze zeroed in on Sadie's head.

"You're a fine one to talk. At least I wash my hair."

"What's with the green streak? It looks like a parrot

crapped on your head."

Sadie ran her hand down one hip before she remembered she had changed into her funeral clothes. "It matches the skirt I had on earlier. Big Leon mixed the color especially to match my outfit."

"Really? It still looks like a parrot crapped on your head."

Sadie picked on her green gelled spikes to make them stand erect. She removed her black suit coat and hung it on the back of her chair. As she tugged her lemon yellow tube top into position, Clay leaned forward to shorten the span between them.

His eyebrows merged over his nose as his eyes reduced to tiny slits. "What's on your gut?"

Sadie patted her tattoo. "That's an asp."

"What's your ass doing up there?"

"I said asp, not ass. A-S-P. It's Cleopatra's asp. Don't you know anything?"

"I know your ass shouldn't be up there. Is that what happens when you turn ninety?"

"Ninety? I'm not ninety. I'm sixty-four. You obviously don't know the first thing about fashion."

"Neither do you." Clay lifted a folder off the desk and opened it.

"Leave Nan's stuff alone." Sadie grabbed the folder. The contents flew across the floor. As she bent down to gather the sheets, she noticed Aanders standing outside the window trying to get her attention. Exasperation etched his face. He beckoned with his hand while trying to remain tucked behind the window frame out of Clay's range of vision.

Moving closer to the window, Sadie raised her eyebrows in question. Aanders responded by spreading his palms upward and shrugging. He shook his head vigorously and repeated the gesture.

"I'll be right back," Sadie said. "Don't touch anything. If anybody comes, be nice to them."

"Okay." Springs squeaked in protest as Clay sat on Sadie's five-dollar garage sale chair and propped both feet on the desk calendar.

"What's wrong," Sadie whispered, after she hurried across the sidewalk.

"It's Sally. I can't find her."

Sadie drew a deep breath. "Where did you last see her?" She had given Aanders one simple task: to keep an eye on Sally. "I don't understand why you can't keep track of Sally."

"She's an escape artist. All I did was look for some dog treats and the next thing I knew, she disappeared."

"You know what she's like. You can't leave her alone for one minute."

"Belly's gone too. I called for him, but he didn't come. He must have followed her."

"They shouldn't be too hard to find." Sadie headed down the path toward the lake. "If we can't find her, she runs the risk of slipping into oblivion. I'll never forgive myself if we lose her."

Aanders hurried to catch up to Sadie.

"Sally doesn't understand the complexity of her death. It's up to us to see she goes through the tunnel with Jed."

"I tried to keep an eye on her. It's not fair I have to do this." Aanders dropped his gaze to the ground as Sadie stopped abruptly in front of him and turned to face him.

"I agree. I didn't ask for this assignment, either. Because we're both death coaches, we've got to make the best of it. You screwed up," Sadie said. "If you're looking for someone to give you an 'A' for effort, it's not going to happen. Now let's find her."

Clay watched Aanders and Sadie trot down the path and out of sight.

"Hey Dude." A man poked Clay's shoulder.

"What?" Clay let out a startled cry as he lurched upright.

"Dude. We're here to see my brother. The funeral lady told me to come early for a private viewing."

"You must be the guy Sadie was expecting. What does your brother look like?" Clay stood and led three leather-clad men into the viewing chapel. "He must be here somewhere."

"Is this the guy?"

"No, Dude. That ain't no Harley rider. That's an old lady. Where's my brother?"

"Maybe he's in the other room." Clay tromped across the floor with two men in black boots and one in pink neon sneakers striding behind him. A heavy chain dangled from the leader's billfold. "Is that him?" Clay pushed through the French doors and led them toward the alcove.

"Yup. That's my bro." The man hung his head and leaned his elbows on the rim of the casket. "He's the best Harley rider I've ever known."

The two other men joined the brother. Heads bowed in respect, one of the men ran his fist under his nose. "Shit man. What a shame. He was the best Harley rider in the county."

Clay looked at a lump under one of the men's shirts. "What you got there?"

"Nothin."

"That don't look like nothin to me." Clay held his arm out. "Hand it over."

"Come on, man. Give me a break," the third mourner said, raising his T-shirt and removing a whiskey bottle. "It's a little something to accompany him on his final ride."

"Let me see." Clay grabbed the bottle. He uncapped it and tipped it to his lips. "Whoa. That's good stuff. Why waste it on him?"

"Cuz he's my brother." The deceased man's brother grabbed the bottle from Clay. Whiskey ran down Clay's chin and dripped onto the floor.

Clay looked toward the door before running the sole of his sandal over the droplets on the carpet. "Give me another swig and I'll let you put the bottle in the casket."

"Deal." The brother grinned and removed the cap. He handed the bottle to Clay.

"What happened to your brother?"

"The doctor told me he had a stroke."

"A stroke?" Clay took a third swing. "I thought he had an accident. He doesn't look old enough to have a stroke."

The brother frowned. "He wasn't. He was twenty-eight. The stroke caused the accident." He pulled the bottle from Clay's hand and screwed the cap into place.

"Are those your bikes out there?" Clay pointed toward the parking lot.

"One of them bikes is his," the brother said. "I thought he'd appreciate having it here for the funeral."

The second mourner said, "We got the dents out and polished it up for the occasion."

"Why leave it out there? Why don't you bring it in and park it by the casket." Clay walked over to the door and held it open while the men descended the stairs toward the bike.

A big rumble erupted from the parking lot as the brother started the Harley and eased it into the funeral home's lobby. "This is great, Dude. Thanks."

"No problem." Clay slapped the brother on the shoulder. "I'll be in the office. I've got an excavation job and I'm waiting to hear when I can start." Clay patted the cell phone clipped to his belt.

The other two mourners gave Clay a thumbs-up and

joined the deceased man's brother at the casket.

Twenty minutes later, Sadie poked her head through the office door. "Dan Avery is looking for you. He said he'd be down by the marina." She indicated she wanted Clay to lean forward. She grabbed her black jacket off the desk chair and slipped her arms through the openings.

"I better get going." Clay stretched and pressed hard against the chair's back. Metal creaked against the weight.

"Are the guys here for their private viewing? I see bikes in the parking lot." Sadie stepped into the office and pushed Clay's feet off the desk onto the floor.

"They're in there." As Clay pointed toward the viewing room a rumble erupted, then mushroomed into an ear-piercing roar.

With the shocked look of a man sorting through a long list of indiscretions, Clay held up his hands. "I didn't do it. They did."

A crashing thud added to the chaos. Sadie hurried toward the viewing room. "What's going on? Shut that thing off," she shouted over the din.

"Dude," the brother said, looking back at the casket and then at his friend, "you must not have hooked it up right."

One of the locked legs on the casket stand had collapsed under the pressure of being pulled forward. The casket lay tipped on its side with the recently departed sprawled next to it, naked from the waist down.

"Oh, my Lord." Sadie gazed at the scene. Liquid dripped from a broken whiskey bottle and pooled on the carpet.

"What?" The brother shrugged. "We wanted him to have one final ride."

"Holy crap," Clay echoed. "What a waste of good booze."

"Lock the doors," Sadie shouted. "We've got to get this

cleaned up before Nan gets back."

"What happened to his pants?" Clay gazed down at the man.

"What happened to the blue shirt and tie I put on him this morning?" Her mouth agape in disbelief, Sadie pointed to a Harley T-shirt. "Where did the shirt come from?"

"I brought it," the brother said. "It's his favorite shirt."

Sadie ran to the lobby and over to a storage closet. She tugged a casket stand from the closet and opened the mechanism, allowing the stand to spring into an upright position. "Help me switch this with the broken one."

Sadie looked up as Clay crossed the lobby and placed his hand on the doorknob. "Get back here. You're not going anywhere until this mess is cleaned up."

"I can't. Nan might catch me here."

"That's the least of your worries. Help them lift the casket back on the stand."

The second mourner edged around Sadie, glancing at her hair.

Once the casket settled into place on the replacement stand, Sadie unlatched the bottom lid. "Lift him into the casket."

The three men shuffled into position. Clay bent down and joined them. He stiffened and stood upright. "I'm not going to pick him up with his dingus staring me in the face."

"Me neither," the third mourner echoed, stepping back to join Clay.

"Yes, you are," Sadie growled. "It's your fault he's down there in the first place."

"The hell it is," the mourner said, pointing at Clay. "He said we should bring the Harley in."

Sadie put her hands on her hips and glared at Clay. She issued instructions to the men easing the corpse back into the casket. After securing the lid, she placed the floral arrangement back into position. "Get the mess wiped up. Be sure to pick up the glass."

As the men crawled on their hands and knees searching for the final shards of glass, a car door slammed and the overhead hearse bay door rose in its tracks.

"Oh, no," Sadie cried.

Clay's cell phone rang. He flipped the lid and listened. "I gotta go. Dan's getting impatient." He sprinted across the lobby and out the front door.

Sadie lifted the waste basket and handed it to the third mourner. "Make it disappear." She stared at the door as footsteps grew louder.

Nan closed the door behind her. She sniffed the air. "It smells like a bar in here. Has Clay been here?"

Peering toward the viewing room, she whispered in anger, "When I told you to change your clothes, I meant get rid of the green hair, too."

"I didn't have time. The brother came for the private viewing sooner than I expected."

"Then do it before the rest of the people get here." Nan crossed the floor and propped open the double doors leading to the viewing room. Three men stood in front of the casket. She walked up behind them. Drawing in a deep sniff, she looked down into the casket and then back at Sadie.

Sadie cringed. Nan had a way of expressing displeasure with her eyebrows. She should take them on the entertainment circuit because they could perform a standup routine all by themselves. This routine meant trouble, but not as much trouble as what she spotted out of the corner of her eye. Sally pushed through Clay's cabin door and sauntered out. A lime-green neckerchief-adorned dog exited behind her.

25

"Quit squirming." Jed resituated Sally on his lap. "Do you have ants in your pants?"

Belly pranced in place at Jed's feet, matching the energy oozing from Sally.

Sadie smiled at the warmth in Sally's giggle. It soothed away the day's stress. Nan's lectures usually inflicted short-term pain, but this one had been a doosie. The words still stung. She shouldn't be surprised, though, because Nan had mastered the art of ambush. Now she knew how Nan's students felt after a semester with the woman who adhered to funeral protocol to the nth degree.

Jane pushed through the screen door carrying a brown paper bag. She turned it over and emptied the contents onto the kitchen table. "Look at all the stuff we got today."

Sadie picked up a few items and dropped them back on the table. "How many rummage sales did you hit?"

"Too many," Bernie said. "She wore me out. I like rummage sales, but usually from the seller's end."

"Looks like junk." Sadie scooped up the items and placed them back in the bag.

"Quit it." Jane batted at her hand. "There's good stuff in there." She held a black knit dickey up to Sadie's neck. "See. This will be perfect when you go ice fishing. It will keep you nice and warm."

"I don't want it." Sadie grabbed it from her and wadded it into a ball.

"What's the matter with it? Don't you like dickeys?"

"It's not that I don't like dickeys. I can think of better

places to wear them than around my neck."

Jed let out a big guffaw before burying his mouth in Sally's hair.

"That's not funny." Jane pointed a finger at Bernie. "Quit grinning. It only encourages her."

Aanders rapped on the screen door before pulling it open. "Hi, Bernie," he said, joining them at the table. "Hi, Mr. Bakke."

"I suppose we better go," Jane whispered to Bernie. "Sadie's got stuff to do."

As Bernie followed Jane to the door, he turned and looked back toward the table. He scrunched his eyes into little slits. His gaze lingered on the empty chair under the clock before Jane yanked him through the door.

"That darn Jane's been blabbing to Bernie. I can tell," Sadie said. "She can't keep the crosser secret for one second."

"He must have accepted what she told him or he'd have fled in the other direction," Jed said. "You have to admit it's incredible. I can see why he's checking it out."

"I knew something smelled fishy. I could tell by the way he's been staring at Aanders. You'd think he expects to see the word death coach branded on Aanders' nose."

"I hear you weren't exactly a good girl, today." Jed picked at a strand of hair caught in Sally's eyelash.

Sally kept her dangling foot in motion, ignoring Jed's comment.

"I thought we agreed you needed to mind Aanders. I can't give you a surprise if you can't follow instructions."

"A surprise?" Sally rotated on Jed's lap. "What surprise?"

"I'm not going to tell you. It's going to have to wait. If you're a good girl, I'll give it to you tomorrow night."

"When we get home from the hospital?"

"Only if you behave."

"I'm getting a surprise, Sadie." Sally jumped down from Jed's lap.

"How about a movie?" Aanders followed Sally toward the inner room.

"I don't want to. I'm taking Belly back to our secret hideout."

"What?" Sadie watched Sally retreat. "What secret hideout?"

Sally tipped her head to one side and kicked at the rug with her bare toes.

"Sally? What secret hideout?"

"It's a secret." She crouched down and buried her face in Belly's neckerchief.

"Remember what we said about going out without permission?"

"I didn't bother anyone."

Sadie put her hand on Sally's head and turned her around. "Where is your secret hiding place?"

"It's not a hiding place. It's a hideout." She drew out the word with exaggerated impatience.

"Same difference," Aanders taunted.

"What do you and Belly do in your secret hideout?" Sadie eased closer to Sally.

"Nothing."

"Can we go with you?"

"You're too big."

Jed and Sadie glanced at each other. "Sadie's pretty small. Are you sure she's too big?"

"You have to be dog size, like me."

"How do you get in your hideout?" Sadie bent down and stooped over. "Like this?"

Sally giggled. "No. You jump in the hole. Then you dig

for pirate's treasure. Just like on TV."

"In the water?"

"No. We dig in the dirt. Belly helps, too. He even found something." Sally glanced toward the kitchen table.

They waited for the miniature culprit to explain, but all they got were lips sealed in stubborn determination. Sally reached over and grabbed at the gyrating hairs on Belly's tail as he circled the group.

"What did you find?" Jed reached out his hand and pulled Sally close.

"Things. I didn't find them, Belly did."

"Where did you put the things?"

Sally glanced toward the table again. "In there."

"Show me," Jed said, tugging on Sally's arm. "Where?"

"They're with Mr. Bakke. He's protecting the treasure." Sally climbed up on a kitchen chair and lifted the lid off Mr. Bakke's urn. Her fingers sifted through the ashes. She frowned. She peered into the dark hole and dug around again. "It's gone."

"Was it a bone?"

"Just like the other one. There's more." Sally dug around again and pulled out a soiled object dangling from a delicate chain.

"A necklace?" Sadie took the chain from Sally and held it over the urn. She flicked dust off the surface before rubbing the half-heart with her thumb to remove the silt. Walking over to the window, she held it so the sun reflected on the necklace. "It's got writing on it. It looks like J-E-D."

"Let me see," Jed said, lifting the chain off Sadie's outstretched palm. He held it up to the window.

"Where did you get this?" Jed spun around and grabbed Sally by the shoulders. Tears sprouted from Sally's eyes and her lower lip quivered.

Jed shook her. "Where did you get this?"

Full blown sobs gushed forth. Sally ran to Sadie and clung to her leg.

"What is it? What's wrong?" Sadie watched as Jed's realization turned to anguish.

Jed's hand trembled as he held it up to Sadie. "It's Celeste's necklace. When we were kids, we bought this heart necklace for our mother. It had two halves. One has *Celeste* engraved on it and the other has *Jed*. Mom gave us each other's half and made us promise we'd always keep them. She wanted us to cherish the love we had for each other."

Jed dropped into Jane's chair. "I put mine away for safe keeping when Celeste disappeared. I wanted the sheriff to have something to match to Celeste's half if it ever surfaced. My half is at my house."

Sadie bent down and wiped Sally's cheeks with her thumbs. "Jed's not mad at you, Sweetheart. He's just worried. Where did you get the pretty necklace? Did you find it in your hideout?"

Sally nodded her head. "Belly dug up some more bones, too. And a pirate's head."

"Will you show us where it is?"

Sally nodded again.

26

"What's taking so long," Dan Avery asked for the second time, pacing the short length of the cabin. "I thought you said a bath would make the kid stop crying."

Dan sat on the bed and cupped his hands over his ears. When the crying grew in intensity, he pushed the hospital blue print onto the floor and yanked a pillow out from beneath the bedspread. "Damn kid," he muttered. He jammed the pillow against his ears with his fists and flopped onto his back. "Can't you do something to shut him up?" He threw the pillow at the bathroom door.

Startled by the door banging against the bathroom wall, the infant wailed in protest.

"Raising your voice certainly won't help," Pam bit back. "I haven't bathed him yet. Quit referring to the baby as a boy. You're going to make a mistake in public. Get over here and hand me a diaper," Pam ordered.

Reaching for the stack of diapers, Dan picked one up and shook it open.

Cool air wafted over the infant. His arms trembled as shrieks of distress added to the tension.

Pam secured the diaper and wrapped the child snugly in the blanket. Drawing the baby to her shoulder, she patted his back and bounced in a smooth, steady rhythm as she joined Dan on the sofa. Within seconds, calm filled the room. Pam whispered, "He apparently doesn't like being cold. We need to remember to keep him bundled." Slapping her forehead with her free hand, she winced. "I mean she."

"Whatever you did, it worked," Dan said. "Keep the kid

quiet." He rotated his neck several times to release the grip of anxiety.

It was just like Dan to barrel headfirst into one of his pouting jags. He did it every time they secured a baby. He criticized her for getting nervous before the abduction, but he fell to pieces when they took possession of the infant.

The customary two-day span the child lived with them sped by too fast for Pam. She loved the feel of a warm infant against her neck. The timing on this abduction forced them to stretch their stay a few days longer to make sure no one suspected anything. She loved the added mothering time.

They'd survived the wait before. They'd survive it again. They? Pam snickered. It wasn't they. It was up to Pam to provide the care. Dan didn't expend any energy fulfilling his end of their arrangement. Unless driving the car and complaining counted. He expected her to function as a drill sergeant and force the babies to behave. She released a jagged sigh as a nagging suspicion resurfaced. Would Dan react the same when they had their own child? She knew the answer.

Placing the child on the bed, Pam pulled a baby bottle and a container of powdered formula from the diaper bag. She scooped powder into the distilled water, shook the lumps out, and lifted the baby into her arms.

Pam gently ran the nipple back and forth over the child's mouth before his lips closed around the object.

"I'm going out for a smoke." Dan let the door slam shut behind him.

Pam looked up when the door slammed a second time.

Sally crossed the floor and peered around the bedroom door frame. "I came to see your baby. I heard her crying."

"There you go," Pam cooed, rubbing her free finger over the infant's warm cheek. "One of these days I'm going to have a baby just like you. She'll be mine. Not one belonging to someone else." Closing her eyes, Pam's thoughts lingered on Dan's promise of starting their own family. She'd make it work. No matter what.

A vision of the house she had dreamed about on Lake Minnetonka filled her mind. A nursery, a library, and a kitchen with every appliance and gadget known to the modern cook would be at her disposal. The need to take risks would no longer be necessary after they earned enough. Cutting out the middle man had been a brilliant inspiration. She didn't want to admit it to Dan, but she now welcomed the next few abductions. If future abductions went as smoothly as this one had, they'd be living in luxury before she had time to sketch floor plans for her dream home.

As the tension from the previous hours drained, Pam slipped into a state of half-sleep. Aware of voices, she didn't rise to full consciousness until a hand tapped her shoulder. She pitched forward.

Dan stood directly in front of Pam with his index finger to his lips. Pointing at the door, he motioned for her to take the baby into the bathroom. His pursed lips trembled in anger. "You should have finished the job before. It'll be your fault if we get caught. Now get in there and don't come out till he looks like a girl."

Pam slipped quietly into the bathroom. Sally followed.

Grabbing a bag from the bed stand, Dan handed it to Pam through the opening. When the bathroom door's latch clicked into place, he headed back toward the porch.

Clay pulled the screen door open and crossed the threshold. With an outstretched arm, he offered Dan a beer. "Here. It's the least I can do for a man who offered me a job." Pulling a chair up, Clay added, "I thought you might like to hear the news."

Bare thighs flowed over the edge of the chair as Clay

leaned back and propped his sandals on the sofa. "There's so much commotion going on at the lodge I had to get the hell out of there. Those cops make a big thing out of nothing. They said a baby's missing. It's just a baby. Now if a car was stolen, that's cause for concern."

Dan pointed at Clay's lap. "Where are your pants?"

Clay looked down and lifted his shirt tails. "I don't know. I must have taken them off when I took a crap."

"You take your pants off to take a crap?"

"I must have." Clay stared up at the ceiling in thought. "Or maybe I left them at the mortuary. A dead guy in the cooler had new jeans. I thought I'd trade with him, but they didn't fit."

A bewildered frown furrowed Dan's forehead as he peered at Clay out of the corner of his eyes.

Clay downed a swig of beer. "That scrawny bitch Sadie is always sticking her nose where it doesn't belong. She's going around telling everybody."

"About your pants?"

"No. About the baby." He emptied the beer bottle. "She reminds me of one of them tight-assed poodles always prancing around. She must be French."

Peeling the paper label off the beer bottle with his thumb, Dan glanced at the bathroom door.

"You still got work for me to do?"

"Tomorrow," Dan responded. He wadded a strip of label paper and shot it across the room. "Unless the kid changes my mind. That crying drives me nuts. Maybe we'll cut our vacation short and head back to Minneapolis."

"I know what you mean. After my divorce, I dated a woman with a kid. We ended up bringing the brat with us on vacation because her babysitter canceled. As far as I'm concerned, the next time I look for a woman, she ain't going to have kids."

"I hear you." As Dan rose from his chair, he handed the empty to Clay and walked toward the door. "Thanks for the beer. I'm going to see if my wife needs help."

Pam placed the sleeping infant on a mattress of towels on the bathroom floor. She gathered a pair of scissors, a can of shaving cream, and a razor from a bag of supplies before arranging them on the floor. Grasping the fine silken hair between her fingers, she snipped at the black wisps until she'd reduced his hair to a jagged quarter-inch in length. Turning him and propping him with her knee, she finished the hair cut.

"My mom cuts my hair. She says she doesn't want to pay for a haircut because it won't make me look better anyway." Sally let out an accepting sigh. "She wishes I wasn't so ugly." Sally stood on her tiptoes trying to catch her image in the mirror. Patting her hair over her ears, she said, "Sadie and Jed told me I'm beautiful. Especially when I wear Sadie's earrings."

Picking at the fallen hair with her fingers, Pam gathered as much as possible and placed it in the wastebasket next to the vanity. She blew across the child's forehead to remove the remaining traces of loose hair.

Pam filled the sink with hot water and floated the can of shaving cream in the basin. After wringing out a white washcloth, she placed it over his scalp. He stirred. His lower lip curled into a pout before he returned to slumber. Pam squirted warm shaving cream onto her palm and rubbed her hands together to distribute the mound.

"Can I help, too?" Sally held her palm out.

Gently drawing the razor from his crown to his forehead, Pam continued until the razor's head overflowed with cream.

The infant flinched at the distraction. She rinsed and shaved until all traces of black hair disappeared.

She ran fresh water in the basin. The child flinched when the warm water washed over him, but didn't protest. Pam cooed gently to the infant during his bath and then patted a dry towel over his body.

Digging in the supply bag, Pam pushed the items around until she found the tiny pink stocking cap. She bit a plastic strip to sever it from the price tag and tossed the pieces into the wastebasket. She placed the stocking cap snugly on the infant's head.

Pam grinned. "You are now officially known as Chelsie. A very bald Chelsie, but still a Chelsie."

The baby whimpered a few times when Pam placed him on her outstretched legs. Digging deeper into the bag, she withdrew the remaining items and laid them on the floor.

"Can I help, too? I know how to take care of babies." Sally edged closer to Pam.

Systematically breaking the seal on each plastic wrapper, Pam removed the tags and stacked the clothing in order of application. After unsnapping the closures on the first item, she lowered the upper portion of the terry towel and pulled on a new pink T-shirt adorned in bunnies. The baby squeaked a protest. She tugged on the new pink booties before the child mustered a second whimper. A diaper and a new soft, pink blanket engulfed him to complete the alteration.

Gathering the plastic wrappers and remaining price tags, Pam dropped them into the wastebasket along with the discarded clothing before unlocking the door and walking over to the bed.

"Wow. That's quite the transformation," Dan said, lifting the edge of the stocking cap. "Looks like a Chelsie to me."

"It's time we introduce him to the world." Pam balled her

fist as she realized her mistake. "I mean her." She nodded toward the screen door. "Let's make the rounds. We need to make sure people see pink everywhere we go."

"You're right. We do, but first, I need to warn you word is out about the abduction. Clay just told me."

Pam drew in a deep breath. "Then the timing is perfect. A boy is missing. People already know we have a girl."

Sally stood on the porch and watched Pam and Dan walk down the path toward the lodge.

27

"We can't just go barging into the sheriff's office," Sadie said. "How are we going to explain how we found two finger bones?"

"I still can't believe it. You mean Sally dug up a body under Clay's cabin?" Jane traipsed back and forth in front of the stove. "How can it be possible? Celeste must have been murdered right under our noses and we didn't even know it."

"We're still not sure it's a human body and we don't know if it's Celeste. Sally said she found a pirate." Sadie paused before she added, "And, we certainly don't know if it's murder."

Bernie's gaze bounced from Sadie to Jane as they discussed the discovery. "Why else would her body be under the cabin if it wasn't murder? I think we need to call the sheriff."

"Me too," Jane replied. "Let's get Lon over here and see what he thinks."

"What do you mean 'we'?" Sadie glared at Bernie. "We don't even know what's going on and you want to bring in the sheriff?"

"I know what's going on. Jane told me. You and Aanders talk to dead people and it's one of the dead who found the bones."

Sadie stared at her sister. "You big blabbermouth. I knew I couldn't trust you. You told Mr. Bakke and now you've told Bernie. Why don't you just put an ad in the newspaper?"

As Jane drew in a sharp breath, Bernie grabbed her hand.

"Actually I'm glad Jane explained it. I wondered about continuing a relationship with Jane because of you, Sadie."

"Me? What do I have to do with your relationship?"

Bernie eased Sadie into the kitchen chair and put his hands on her shoulders. "To be honest, I thought you were, well, a bit unstable."

"Unstable? Unstable? I'm not the one who has to have everything in order every second of every day." Sadie pointed at Jane. "She even insists I have tidy thoughts before I speak."

"I happen to like tidy," Bernie said. "I'm anal just like Jane and understand where she's coming from. I'm not one to believe in supernatural powers. Bernie indicated quotation marks around the word 'powers' with his fingers. "After hearing the story about Mr. Bakke's death and all the comings and goings of your crossers, it makes sense."

"My crossers are none of your concern. That's confidential information. I want it to stay that way. If word got out, every lunatic in the country would be camping on my doorstep searching for their dead relatives. It's difficult enough guiding the crossers without added distractions."

"I appreciate what you're doing. Everyone's got secrets."

"I don't." Jane beamed up at Bernie.

"This isn't a secret. It goes way beyond secrets." Sadie gestured with her hand. "I don't need to explain this. You're interfering where you don't belong."

"I disagree. I want to help." He sat next to Jane and cupped her hand in his. "Right now the two of you have a bigger problem than the crossers. You've got two bones and a necklace. You should have gone to the sheriff with the first bone."

"I thought it was an animal bone," Sadie said.

"Well, what are you going to do about it now you know it's a human bone?"

"Check it out, that's what I'm going to do. The whole law enforcement crew is busy trying to locate the baby. By the time they find him, we'll be done with our own research. That's when I'll tell Lon."

The screen door banged and Aanders followed Jed into the cabin. "Dad's still sleeping on his porch swing."

"More like passed out," Sadie mumbled.

"Whatever it is, he's dead to the world. Sally's painting his toenails," Jed said.

"She'd better not be using my new polish. I haven't even used it yet." Sadie hurried to her bedroom. A muffled shout came from the corner of her closet. "That little thief. I thought I hid it where she wouldn't find it."

"Who's all here?" Bernie looked at the chair under the clock.

"As far as crossers go, just Jed." Sadie returned to her chair.

Jed looked from Bernie to Sadie. "You're right. Jane blabbed."

"She blabbed all right. Couldn't keep her flappers shut."

Aanders gaped in disbelief. "You mean Bernie knows about the crossers? He seems to be taking it pretty well."

"He doesn't have much choice. He had the nerve to tell me he thought I was unstable. Can you imagine?"

Jed's eyebrows twitched as he looked at Aanders.

"You need to quit dwelling on what I said." Bernie held a hand toward Sadie. "I accept it. I understand. If you notice, I'm still here."

"Just ignore her," Jane huffed. "She's a legend in her own mind. She can't take criticism."

Jed and Aanders slumped against the backs of their chairs and peered at Sadie.

"What is this? Kick her while she's down day? We've got

more important things to deal with." Sadie glared at Jane. "If you're so smart, what would you do?"

"I have an idea." Aanders sat upright and leaned against the table. "Maybe I can sneak down into the crawlspace while Dad's sleeping."

"We can't risk it," Jed said.

"I know what we can do." Bernie gestured with excitement. "I'll invite Clay to go fishing. Just tell me how long you want me to stay on the lake."

"That will work." Sadie turned toward Aanders. Ask one of the dock boys to get a boat gassed up and ready to go. Make sure all the fishing gear is in it, too."

A half hour later, Sadie and her collaborators watched listless Clay follow Bernie down to the dock.

"He sure doesn't look like he wants to go fishing. He looks puny." The boat motor roared to life and sped away from the dock. Jane smiled and threw a kiss back to Bernie.

The screen door banged against the frame. A breathless Aanders stumbled into the cabin. "I found a shovel and some boxes."

"A shovel?" Jed met Sadie's gaze. "You can't use a shovel. You've got to keep everything intact for the deputies."

"I know," Sadie said. "Aanders just wants to help. I need to see for myself what's down there before I tell Lon."

When they entered Clay's cabin, Sally looked up and grinned. "Look. I did it myself." She held up her foot. Red glitter nail polish adorned each toenail, three toe knuckles, and several spots on the wood flooring. The hairs on the applicator brush had dried into a rubbery clump adhered to the braided rug.

Jed whispered a fearful, "Oh, dear." He scooped Sally off the floor. "Sadie's not going to be happy." He shifted a hammer and screwdriver into his free hand. "You're coming outside with me so we can keep watch."

Jane lifted the trap door and eased it back against the rug. "Are you sure you want to go down there? It looks awfully small?"

"I need to see what's down there," Sadie said. "Aanders will help me. You go outside and keep watch with Jed. He's going to remove the screen in case I need to pass anything through the air vent."

"Maybe I should go down there with you."

"You're too big. Besides, it's nothing but dirt and spiders down there."

"Aanders is taller than me," Jane argued.

"I wasn't talking about height." Sadie shooed Jane away with a wave of her hand.

Belly snorted as he whined into the hole. His tail jerked frantically. Tail hairs darted in an irregular circle before he finally took the plunge.

"Come back here," Sadie ordered. "I don't want you disturbing anything." Sadie pointed at Aanders. "Get him out of there."

Aanders dropped into the hole. He flicked his flashlight on and crawled under the floorboards. A muffled comment wafted back toward Sadie. "It's okay. Jed already took the screen off and Belly went out through the vent."

Jane poked her head into the vent opening. "Belly had something in his mouth, but he got away. It looked like a bone."

Sadie sat on the edge of the hole and lowered her feet through the opening. She strained to reach the dirt with her toe. "Shine your light this way," she ordered. After both feet landed on the dirt, she thumbed the flashlight's on switch.

"What you doing, Jane?" Clay rounded the side of the cabin.

Jane let out a cry as her hand flew to her chest. "Clay. What are you doing here?"

"He forgot his fishing license in his glove compartment," Bernie said, hurrying Clay past the opening and over to his car.

Sadie and Aanders turned off their flashlights simultaneously and edged into the crawlspace darkness. They hugged the wall.

Bernie kept his hand firmly on Clay's arm guiding him back past the air vent opening. He stumbled against Clay when Clay stopped in his tracks.

Clay bent down and peered into the crawlspace. He held his hand over his eyes to shield the sun. "What you doing in there, Sadie?"

"Planting potatoes," Sadie shouted as she waved at Clay.

"Really? I'd help you, but I'm going fishing."

"That's okay. I don't need any help. I'm almost done."

Clay straightened. "See you later, Jane."

As the two fishermen neared the dock, Clay looked back toward the cabin. "What a lamebrain. Everybody knows you need sun to grow potatoes."

Sadie squatted near the bones. She brushed loose dirt away with her fingers, taking care not to disturb the skeleton.

"Do you see the pirate?" Sally bent low and shouted through the air vent.

"I do," Sadie answered.

"Can you tell if it's a woman?" Jed strained to see into the darkness. "Can you tell if it's Celeste?"

"It's hard to tell. The skull has lots of hair. There's dirt caked in it, but it looks like it could be black."

"It's Celeste. I know it is." Jed rocked back on his heels.

As Sadie felt along the folds of fabric, chunks of material broke loose and flittered into the rib cage. "Aanders, shine your flashlight over here."

Sadie turned toward the air vent. "There's a notebook in here. I'm going to take it back to the cabin so we can look at it."

"You better not remove anything in case it's evidence," Jane said.

"I agree. Let the sheriff take care of it." Jed cupped his hands megaphone style and leaned into the opening. "Don't get your fingerprints on it."

Sadie held her finger to her lips and whispered to Aanders. "What they don't know won't matter." She lifted the notebook cover with her fingernail. She shined the flashlights beam on the pages and fanned through them. Sadie paused as she stated at one of the pages. "Oh good Lord."

28

Sadie shifted in her chair, tugging on the black fabric sticking to the back of her legs. Not only had the thermometer reached eighty-seven degrees and the humidity had turned unbearable, but Nan had insisted she dress in her best funeral attire. How disgusting. She looked like an old lady. Tempted to hoist her skirt up above her knees so her skin could cool against the metal chair, Sadie decided against it. It would only bring on another lecture.

It wasn't every day State dignitaries came to Pinecone Landing to pay their final respects. A senator from St. Paul, who had served his constituents for over thirty-seven years, had requested he be interred in his home town. Nan arranged a memorial service in Pinecone Landing prior to the burial. The official funeral with all the pomp and circumstance had taken place a day earlier in St. Paul, but with campaigning for fall elections in full swing, campaign managers had made sure their candidates accompanied the senator all the way to the grave. Tearful publicity never hurts. Especially with the cameras rolling.

The heat generated from so many attendees crowded into the mortuary added to the discomfort. Sadie fanned the neck of her blouse. Clay and Aanders demonstrated equal distress by squirming, scratching, and sighing deeply while their eyes glazed over with boredom.

Sadie scanned the crowd. The majority of mourners flicked their funeral brochures in rhythmic harmony to keep air circulating around their shoulders. A sea of black suits. Three hundred to be exact. She should know. She helped

Aanders and Clay count and arrange the chairs.

The essence of influence and superiority generated by the attendees turned palpable. Minnesota's finest. All except for Kimmer, who straddled one and a half chairs next to his wife in the fourth row. Sadie noticed him hobnobbing with the politicians before the ceremony, as only Judge Kimmer could do. That would soon change. She could already imagine the whispers.

Sadie had tried to talk to Lon earlier about her discovery, but he had been dispatched to an altercation at one of the boat landings. She also tried to tell Nan, but when the air conditioning went out in the chapel, Nan wasn't in the mood to listen to anything but the sound of a repair truck pulling into the parking lot. She'd tell them as soon as they returned from the cemetery.

Before the mourners had arrived for the ceremony, Nan frantically tried to locate an air-conditioning repair man. While Nan used the phone, she shouted instructions to Clay on where to situate the casket in the viewing alcove. Because of the large crowd anticipated, Nan had hired Clay for the day. She loaned him a white shirt, a black tie, black shoes, and black pants from her stash of funeral burial clothes.

For once, Clay looked almost human. Almost. Sadie had Jane to thank for the metamorphosis. Jane's passion for browsing rummage sales for cast-off clothing paid off. Jane's purchases over the years had also provided clothing for families who couldn't afford proper burial outfits for their loved ones.

Sadie's gaze drifted to the window. She had never seen so many black limousines in one gathering. The high school prom held a close second, but it couldn't top this display of citizens' tax dollars gone astray.

* * *

Nan approached the front of the room and stood next to the casket. Her striking presence caused mourners' heads to rotate in unison while they watched her cross the chapel floor. They quickly averted their eyes by dabbing with tissues to make sure no one noticed their lustful stares. A twinge of jealousy tickled Sadie. Nan radiated compassion. Her Scandinavian features contrasted sharply against her black suit, adding an aura to the mix.

Nan closed the lid and motioned to Clay. He joined her and released the brakes on the casket stand. Nan signaled for the audience to rise as Clay pushed the casket down the aisle. A faint ring tone began to play *Ninety-Nine Bottles of Beer on the Wall*. Nan's gaze darted toward Clay. He frowned and patted his shirt pocket, then his pants pockets. The cell phone repeated the melodic ditty two more times before it stopped.

Eyes wide with panic, Nan led the casket procession down the aisle and into the lobby. Clay followed behind Nan, bending every few feet to peer under the casket. As the mourners emptied the aisles and fell into place behind the casket, the ring tone began again. Nan kept her eyes straight ahead. She set her jaw and held her breath. Picking up the pace, she passed Lon who stood with seven other uniformed deputies. They saluted the casket and stared at it in disbelief.

Lon glared at his cousin. Clay shrugged in panic. He patted his pockets and shot Lon a contorted 'I can't find my cell phone' expression. The desire to wring Clay's neck etched Lon's face.

Lon stood beside Nan at the hearse. "See if you can get the pallbearers away from the car and I'll try to find the phone."

Nan clustered the pallbearers in front of the hearse and gave instructions as to what would take place at the interment.

Lon released the casket latch and signaled to Clay. "Close the hearse door behind me. Don't open it until I signal." Lon climbed into the hearse.

Nan rapped on the hearse door before pulling it open.

"I can't find it." Lon removed his hands from beneath the body.

"What's the hold up," one of the senator's sons demanded.

"I can't find it," Lon whispered again.

Nan drew a jagged breath. "Just close the lid and pray it doesn't ring while we're at the cemetery."

Lon climbed out of the hearse. He squeezed Nan's hand and quickly bussed her cheek in passing. Pulling the squad car forward, he tapped the switch to activate his overhead flashers.

Nan followed behind Lon's squad car, assuming the pace set by the deputy. The limousine containing pallbearers fell into place behind the hearse while family members, dignitaries and friends pulled out of the parking lot and lined up for the trip to the cemetery. Lon nodded at his fellow deputies who blocked intersections along the route to assure the funeral procession could pass unimpeded.

Sitting between Nan and Clay in the front seat of the hearse, Sadie fidgeted. The air dripped with tension. Clay feigned indifference. Sadie braced for a tongue lashing, but not one word escaped Nan's lips. Three distraught people stared straight ahead while Clay drummed his fingers against the armrest and tapped his shoe on the rubber mat.

The penetrating summer sun encouraged many to remove their suit coats before approaching the gravesite. Lon directed the last of the mourners' cars while Clay helped the pallbearers lift the casket from the hearse and place it over the grave. Sadie arranged a large spray of flowers on the casket. The immediate family sat in white chairs surrounding the grave in the same order they had assumed during the exit procession at the church. The others gathered behind the senator's grieving widow.

After the ceremony, Lon remained in the background while Nan gave final instructions to the family and presented the option of attending the body as the grave crew lowered the casket into the grave.

Sadie sighed with relief as the family declined observing the final committal. Nan accompanied the senator's widow to her limousine. Sadie discretely signaled to the grave crew to lower the casket while the silent procession of mourners inched slowly toward their cars. *Ninety-Nine Bottles of Beer on the Wall* interrupted the somber scene. Gazes turned in unison to watch the senator's casket sink into darkness accompanied by a toe-tapping ditty.

"Where's Clay?" Lon stormed into the mortuary lobby. "I need to have a long talk with my cousin."

Nan handed two ends of the casket drape to Sadie and together they folded it into a square. "He skipped out as soon as we returned from the cemetery."

Lon grinned at Nan.

"Don't you dare grin at me. I've never been so humiliated in all my life. That man's going to be the death of me." Nan dropped onto the sofa and buried her face in her hands.

Lon put his arm around her. "That's one funeral they'll never forget. If the senator appreciated a good bottle of beer, he probably got a kick out of it."

Nan moaned. "How could I have been so stupid? Every time I ask Clay to help, it turns into a disaster."

"Did you see the senator's wife?" Sadie grinned at Lon.

"She turned so white I thought she'd faint."

"I'll never live this down. Don't ever bring it up again. Ever."

Jane opened the lobby door and poked her head through the opening. "You're back." She strode across the lobby floor with Bernie close behind. "Did you tell them yet?"

"Tell us what?" Nan looked up at Jane and then at Sadie. "Now what did Clay do?"

"Hopefully nothing," Sadie said. "We're not sure yet. As soon as you finish, why don't you come over to the cabin. You're not going to believe what we've got to tell you."

Sadie leaned her head back, closed her eyes, and ticked items off her mental checklist as she waited for Nan and Lon to join them. "If I leave anything important out, be sure to tell me. It has to make sense if Lon's going to believe it."

Jed nodded. "Don't worry. I will. Somebody's going to pay for what happened to Celeste." As Sally's head bobbed in slumber, he shifted her to his other shoulder and tucked her head against his neck.

Aanders opened the screen door and walked over to the cookie jar. He lifted a cookie out of the container. "What is this?" He sniffed the cookie and looked at Bernie.

Bernie held up his hand in warning. "Don't eat it. It's one of Jane's experiments. I think she did something wrong."

A voice from the bedroom wafted into the kitchen. "Fresh cookies in the cookie jar, Aanders."

"Okay, Jane," Aanders shouted, placing his cookie on the floor for Belly. "I thought she had a new cookbook."

"She does," Bernie replied in a hushed tone. "She obviously didn't follow it."

Belly licked it, snorted, licked it again, and walked away.

"Your mom and Lon will be here in a few minutes," Sadie said. "Let me do the talking."

"You're going to lie, aren't you?" Aanders picked up the remote and switched on the television.

Sadie took the remote away from him and pressed the off button. "Not exactly. I'm going to fudge the truth."

"It's wrong. You're always telling me I can't lie to the crossers. The only way they accept death is by telling the truth. How come you can lie and I can't?"

"Because I'm the boss. Because we're dealing with a crime, not a fairy tale."

"Then tell the truth. When you lie the cops always figure it out, anyway. I watch TV. I know what happens." Aanders' lip curled in rebellion.

Toying with an earring, Sadie walked around her chair and leaned on the back with her elbows. "Okay, Aanders. When Lon gets here, I'm going to let you tell him. Be sure to tell him we take care of crossers and there's a dead man sitting at the kitchen table." Pointing a finger at him, she added, "What do you think your mother's going to say?"

"About what?" Nan opened the screen door. She tapped the lid on Mr. Bakke's urn. "How you doing, Mr. Bakke?"

Sadie motioned to Aanders to begin, watching his incensed glare turn sheepish.

"You tell her." Aanders went limp against the back of his chair.

"Tell me what?" Nan pulled out a chair and sat next to Lon.

Jane sat in the final chair and watched Sadie spread a napkin out on the table.

"We've got something to show you." Sadie opened a small box and laid two bones and a necklace on the napkin.

"Bones? Chicken bones?" Lon picked up one of the

bones and rolled it over in his hand.

"They're human bones," Sadie said. "Finger bones to be exact."

"Where did you get these?" Lon looked at Aanders, then at Sadie.

The corner of Aanders' lips twitched as he opened his mouth.

"They're mine." Sadie waved her hand. "Well, not my personal bones, but I found them. Aanders helped me."

"What's this?" Lon held up the necklace and blinked twice at the tiny letters. "What does it say?"

Nan took the necklace and held it toward the window. "It looks like J-E-D."

"That's what it looks like to me, too," Sadie indicated. "We've discovered a skeleton under Clay's cabin. I think I know who it is."

"What?" Lon's mouth stayed open as he drew in a quick breath. "You've got to be kidding. Are you saying Jed Perry's skeleton is under Clay's cabin? It can't be Jed. We buried him last week."

"It's not Jed. Good grief. How dumb do you think I am? It's Jed's sister."

"Celeste?"

"I think so. I can't prove it, but the evidence points to it. Do you remember when Celeste disappeared?"

"Of course I do. That's got to be over ten years ago," Lon said.

"Fifteen years ago." Jane held her hand over her chest. "I remember the heart ache I felt when her parents offered the big reward and no one came forward. For that kind of money I thought for sure someone would talk."

The half-heart dangled from the chain as Nan handed it back to Lon.

Lon squinted at the lettering. "Where did you say you found this?" He set the chain on the table. "If this is evidence, we shouldn't touch it. What were you doing under Clay's cabin?"

Sadie pointed at Belly. "Our little friend uncovered it."

"How'd he get under there?"

"I've seen Belly clawing at the air vent on Clay's cabin," Nan said. "He must have gotten it loose."

Belly placed his head on Sadie's lap and blinked his eyes in adoration.

Sadie scratched behind his ears. "You get blamed for everything, don't you?"

"Bless his soul." Bernie winked at Jane. "He can't help it if he's nosey."

"You mean Belly actually brought this to you?"

"You could say that." Sadie placed the bones side by side on the napkin. "There's more. I also found a notebook."

"You didn't get fingerprints on it, did you?"

"Well I didn't leave my fingerprints at home."

Lon ran his hands through his hair. "Sadie. You know better than that. Nan's told you a million times if you suspect anything when you're prepping a body you should contact the authorities. Finding a skeleton is no different."

"I didn't do anything wrong." Sadie's voice rose. "It's a skeleton. A very old skeleton. It's been there a long time. When I saw the necklace with Jed etched on it, I remembered when Celeste disappeared and put two and two together. You have to admit it's a possibility."

Lon looked at Sadie and shook his head in disbelief. "Why didn't you come and get me right away? If this is a crime scene, we've got to get the forensics team out here right away."

"We know that, Lon. That's why we contacted you now."

Jane leaned back against Bernie's arm. "We can't be sure, but maybe the skeleton was there when we bought the cabin from Kimmer's folks."

As if lightning struck, Nan blurted, "Do you think Clay had something to do with this?"

"I don't think so. I'm still puzzled why Kimmer rented the cabin for Clay," Sadie explained. "I'm guessing neither Kimmer nor his folks knew about the skeleton. Judging by the decayed clothing and mouse droppings, it's been there a long time."

"The sheriff isn't going to be happy you waited to tell me."

"You were busy with the missing baby. By the way, how is the search going?"

"Not good. It's got similarities to the abduction last summer. Somebody knew exactly what they were doing. The abduction was too calculated to be pulled off by an amateur."

"You're in big trouble, young man." Nan shook her head from side to side. "You should have told me about the skeleton."

"I made him promise not to," Sadie said. "I needed to think it through before I told Lon. There's stuff in the notebook that didn't make sense. If it is Celeste, why would she have the notebook?"

"What was in it?" Lon stared at the diminutive sleuth. "Sadie, what was in the notebook?"

Sadie lowered her head and looked at Lon over the top of her glasses. "You've got to promise you won't yell. If you do, I won't show you."

Lon's mouth dropped open. "You mean you removed the notebook?"

"Don't show him if he's going to get huffy," Jane said. "You're darn lucky Sadie's sharing this with you. If it wasn't for her, poor Celeste would never have been found."

"We've all touched it," Bernie admitted, "so our fingerprints are on it too. Jane tried to help Sadie make sense of the names and numbers."

Nan put her hand on Lon's arm. "Let her get the notebook. It's already compromised."

Lon returned from his squad car pulling on a pair of Latex gloves. "A lot of good this is going to do. You've already contaminated the evidence." He placed a plastic bag on the table. Sadie, Nan, Jane, and Bernie stood behind him as he opened the notebook.

Sadie pointed at the name on the first page. "His name is in there several times." Pointing at a column next to the name she added, "There's a dollar amount and date after his name each time, too."

"Who's Reginald Carson? And look at this." Lon pointed at another name.

"Oh, dear," Nan said.

Lon looked at Sadie and then at Nan. "Does the name mean anything to you?"

"It does to me. It's the name of the family whose baby was abducted about twenty years ago." Nan put her hand over her mouth in disbelief. "I went to school with one of their kids."

"Now do you see why I wanted to be sure before I told you?" Sadie pointed at the notebook. "If you follow the line across the page, you'll see a dollar amount and a check mark. It looks like the beginning and end of a transaction. Either Celeste was involved in the crime or she was killed because she knew too much."

29

"I want to go to my secret hideout." Sally tugged on Jed's hand. "I want to see what they're doing."

"You can't. The sheriff's deputies are there and we need to stay out of their way." Jed nodded toward the inner room. "Sadie put some jewelry on your bed. Why don't you play with it?"

"I don't want to. I want to go to my secret hideout."

"The answer is no. Quit trying my patience."

Sally sank back against the chair rungs and dropped her hands into her lap. "I don't like you anymore. You're mean."

"If you don't like me, I'll have to give your surprise to someone else."

"I think you're full of bull."

"Bull?" Jed grinned broadly.

Sally tightened her arms over her chest. "That's right."

"What exactly does full of bull mean?"

Sally's bare heel tapped against the wooden leg. "It means you're lying. Mom says Dad is full of bull."

"I'll bet it's not true." Jed patted his lap. "Come and tell me about your dad."

Sally hesitated. "Mom said Dad didn't love us. I don't believe her. Dad told me every day how much he loved me."

"He loves you, Sally. Your dad's a good man."

"I wish he'd find me so we can go home. I don't know what's taking so long."

Jed lifted her off the floor and Sally snuggled against his massive chest. "You're like a big lion." She spread her arms out to embrace him. "I miss my dad."

The screen door banged against the frame as Lon, Sadie, and Bernie entered the cabin. Lon lifted the lid off the cookie jar.

"I wouldn't do it if I were you," Sadie said. "You might have to arrest Jane for murder."

"Was she experimenting again?" Lon replaced the lid and looked toward the screen door.

"Unfortunately, she varied the recipe. I bought her two new cookbooks, but she doesn't bother to read them." Bernie looked at Sadie. "Has she always experimented like this?"

"Always," Sadie and Lon replied in sync.

"Jane cooked at the resort's restaurant three summers ago. A disaster. A complete disaster." Sadie shook her head remembering the dismal summer. "Word-of-mouth is a killer in a resort community."

"Bless her soul," Bernie said. "She means well."

Jane placed her nose against the screen and peered into the cabin. "There you are. I got sidetracked by a guest asking questions about the deputies' cars parked at Cabin 12. We need to do rumor control before we lose our guests."

"We're trying to keep it as low-key as possible," Lon indicated. "I've gone cabin to cabin telling your guests there's nothing to worry about."

"That's not what it looked like. Four squad cars and a forensic van is enough to scare people away."

"They shouldn't have much left to do. As soon as they're done, Clay can move back in."

"That will make Nan happy," Sadie said. "She isn't thrilled Clay had to sleep on her couch."

"Neither am I."

Lon's hostile tone surprised Sadie. "You can't possibly think Nan would give Clay a second chance?"

"Of course not, but I don't trust the man. Nan doesn't

need the added stress."

Sadie nodded in agreement. "How are Celeste's folks dealing with the news?"

Lon removed his cap and hung it on a chair spindle. "They're real troopers. They identified the necklace as belonging to Celeste. Mrs. Perry remembered seeing the notebook on Celeste's night stand, but said it wasn't Celeste's handwriting. Actually, I think they're relieved. They can finally put her to rest."

Sadie glanced at the chair under the clock. Jed winked back and nodded.

"I trust you won't leak information to the press. There's bound to be a clue in the notebook and I don't want anyone knowing about it."

Jane set a plate of cookies on the table. "I thought these would have disappeared by now. Eat up. There's more in the cookie jar."

"I'm guessing Nan will have a full chapel for Celeste's memorial," Lon said. "It's a shame they just buried Jed and now they have to deal with this."

"Or," Sadie added, "they'll find comfort knowing Jed and his sister are finally together."

Jed wiped at a tear rolling down his cheek.

"You're probably right." Lon patted Sadie's shoulder and rose. "You make me look at things from a different angle. I appreciate the new perspective. I'm afraid pessimism comes with my job." He shouted back through the screen door as he stepped off the porch, "I'm going to the sheriff's office. I'll see you later."

Sadie closed the door to the chapel when the minister began to speak. She tiptoed across the lobby and into the office as the phone rang. "This would be Sadie."

"I'm out in the parking lot. You'd better keep an eye on Clay. He just sneaked in the back door," Lon said. "I'll be back in a few minutes."

Sadie looked out the window and saw Lon flip the lid on his cell phone. She dug through the drawer for the stack of *Please Turn on Headlights* cards.

Every parking space in the parking lot held a vehicle. Thirty-eight to be exact. Scanning the street in both directions, Sadie figured the twenty additional vehicles parked on the street would join the funeral procession. She fanned the headlight cards. Selecting a hundred or so, Sadie placed them on the credenza.

The memorial basket situated on the lobby podium held a stack of sympathy cards containing memorials for the deceased's family. The Perry family had indicated they would add the funds from Celeste's memorial to those from Jed's funeral and initiate a yearly scholarship. Sadie aligned the guest book, the pen, and the basket. Nice and tidy. Nan would be pleased.

Jane walked out of the chapel as organ music filtered into the lobby. A vocalist sang the hymn's last refrain. "Need any help? It's so crowded in there, I couldn't breathe."

Sadie handed Jane half the *Please Turn on Headlights* cards. "You take the street and I'll take the parking lot."

Sadie weaved between each car, tucking headlight cards carefully under the driver's wiper. Saving the best car for last, she slipped a card under a neon-purple wiper matching the car's psychedelic paint job. She gazed at the interior as she waited for Jane.

"I should have bought the car last year when she had it for sale," Sadie said. "Don't you just love those lavender fur seats? That's the nicest car I've ever seen." Sadie took the remainder of the cards from Jane. "I still don't know why she backed out of our deal. She was all set to sell it to me and suddenly changed her mind. I wonder why she never told me who bought it."

Jane shot a side-glance at Sadie and hurried toward the lobby door.

Organ music filtered into the lobby and mourners began to sing. "Bernie's in there singing his heart out." Jane said. "He won't notice I'm gone. He sure has a beautiful voice."

Sadie followed Jane into the office, but stopped short when she spotted Clay reaching into the memorial basket. He pulled out a sympathy card.

Seeing Sadie approach, Clay hastily tucked the sympathy card into the seat of his pants and backed against the wall. He crossed his arms over his chest.

"Give me the card, you worthless crook." The veins stood out in Sadie's neck, contempt flaring in her eyes.

Clay raised his empty hands. "What card?" After scanning the floor around him, he looked up and shrugged. He gazed at his palms.

The confident grin disappeared when Jane stepped forward and grabbed Clay's outstretched arm. "Give me the card or I'll tell Nan."

"Don't tell Nan," Clay whined. "You're going to ruin everything. I'm short on cash. Nan will kill me if she finds out."

Jane's gray bob swung forward as she thrust her nose under Clay's chin. "Give me the card."

"I can't. You don't want me to go hungry, do you? If I don't eat, I'm gonna end up in a casket." Clay wavered as he pointed toward the viewing room. "I had a job, but Dan cancelled it. He's heading back to Minneapolis, instead. Ain't it the shits?"

Before Clay could whine further, Jane spun him around,

tugged at his loose waistband, and plunged her hand into Clay's pants.

Lon stepped up to the jostling pair. "Jane. I'm shocked. The things you don't know about your friends."

"Don't tell me you called the cops." Clay's whine rose higher with each word.

As Clay tried to wriggle free, Lon squeezed the back of his neck and pressed him against the wall.

Jane grimaced and held the sympathy card at arm's length between her thumb and forefinger. Turning her head away from the recovery, she dropped it into the memorial basket. "This insult to the human race is a thief."

"Now we know why you show up at every funeral. I actually thought you had one redeeming quality." Lon released his grip. "Does Nan know you steal cards from the basket?"

"Don't tell Nan," Clay begged. "She'll have me put in jail again. She'll kill me."

"What a shame that would be." Sadie faked a pout.

Lifting the envelope from the basket with two fingers, Jane peeked under the unsealed flap. "Look at this. There's fifty dollars in there."

"Fifty bucks?" Clay's disbelieving shout rebounded across the lobby. "Damn. It's usually only twenty." Clay glared at Jane. "You're just as nasty as your sister."

Turning Clay toward the front door, Lon said, "Now get out of here. If I hear you've taken money again, I'll file charges."

"I can't for the life of me understand why Nan married a pig like Clay." A smile crossed Jane's face. "Come to think of it, she seems to be a swine connoisseur."

"Jane!" Lon looked at Sadie. "Who lit Jane's fuse?"

Jane cocked her head. "What makes you think I don't

have a few good zingers? You have to admit he's truly a revolting wretch. Can't you keep him away from the mortuary?"

"He may be a wretch, but he's a creative wretch. I never thought of stealing money from the memorial basket."

"He's not in the least bit creative. He's pickled, he's repulsive, and he's Kimmer's puppet."

"He didn't think you'd dig for the card. I don't think I would have stuck my hand down there. In fact, I know I wouldn't have. We all have secret desires."

The chapel doors swung open. Nan glared at Sadie. Sadie hurried over and helped Nan prepare the casket before the pallbearers accompanied it to the hearse.

Celeste's parents wept in silence as they walked behind the casket. Jed placed his hand on his mother's shoulder as he followed behind her. He held on to Sally with his other hand. Tears rolled freely down his face.

After the mourners returned from the cemetery, they gathered for a luncheon in the Community Center. Sadie reached across the table and put her hand on Jed's arm. "How are you doing?"

"I'm at peace. Thanks for suggesting I ride with my parents to the cemetery. It's like they knew I sat next to them. Dad told Mom he was proud of me because I insisted they'd someday find out what happened to Celeste."

Sadie patted his arm. "You're ready to go back through the light now, aren't you?"

"I am. I'm going to miss you." Jed smiled. "If only I could tell everyone the real truth about Sadie Witt's imaginary friends."

"I'm afraid that's something I'll take to my grave. I don't like it when they talk behind my back, but there's nothing I can do about it. I can't quit guiding the dead because my feelings get hurt. Aanders will experience the same frustration."

"That's a shame," Jed said. "You're accused of being crazy when it's completely the opposite. Where's the fairness in that?"

"Indeed," Sadie replied. She glanced up at Jed over the top of her glasses. "Have you made your declaration?"

"I'm going to the parallel world. I'm taking Sally with me."

A huge sigh of relief surged from Sadie's lips. "Thank you. I hoped I'd hear you say those words. Now you have to find someone on the brink before it's too late." Sadie brushed a tear from her eyelid. "I've become quite fond of you. If all my crossers were as compassionate as you, it would make my job a lot more tolerable."

Lon and Aanders strolled up to the table. Lon pulled a chair out with his foot, balancing a plate in one hand and a cup of coffee in the other. "You okay, Sadie?"

"I'm fine. Just tired, I guess." Sadie patted the chair next to her and pulled it out for Aanders.

Jed grabbed Sally's arm as she skipped down the row between the tables. "Not so fast. Be careful, or I'll make you sit down until it's time to go."

Lon set his coffee cup on the table and mumbled out the side of his mouth. "Don't look up."

Sadie's head shot up.

"I said don't look up. Kimmer's looking at us. Pretend you don't see him or he'll sit with us." Lon placed a forkful of macaroni salad in his mouth.

"You don't mind if I join you, do you?" Kimmer set his plate on the table and unbuttoned his suit coat. "I'd prefer to sit where I can have an intelligent conversation, but there's no other chair available."

Sadie set her fork on her plate and pushed it toward the center of the table. "By all means. We don't mind if Humpty Dumpty joins us, do we Lon?"

Lon coughed and shoved in another forkful.

"Oh, it's you, Sadie." Kimmer stretched his neck and looked down at Sadie. "They must not have booster seats here." He buttered the front of his roll. "I see your boss dressed you today. Either that or you've come to your senses."

"You're a fine one to talk about fashion. You look like you…" Sadie jerked as Lon's boot connected with her shin.

"How's the investigation coming, Lon?" Kimmer buttered the back of his roll. "Any idea what happened to Celeste?"

"Not yet." Lon glanced at Aanders, then at Sadie.

"Do you think they'll classify it as murder?"

"I'm not sure."

"Well I don't think those bones ended up the cabin all by themselves." Kimmer cocked his head. "Even an idiot can figure that out."

Lon kept his gaze on his plate. "The investigators are doing the best they can."

"I'm sure. Did you find anything with the body?"

"Like what?"

"Evidence." The chair creaked as Kimmer shifted. "Anything that will help the case."

"I'm not sure what the forensic team found. I wasn't there." Lon stood and signaled to Aanders. "We'd better see if your mom needs help."

As Lon rounded the table he turned back toward Kimmer. "Come to think of it, they did find something with the body, but I can't talk about it."

30

"I want to thank everyone for gathering on such short notice," Sadie said, while curious murmurs floated through the crowd. She had knocked on every cabin door earlier to notify resort guests a sheriff's deputy would make an announcement at 10:00 AM. The guests clustered behind her as she stood next to the porch railing.

Lon climbed out of his squad car and joined Sadie. She introduced him. Unrolling a bright neon-orange poster, he handed it to Jane. The sisters gazed at the sheet intently while Lon waved everyone closer to the porch railing. "I felt it's important to inform everyone an infant has been abducted from our local hospital."

An undertone rose from the crowd. Guests looked at one another and then back at Lon with apprehension. "I don't think there's cause for alarm. We believe the abductors have left the area."

Sadie watched Pam Avery lift the blanket off Chelsie's face as she held her close. Dan put his arm around Pam. Sadie sympathized with their concerned expressions.

The Witt sisters listened to Lon's explanation while parents reached for their children's hands. Belly sidled up to Lon. He leaned against Lon's left leg and jerked his gaze back and forth with every gesture Lon made. "Just so you know, during the past two summers similar infant abductions have taken place in neighboring towns. I want to make it clear someone abducted the infants from hospitals and not from any other location."

Venting her concern, a young mother standing at the

back of the crowd said, "Were the babies found?"

"I'm not at liberty to say, Ma'am."

Another wave of concern issued from the group.

Heads turned to the right as a car pulled into the parking lot. A gentleman of Asian descent opened the driver's door and lingered in position, studying the crowd gathered at the railing. He rummaged through the items on the back seat before layering two cameras around his neck.

"Are our children in danger?" Dan Avery's question piqued the crowd's interest. "What kind of protection are you providing?" Reinforcing echoes rolled through the group as others insisted on an answer.

"I don't believe your children are in danger at this point. Like I said, the sheriff feels certain the abductors left the county. All surveillance film is being reviewed and there will be a press conference this evening."

"How do you know the abductor left the area? How can you be sure?" Two separate guests shouted out questions.

"Because there are patterns to this type of crime. An infant would be a hindrance to the perpetrator. It would be reasonable he'd head away from the area where he could pass the child off to an accomplice."

Heads nodded in agreement.

Shoulders and arms jostled as the oriental man pushed his way through the crowd and stepped up onto the porch. Short in stature with close-cropped, sparse, silver hair, the Asian man wore black slacks, a white button-down shirt, and black leather sandals. One of the cameras dangling from his neck sported a long telephoto lens and swung widely with each step.

Lon looked down at the intruder and scowled before continuing to address the questions.

Jane and Sadie stood next to the cabin wall behind Lon

and watched the Asian gentleman survey the area.

A favorable smile crossed the man's lips as he noticed the sisters. Bowing with grace, he bobbed in place several times before stepping between Lon and the Witt sisters. He pulled a folded sheet of paper from his pants pocket.

Jane whispered in the man's direction. "Can we help you?"

Belly joined the sisters. Wagging his tail in delight he sniffed the man's sandals.

Bowing again, the gentleman pointed at the sheet in his hand.

Lon waved toward the orange poster Jane held. "Our telephone numbers are listed on the poster. We're available to answer questions and are only a few minutes away if you need us. You can be a great help by reporting anything suspicious."

Jane held the poster toward the crowd, but had to walk around the man who blocked their view. "I'll post this in the lodge lobby in case you need the number," Jane informed the crowd. She stepped back to rejoin her sister and bumped into the man.

"Do you have a reservation?" Sadie placed her hand around the man's upper arm and tried to reposition him closer to the wall.

Jane watched the gentleman bow and point to the sheet in his hand. "Maybe he doesn't speak English."

Lon glared at the Asian man and bristled with impatience before he continued addressing the crowd. "The abducted infant is a seven-pound, four-ounce male with black hair. He was wrapped in a blue blanket. He wore a white T-shirt and a newborn-sized diaper. He also wore a blue stocking cap and booties."

Jane leaned toward Sadie and whispered in her ear. "Do

you think he has a reservation?"

Stretching in the opposite direction, Sadie leaned toward the man and asked in carefully spaced words, "What do you want?"

Pointing at Jane's crotch, the man bowed lower than he had previously bowed and came up nodding with excitement.

Two pair of eyes stared at the man and grew wide with alarm. The sisters simultaneously looked sideways at Lon.

"I think I know who he is," Sadie mumbled, poking Jane with her elbow. "I think he's the Chinese man who wanted a date with you. It's Mr. Hahn, the guy from the dating site."

Jane turned to stare at the man. "Are you crazy? He's too short."

"That's not your biggest problem. How are you going to get rid of him?"

"Me? What do you mean me?" The abrasive words spilled over Jane's lips. "How did he find me?"

"Beats me. You can research anything on the internet."

"He's pointing again." A choke escaped Jane's lips. "Did he point at what I think he pointed at?"

"Are you Mr. Hahn?" Sadie stepped closer to the man.

"Did you see what's in his hand?" Jane's whisper grew in intensity. "He's got my picture on a piece of paper."

"That's from the website," Sadie said. "He must have printed it."

Through clamped teeth, Jane warned, "Get him out of here before Bernie gets wind of this."

Taking the elderly man's arm, Sadie led him down the steps, away from the gathering. Belly followed the pair while they made their way toward the lodge.

A resort guest looked at Jane. "Do you think we'd be safer leaving the area and returning to our homes?"

Jane clutched the orange poster to her chest. "I don't

think it's necessary. You're safe at Witt's End. There's no need to leave."

Dan Avery stepped forward. "I think Miss Witt is right. It's safe here. I'm staying. I hope the rest of you will, too." Dan pulled his wife close. They walked away from the crowd and headed toward their cabin.

After Lon answered a few more questions, the crowd slowly dispersed.

When Sadie returned to the cabin, Jane said, "Did you get rid of the Chinese guy?" She reached under the sink and pulled out her spray bottle. "I'm a nervous wreck. I need to clean." She waved at Jed's chair. "I'm going to clean your chair, Jed. If you're in it, you'd better move." She spritzed the chair.

"I got rid of him, but it took some doing. Thank goodness his son met us at the lodge."

Aanders entered the cabin, letting the door slam behind him. "You mean the Chinese man? I think he wanted to talk to Jane yesterday, but I couldn't understand him. He had a picture of Jane in his hand. He kept shoving it in my face."

Jane's hair swung free around her face as she concentrated on scrubbing the wooden seat. "Did you find out what he wanted?"

"He obviously wanted you." Sadie chuckled. "It wasn't my crotch he pointed at."

"That's ridiculous. He doesn't even know me."

Sadie pulled a photo envelope from her skirt pocket. "I think he knows you better than you realize. He's quite the photographer." Sadie laid six photos in a row on the kitchen table. "He wants you to have these. Apparently he had them developed on his way over this morning. Mr. Hahn and his son are staying at the resort across the lake, but they've spent most of their time fishing in our bay."

Jane tapped on one of the photos. "That's terrible. My rear end isn't that wide."

Aanders leaned over and peered at the photos. "Yes it is. It looks just like you."

"What?" Jane's shriek caused Aanders arm to lurch as he pulled two other photos to the edge of the table.

"That shouldn't surprise you," Sadie said. "Anyone who wears a bra big enough to double as a porch swing should know their ass is wide."

"How come none of these pictures show Jane's face?" Aanders lifted one of the photos off the table and held it under his nose. "Look." He pointed to the left corner. "There's Judge Kimmer coming out of the Avery's cabin."

"What?" Sadie grabbed the photo. "Kimmer? That's odd. I didn't know he had been here again. He usually parks it in front of our cabin to harass us."

Jane tapped on the photo. "Isn't that the same shirt Dan wore this morning? That means Kimmer was here this morning."

Jane dropped into her chair. "Kimmer, a Chinese man, and photos making make me look like a walrus is more than I can handle. Why does everything happen at once?"

"A walrus and a Chinese man? Do I even want to know what you're talking about?" Bernie closed the screen door and walked over to the table.

"Jane's overwhelmed. Why don't you take her for a pontoon ride to calm her down," Sadie said.

"Is she complaining about the crossers again?"

Sadie frowned at Bernie. "How come you're taking the crossers so calmly? Most people would have bolted and never looked back. Don't you think it's odd you're sitting at a table with dead people?"

"Dead or alive, we're all equal."

"There you go again. That's a cop-out. Why don't you admit it gives you the willies and quit being a know-it-all?"

"Don't be so hard on him," Jane said.

"I'm trying to fit in," Bernie responded. "Having to accept what goes against everything I believe isn't easy."

Sadie removed her purple-glitter glasses and ran her thumb and forefinger over one of the lenses before slipping them back on. "Look." She tapped the newspaper. "Every square inch of this morning's newspaper is about the infant abduction."

"Sally, can you scoot over so Sadie can spread the paper on the table?" Jed leaned toward the table.

"It even made national news." Jane leaned into Sadie's shoulder. "I heard it on the *Today* show. They showed a photo of the baby. It's a good thing the hospital takes photos of all the newborns."

"Can I stay here when you go to the hospital?" Sally looked up at Jed.

"I wish you could, but we've got business to take care of." Jed smiled down at her.

"I want to wait here in case my dad comes."

"I'll tell you what," Jed said. "Go to the inner room and bring me the box from the closet."

Sally skipped into the bedroom.

"Mom told me most newborns look alike," Aanders said. "Putting his photo in the paper isn't going to help, is it?"

Sadie ran her finger under the print. "It says he's got a distinguishing birthmark on his hip. I'm sure the sheriff wants the public to be aware of anything that might identify him."

"This one?" Sally ran up to Jed and handed him the box.

"If you're a good girl while we're at the hospital, you can have it." Jed set the box on the table.

"What's in it?"

"Remember the surprise I promised you?"

Sally climbed up on Jed's lap. "Can I open it now?"

"No. We'll open it later." Jed lifted the box. "I'll let you hold it if you want."

Sally snuggled back against Jed's chest and smiled up at him. She cradled the box on her lap.

Sadie turned the newspaper page. "I can't imagine how the mother must feel." She tapped the woman's photo. "She was on the news last night pleading for the return of her baby."

"That's the baby that lives over there." Sally pointed toward the Avery's cabin.

Jed redirected Sally's finger and brought it to his lips. He gently kissed the tip of her index finger. "I don't think it is. All babies look alike when they're born. Besides, the Avery baby is a little girl."

"It's a boy. He's got a penis."

"I don't think so. Only boy babies have penises," Sadie said.

"He does. He's a boy." Sally leaned her elbow on the table and turned the paper back to the front page. "That's him."

"You've never seen the baby with her clothes off. How could you see a penis?" Jed placed his fingers on her cheek and turned her face toward him.

With exaggerated hand movements, Sally said, "I saw him. I saw his penis."

Sadie leaned back against the chair slats. "When exactly did you see the baby with her clothes off?"

"It's…a…boy."

Sadie took one of Sally's hands. She smiled. "How do you know it's a boy? Were you in the Avery's cabin?"

Sally traced her fingers along the flowers adorning the

box lid.

"Sally? Tell me how you know the baby is a boy."

"Can I go to the inner room now?" Sally looked up at Jed.

Sadie lifted Sally's chin to get her attention. "I'm not going to get mad at you. You're my friend and friends don't get mad at one another. Just tell me why you think it's a boy."

Belly's toenails clicked against the wooden planking as he trotted across the floor and nosed Sadie's leg. She held her hand out and ran her fingers through his fur.

Sally copied Sadie and scrunched her fingers through the hair on Belly's neck. "First I saw the baby through the window. Then I went in and watched the mom cut his hair. She washed the hair off when she gave him a bath in the sink."

Sally looked up with an amazed expression. "Did you know I used to fit in the bathroom sink? Mom used to put me in there when I was a baby. She told me she should have pulled the plug and let me go down the drain. It's a good thing she didn't."

"I think your mom was teasing." Jed ruffled Sally's hair and gave her a hug. "Babies can't really fit down sink drains."

"I know. I'm not ascared of sinks anymore."

"You said Pam gave the baby a haircut," Sadie said.

"I did? What are you talking about?" Jane folded the newspaper and placed it next to Mr. Bakke's urn.

"Hang on a second." Sadie patted the air impatiently. "I'm talking to Sally."

"She gave him new clothes from the store, too. She had them in a bag." Sally pointed toward the inner room door. "I kept some tags so I could play store lady. I played store with Belly yesterday."

Jed glanced at Sadie. He nodded toward the inner room.

Sadie leaned toward Sally and spoke gently. "Will you show me the tags?"

Sally jumped down and ran to the inner room.

"What's going on?"

"I said hold your horses, Jane. I think Sally just put us on to something, and it's not good."

Bernie put his hand on Jane's shoulder as he looked at Sadie. "Is there anything I can do?"

"Not yet."

Sally handed Sadie four merchandise tags and three plastic stems removed from the tags. "Here's a bag, too. This one had pink socks in it." Sally pointed at a bootie outline sketched in black on a white label.

Aanders picked up a tag and looked at Sally. "How do you play store with a dog? That's dumb."

Jed lifted Sally back onto his lap. "Maybe Pam bought new clothes for Chelsie."

"No she didn't. Chelsie was in a box under the desk." Sally tilted sideways and tucked the tags in her hip pocket. "That baby sure cries a lot."

"She sure does," Sadie said. "The first few days the Averys were at the resort, I didn't hear a peep. Then all of a sudden, Chelsea cried nonstop. I wonder if she developed colic."

"Are you talking about Pam's baby?" Jane looked at Sadie.

"I noticed she's been crying a lot, too."

"Not Chelsie," Sally said. "Chelsie can't cry. She's a doll. See?" Sally pointed at one of the photos from Mr. Hahn's envelope.

Sadie lifted the photo and held it to the light. "I don't see what you mean?"

"There." Sally placed her finger on a shadow. "That's

Chelsie."

On one of the photo's Mr. Hahn had taken of Jane, Dan Avery stood peering out through the cabin door. His right hand clutched an item as it dangled at his side. "See. Chelsie's not wearing new clothes. She's BA."

Sadie and Jed squinted as they strained to see the object.

Jane said, "Why are you looking at my picture?"

Sadie held it up to Jane. "I'm not looking at you, I'm looking at what Dan Avery is holding. Sally says it's Chelsie."

"Chelsie?" Bernie raised his glasses above his eyes and leaned closer to the photo. "If it is, he's holding her by her leg."

"He was." Sally nodded in agreement. "She's BA. Just like Jed." Her hand shot to her mouth as she giggled.

"Sally said that's exactly what Dan was doing. Holding Chelsie by her leg." Sadie looked at Jane and Jed in disbelief.

"I don't get it." Bernie frowned. "What did I miss?"

"Sally's claiming Chelsie is a doll and the baby Pam's been carrying around is a boy."

"I saw her. She's a girl," Jane argued. "All you have to do is look at her."

"Look at what? Pink?" Jed tapped his temple. "Think about it."

Sadie turned from Jed to Jane. "That's exactly what they wanted us to see. Pink."

Bernie drew a deep breath as his eyes grew larger. "Do you mean to tell me you suspect the Averys of child abduction? Are you out of your mind?"

"Do you have a better explanation?" Sadie glared at Bernie.

"I certainly wouldn't take the word of a child," Bernie said. "Especially when she's a crosser. How are you going to get Lon to believe you? You'd better have proof before you make an unfounded accusation."

"I intend to. I need to find a way to get into the Avery's cabin." Sadie pointed at Bernie as she walked toward the door. "And you're going to help me."

31

The printer hummed as it spit out a spreadsheet. Draining the last drop of coffee from his mug, Lon stood, stretched, and reached for the coffee pot. Empty. Didn't anyone have the competence to brew another pot?

Lon had spent the last three hours creating a spreadsheet listing each hand-written entry from the notebook Sadie had discovered with Celeste's body. He carefully traced the lines connecting one name to another. Nan and Sadie had recognized one of the names as a parent of an abducted child. Maybe a coincidence. Maybe not. Each connection began and ended within a short timeframe.

The muscles in his back burned. Time for a fresh shot of caffeine. He also needed a firm-handed masseuse to get the kinks out.

The writing in the notebook looked familiar. Lon had sat so long staring at it, his brain had gone fuzzy. Where had he seen the scrawl before? When Lon visited Celeste's parents to find out if it was their daughter's penmanship, Celeste's mother confirmed it wasn't. When she provided one of Celeste's old letters for comparison, the writing appeared nothing like the nearly illegible writing in the notebook. Celeste's writing was the opposite. Practice-sheet perfect.

"What are you smiling for?" Deputy Wayne joined Lon at the coffee station and watched while fresh coffee ran through the filter into the pot.

"You don't want to know."

"Try me."

"I have this image of Sadie on her hands and knees in a

mini skirt under Clay's cabin and I can't get it out of my mind."

"Ouch." Deputy Wayne poured a cup of coffee. "Sadie in a mini skirt isn't something I care to think about." He grimaced. "In fact, the thought scorched the right side of my brain."

Lon laughed. "Sadie means well."

"No she doesn't. She's a busy body. She's also loonytoons."

"No she's not. She's actually very smart. If you knew her better, you'd agree."

"That woman has imaginary friends. She's got a tat on her belly."

"So?" Lon grinned at Deputy Wayne and raised an eyebrow. "I seem to remember your wife got a tattoo on her boob last year. You gave it to her for her birthday."

"That's private information. Besides I didn't think you were listening. Do you remember everything?"

Lon sat back in his chair and put his hands behind his head. "I wish I could." He held the notebook up. "This is driving me nuts. I've seen this writing before, but I can't place it."

"Let me see." Deputy Wayne turned the notebook around. "Looks like hen scratch."

"I agree it's pretty bad. I couldn't read some of the names. At least I didn't recognize any as being from Pinecone Landing." Lon laid the spreadsheet on his desk. "I thought if I organized it by date, we could make sense out of the notebook. If you think of something better, let me know."

Static erupted from the speaker clipped to Deputy Wayne's shoulder. He shouted to the dispatcher, "I'm standing right here. You don't need to broadcast."

A muffled voice came from the dispatch center, "Sorry. I

didn't know you came back."

"I've been chasing my tail following up on all the sightings," Deputy Wayne said. "Everybody and their mother think they've spotted the abducted baby."

"I know what you mean. Dispatch called me at midnight to go to the Fertile Turtle. One of their regulars insisted the baby was sleeping in the back seat of his car. It turned out to be a bag of groceries."

Lon tapped on the date column with his pen. "From the dates in the notebook, it looks like it covers twenty-one years. Whoever made the entries wrote it hit and miss at first. Then they started adding more details about four years before Celeste went missing."

Lon ran his finger down the date column. "Here's where the frequency increased." He moved his finger to the dollar column. "The amount increased, too. Whatever they sold got more expensive."

"What's that?" Deputy Wayne pointed at a right hand column containing names.

"I haven't figured it out. The notebook had lines drawn from one name to the other, so I figured it must be part of a transaction. Actually, that's what Sadie figured it meant when she handed over the notebook. Sometimes the lines spanned two pages, but a line and an arrow always ended in the same column."

"When did Celeste go missing? Ten years ago? Or was it earlier?"

"She disappeared fifteen years ago during the summer. Fifteen years as of last week. I pulled the old file so I could compare dates with the notebook."

"It's too bad Jed didn't live long enough to find out what happened." Deputy Wayne shook his head. "He'd have been pleased his parents finally put her to rest."

"It is a shame," Lon said. "Nan and Sadie shed a lot of tears over Jed's death. Everybody did."

"So, did you ask her to marry you yet?"

Lon crossed his arms over his chest. "Who? Nan or Sadie?"

Deputy Wayne stopped tipping his coffee mug in mid-motion. "That thought scorched the other side of my brain."

"I asked Nan more than once. She's afraid Clay will drive a wedge between us."

"Then get rid of him. He left town once, maybe he'd leave again."

"I'm trying. First I need to sort a few things out."

"Nan's too skeptical."

"You'd be skeptical, too, if you'd picked a loser," Lon said.

Deputy Wayne held up two fingers. "Two. Don't forget she planned to marry Paul Brinks last year."

Lon turned his head from side to side trying to loosen the knots in his shoulders. Deputy Wayne had covered his back more times than he cared to remember. Working side-by-side over the years, his partner understood the depth of his love for Nan. They had more than a partnership. It was a relationship based on complete trust. The day Lon learned Nan intended to divorce Clay, Deputy Wayne encouraged him to quit striding the fence and make his feelings known.

After Nan's divorce, Lon moved forward with the fervor of a hungry lion. Then Paul Brinks entered the scene and shattered Nan's life. Now the lion circled once again had no intention of losing sight of his prey. He needed something more. His falling in love with Nan years earlier hadn't been an accident. Everything happened for a reason.

Lon pointed at Deputy Wayne. "Don't forget the other man in Nan's life. Aanders plays a big part in this. He's a great kid. He's been through a lot and I don't want to screw it up for him."

"That poor kid," Deputy Wayne said. "He's probably as skeptical as Nan. How come he never plays with kids his own age? Every time I see him he's with Sadie."

"He likes the Witt sisters. Sadie and Jane are like his grandmothers," Lon explained. "He's lucky to have them. So is Nan."

Lon rubbed his eyes. His eyes burned from staring at the notebook too long. Fifteen more minutes of this and they'd pop out and roll on the desk. "I think Aanders has an identity problem. Nobody likes death. People tend to think a kid who grows up around caskets must be a weirdo, and that's why he doesn't have friends. It could be why he hangs with Sadie."

"I suppose. It also doesn't help he talks to Sadie's imaginary friends."

"What?" Lon stared at his partner.

"When the crowd walked back to their cars after Celeste's burial, Aanders walked all the way to the hearse talking and waving his arms."

"So?"

"He walked alone. I didn't get the impression he was talking to the people in front of him, because they chatted to each other."

The sheriff peeked around the bullet-proof glass partition separating the dispatch office from the deputies' desks. "What are you working on?" He pointed at the spreadsheet.

"I'm trying to make sense out of the names in this notebook Sadie found with Celeste's body."

"Any luck yet?" The sheriff scanned the sheet.

"Nope. I know I've seen this writing before, but I can't place it. There's something about this name that keeps raising a red flag." Lon looked up at the sheriff. "The next step is to Google these names and see what comes up. I'll run them through the missing-person data base, too."

Lon waited for the search engine bar to appear. After he keyed the name in the search field, he hit enter and waited. The three men stared at the listings as they appeared on the screen.

"Oh, oh," the sheriff whispered. "That better be a coincidence, or somebody's got a lot of explaining to do."

32

Sadie parted the curtains and peered out the window. "What's taking so long? Our manager said the Avery's planned to leave for Itasca State Park at 10:00 AM. They got directions and a map earlier this morning." Sadie looked at her watch. "It's almost 10:30."

"Maybe the baby's not feeling well." Jane joined her sister and peeked between the white muslin panels.

Sadie picked at her blond gel-tipped spikes. She looked at Bernie. "Why do you keep staring at my hair?"

"Because it looks like you've got a skunk on your head." Jane reached out to touch Sadie's hair. "That's the second time Big Leon made you look like a skunk."

Sadie turned her head back and forth and gazed at her reflection in the window. "I can't help it if most of the highlights ended up in a row." She picked at the spikes and tried to move some of them sideways. "Big Leon said it'll look better after he trims some of the streak."

"I'd schedule the appointment if I were you," Jed murmured.

"I should have known better. Big Leon was in a hurry. He had a date with his cousin."

"You mean as in a romantic date?" Jane scrunched her nose. "Ohhhh. Gross."

"I guess so. Apparently in his family they date their relatives. He couldn't keep his mind on his business.

"Instead of staring at my head, Bernie, why didn't you notice my new bra?" Sadie cupped her hands under her breasts. "I got it yesterday."

"Sadie. Shame on you," Jane shouted. "Bernie doesn't want to look at your breasts."

"Actually, I did notice them. The fact they're considerably higher than yesterday makes it hard to ignore. Maybe you should lower them a tad. That looks uncomfortable."

"It is. I'm getting ready for tonight. I'm going to the Fertile Turtle and I want to look super sexy."

Holding Sadie's gaze, Bernie said, "Have you ever been diagnosed with personality disorder?"

"Not yet, but I've been diagnosed with hemorrhoids. I got it from Jane's cooking."

Sadie ignored Jane's disproving stare. "Bernie and I talked about what Sally saw at the Avery's cabin. It makes sense." Sadie tapped the table with a bright yellow fingernail while she looked at her sister. "If you think back on when the Avery's checked in, they bundled their baby way too warm for a hot summer day. Think about the rigid bundle. I never noticed any hands or feet moving and the covers never slipped out of place. I know you don't want to believe it, but I think Sally's on to something."

"Sadie said the Averys sat on their porch without the baby, but the minute someone stopped by, Pam got the baby and held her while they visited." Bernie tapped a long finger on the table. "This all took place without a single cry from the baby."

"Maybe the baby slept most of the time?" A skeptical frown caused Jane's chin to dimple.

"Maybe," Sadie said. "But I never heard a single peep out of their child for the first few days. Usually babies cry when they're hungry. Either Chelsie has no vocal cords, or Pam has ESP. Chelsie didn't make a sound until shortly after the infant abduction."

"Think about it, Jane." Bernie cupped his hand over Jane's hand and held it. "When the Averys visited with other guests, the baby was completely covered and they did everything to shield her from curious eyes. They didn't want to disturb her."

Sadie paced. "After the infant abduction, the Averys went out of their way to show her off and introduce her to everyone."

Jane tugged at her lower lip. "This is unbelievable. Do you think we've seen too many movies?"

"I keep drifting back to why Sally thought the baby had a penis," Bernie said.

"Because, it's exactly what she saw." Sadie's voice rose with excitement. "She's too young to make it up. Now it's up to us to prove it."

"Oh, no, Sadie." Bernie rose quickly. "I don't like your idea. It's too dangerous. If the Avery's have the abducted child, we need to contact Lon."

"If we took what we've got to the authorities, they'd think we were crazy. Remember, it's one of my crossers who discovered the evidence. The Averys will be gone until later this afternoon, so you and I are going to do some detective work."

Bernie's eyes fill with unease. "Me? I thought you were kidding earlier. I'm not going to help you. Why can't Jane do it?"

"I'm not going to help you, either. I refuse to commit a crime. I'll stand guard and let you know if anyone's coming." Jane nodded sharply to affirm her position. "You aren't really going to snoop in their cabin, are you?"

"You already know the answer. If there's a sign that says do not enter, I'll be the first one through the door. I need to know what's on the other side."

Bernie said, "What if they come back and catch you?"

"Then we'll make something up. Like we smelled a gas leak, or we smelled smoke. Something legitimate."

"I won't do it. I simply refuse."

"You're such a wuss. Haven't you ever broken the law?"

"Not exactly. I have an aversion to handcuffs, and I'm confident I'm in the majority."

"We'll there's always a first. I'll scout it out by looking through the window. If someone comes near the cabin, holler."

"You mean like, 'Somebody's coming. Quit looking in the cabin window or they'll know you're sneaking around?'"

Balling her hands on her hips and grunting in disgust, Sadie said, "That's not funny. You're not helping one bit. Act like a detective or at least try to think like one. If someone comes, pretend you're calling the dog. We'll use Belly's name as our code."

"I'm not going to be a part of this, Sadie." Bernie walked toward the screen door.

"You already are. You're an accessory."

"The Averys just got in their car," Jane whispered, stepping back from the window.

"Did they have their suitcases with them?" Sadie peered over Jane's shoulder.

"It didn't look like it."

"Thank goodness. I'm afraid they'll sneak away before we can prove anything. We'll wait ten minutes before we check it out."

Mustering the energy to follow Sadie, Belly waddled slowly behind her as she led Bernie across the pine needle strewn ground.

"I don't like this one bit. I feel like I'm going to the gallows." Bernie matched Sadie stride for stride.

"Don't be silly. The Averys committed the crime, not us. I own the cabin and we have every right to go in there. We smell gas, remember?"

As Sadie and Bernie stepped onto the paved path, a woman shouted, "Father Johnson. Is that you?"

Bernie stiffened, but kept walking.

"Yoo-hoo. Father Johnson. Is that you?" The woman hurried to satisfy her question and fell into place next to him. "It is you. What a pleasant surprise." She waved at her husband. "Look who's here. It's Father Johnson."

"Well I'll be darned." The husband caught up and shook Bernie's hand vigorously. "What a surprise. I heard you had left on vacation but I had no idea you were at Witt's End."

The woman looked at Sadie's hair, at Sadie's breasts, and back at Bernie. "We arrived two days ago. We love it."

Bernie cleared his throat. "This is Sadie Witt. She owns the resort."

Sadie smiled at the woman. "I hope you're enjoying your stay. If there's anything you need, let the manager know."

"We will. We're going on a pontoon ride for senior citizens. You're not going on it, are you?"

"Not this time," Sadie said. "We've got business to attend to."

"Good," the woman muttered as she grabbed her husband's hand. "We look forward to having you back at church, Father. The interim priest isn't filling the pews, if you know what I mean." The woman jerked her husband away, shooting Sadie a disapproving glare.

Sadie and Bernie watched the couple walk toward the beach.

In a broken whisper, Bernie said, "I can explain."

Sadie clenched her hands against her chest. "I can't believe what I just heard. I'm furious with you. How could you do this to Jane?" She shook a trembling finger at Bernie. "If you hurt my sister, I'll make sure everyone knows what you've been up to. I'll interrupt one of your Sunday sermons and announce it to the world." She stormed off toward the Avery's cabin.

What a fine mess. Jane would have her head when she found out. Aanders had been right. She should have stayed away from the dating site. A serial killer? Maybe. A snake charmer? Could be. But a priest? What were the odds of something so absurd? She'd make him pay. Boy, how she'd make him pay.

Balancing on her tiptoes, Sadie grasped the window ledge with her fingers while she peered into the Avery's living room. She jerked with fright when Belly's nose brushed against her leg. She attempted to wave him off with a backward motion. "Scram. Go find Jane," tumbled out in an airy whisper. She nudged the dog with her leg.

Looking toward a Norway pine standing between Cabin 14 and the Avery's cabin, Sadie pointed frantically down at the dog. She stabbed her finger in Belly's direction and swept her arm toward Jane. Sensing a lack of understanding from the watch person who was supposed to be incognito behind the tree, but whose boobs and rounded butt cheeks protruded from both sides of the trunk, Sadie repeated the sweeping motion two more times.

Exasperated, she mumbled, "Do I have to do everything?" Faking a morsel of food in her hand, Sadie made smacking sounds with her lips to attract Belly's attention.

Alerted by his favorite sound, Belly perked and readied while he watched Sadie wind up and throw the invisible morsel across the yard.

The instant the dog took off to ferret out the prize, Sadie

disappeared around the cabin's corner. Straining to take a mental inventory, Sadie peered through the bathroom window. She cupped her hands over her eyes to shut out the sun's glare while she edged along and peeked through two more windows.

Sadie tested the doorknob. Locked. She inserted the master key and the knob turned in her hand. Nonchalantly glancing from side to side, she pushed the door open with her knee and waited. Hearing nothing from within, she scurried into the Avery's cabin. She waved Bernie in.

Bernie failed to follow. Sadie made her way back to where he hid behind a brick fireplace. "Didn't you see my signal?"

A startled cry issued from Bernie's lips.

"Sherlock Holmes you're not. You're afraid of your own shadow." Sadie retreated back toward the door. "Now hurry up and follow me."

"I'm not accustomed to helping someone who's breaking and entering," Bernie said. His long limbs resembled grasshopper legs as he crouched low and crossed to the stoop. "I watch television. I know what you just did is against the law. I don't care if you own the place. You rented it to them in good faith."

"You had me so nervous when you were in there, I almost peed my pants." Jane pulled a chair out and joined Sadie and Bernie at the kitchen table. "Clay came by looking for the Averys. I had to distract him. He said Dan changed his mind and decided to check out early."

"Did he say when?"

"No. Clay told me Dan cheated him out of a job. Something about the plans changing."

"That's what I'm afraid of." Sadie handed Jane a tablet

and a pen. "We've got to get this on paper while it's fresh in our minds."

Jane patted Bernie's hand. "I'm proud of you. I didn't think you'd go through with it."

Sadie glanced at Bernie over the top of her glasses. "Bernie was more than willing to help. He's a man of many talents."

"Everything Sally told us is credible. The evidence is in the Avery's cabin, just like she said. We wanted to bag it and take it with us, but they might realize it's gone."

"You put stuff back exactly where you found it, didn't you?"

"Of course I did, Jane. I'm not stupid." Sadie leaned toward her antsy sister and relayed the sequence of events.

"When I looked in the living room window, I saw pink baby outfits on the sofa and a box of diapers on the coffee table. The normal stuff. When I looked in the bathroom window, I saw a portion of a green-striped bag sticking out of the wastebasket. It looked like the kind the hospital gift shop uses."

Jane impatiently tapped her pen on the table as Sadie organized her thoughts.

"When we walked through the kitchen, it didn't seem to have much other than baby bottles and formula containers on the counter. When we checked the bathroom, our luck changed. The green-striped bag actually had the hospital logo printed on its surface."

"The Averys could have been visiting someone at the hospital. That bag doesn't prove anything," Jane said.

Sadie grabbed Jane's free hand and squeezed it. "That's just the beginning. When I looked through the wastebasket, I found several price tags and a receipt for baby's clothing."

"It's not unusual to buy baby clothes. I don't think you

can consider the clothes as evidence."

"That's what Bernie said, too. When we found the rest of the stuff, it made sense. When I checked the bedroom, I tripped on something sticking out from under the bed. I tried to push it back with my toe, but it crinkled. It was a thick roll of paper. When Bernie and I unrolled it, guess what we discovered?"

Jane's eyes grew large with anticipation. "Quit keeping me in suspense. Tell me."

"A floor plan of the hospital."

"What?"

Jane's incredulous cry bolstered Sadie's pride in her discovery. "Someone had marked the nursery floor plan with yellow highlighter and red lines and had made notes in the margins." Sadie pointed to the tablet. "You've got to write this down. We'll need it when we talk to Lon."

"Arrows leading from the elevator, the nursery, the restrooms, and the stairways were marked in red with times indicated in each hallway. Pam and Dan must have timed how long it would take to get from one point to another," Bernie explained.

Scribbling as she tried to remember everything, Jane shook her head in disbelief.

Sadie pointed to Bernie's back pocket. Bernie removed a large wad of paper. He unfolded it and placed it on the table.

"You took it?"

"We had to," Bernie replied. "This is the best piece of evidence we found. They won't realize it's missing unless they unfold the blueprints. We're hoping they won't because the abduction is already done."

"Second best piece of evidence," Sadie interrupted. "Wait till you hear the rest."

"After we found the blueprint, I decided to check out

their closet. Most of the things were what you'd expect for a family on vacation, except for a half-full garbage bag on the floor."

"You opened their garbage? That's private. You shouldn't have done it."

"Jane. What's the matter with you? That's what detectives do. They snoop. Actually I made Bernie open it in case it had yucky stuff in it. Guess what he found."

Leaning her forehead against her fingertips, Jane peeked sideways at Bernie. "Do I really want to know?"

"Evidence. The bag held lots of evidence." Using finger tabulation, Sadie listed the items. "What do you think I discovered balled up on the bottom of the bag? A nurse's uniform with a photo ID and guess whose picture was on the tag. Pam Avery's."

"I can't believe it," Jane uttered.

"Write it down. Write it down," Sadie ordered, wagging her finger at the tablet. "I also found white shoes and some kind of denim shoulder tote jammed in the garbage bag, too." Placing her hands squarely on the table Sadie announced, "Then we found the most important piece of all. A paper towel wadded up on the bottom of the bag. When I unrolled it, I found several tiny clumps of fine, black, baby hair."

"The abducted baby had black hair." Jane's words faded as she mulled the prospect.

"Yes, and when the Averys showed their baby off around the resort, she was as bald as a bowling pin."

Jane moaned, "That poor child. Can you imagine what he's been through? What kind of maniacs would jeopardize an infant?"

"That's what I wondered," Bernie said.

"I think you need to call Lon right away." Jane laid her pen on the tablet.

"That's exactly what I intend to do." Sadie headed toward the door. She stepped off the last porch step, bent low, and reached under the step. Cupping her fingers together, she stuck them into the center of a beer glass. "Fingerprint evidence. We've got to get this to Lon. Who knows, it might help." She wriggled her fingers through the inverted glass. "You know what else scares me? The Averys might have been involved in those other abductions. They know exactly what they're doing and it makes them dangerous. Especially with the pistol in their nightstand."

33

"Look." Lon pulled the computer screen closer, and strained to read the small print. "I knew the name sounded familiar. Reginald Carson is a big-shot lawyer who arranges adoptions. Remember? He got in hot water a while back over a botched adoption in Hollywood."

"I don't remember," Deputy Wayne said. "I can't look at the screen any more. I'm going blind. Between the computer information and your spreadsheet, don't you have enough? We checked on most of the names listed in the left hand column and found out they're parents of abducted children. Chances are the ones we couldn't locate are in the same situation."

"What about this list?" Lon pointed at the names in the right hand column. "We only found two of them."

"At this point, what does it matter? The FBI is on their way because you think you have a connection between the names and dates. If you're right, and the transactions crossed state lines, it's out of our hands."

"There's something gnawing at me. How did Celeste end up dead under Cabin 12? I can't imagine she'd be involved in anything illegal."

"She probably wasn't, but I'll bet Kimmer had a hand in it. If you think the sheriff complained about his ulcer before he connected Kimmer with Reginald Carson and the abductions, you should hear him now. I've never seen anyone get so pale so fast. He's in a world of hurt." Deputy Wayne glanced toward the Sheriff's desk. "He's trying to figure out how to approach the Judge and question him. If the Judge isn't involved, the sheriff risks losing his job. If he is involved, he's worried about the publicity."

"He's involved, all right, but to what extent? There's too much coincidence, especially during the time frame."

"I think Celeste found out about the abductions and was ready to turn someone in. Maybe the notebook belongs to Reginald and he had her killed because he couldn't risk it."

"I agree," Lon said. "Maybe because Kimmer and Reginald are connected and because Celeste worked for Kimmer, Reginald had Kimmer arrange it. Maybe Kimmer had no choice."

"My brain's scrambled. I need to eat. See if you can find anything else linking Kimmer to Reginald Carson. I'm going to lunch." Deputy Wayne poked his head around the bullet-proof partition and tapped the dispatcher's shoulder. "I'll be home for about a half-hour. Call if you need me."

Lon searched the internet by including word variations with Reginald Carson's name in the search engine, but each search retrieved the same articles he had already read. When he slanted his search toward legal issues, several results containing Reginald's name appeared. Many also contained Kimmer's name. The hair on Lon's neck prickled. He read an article featuring Kimmer and Reginald Carson promoting private adoptions. The article, dated two years prior to Kimmer's appointment as a judge, touted the safety of adopting through private channels to guarantee the birth parent's heritage and credibility.

Lon tapped absentmindedly against the edge of his desk. The first column on his spreadsheet listed families who lost infants to abduction. The last column listed at least two families who had adopted during the time frame listed in the notebook. As Lon researched each name on the internet, one search yielded forty-eight identical names. Time to place phone calls. The twenty-third call netted results with the man's wife verifying they had adopted through private means seventeen years earlier.

Lon now possessed evidence related to an abduction ring. Why Celeste had the notebook when she died remained a puzzle he had to solve.

When Lon had tried to locate people in the adoptive parent's column, they were by far more difficult to locate. Maybe they no longer existed. Or, maybe their affluent status allowed the use of assumed names to maintain anonymity.

Lon keyed the name of the first adoptive party into a different search engine to see if he could find any connection to Minnesota. Fourteen results appeared on the screen. The first ten proved the same as when he'd originally researched the name.

The dispatcher rapped softly on Lon's door. "You need to take a break. I can hear you cussing all the way down the hall."

"Sorry. I'm getting nowhere and it's driving me crazy."

"Get some fresh air. Maybe it'll make sense when you come back." The dispatcher ran back to the console to answer a call.

Lon clicked on the eleventh entry. A glitzy Los Angeles corporate website radiated across the screen expounding a recent multi-million dollar lawsuit settlement in their favor. A photo of the corporation's attorney, Reginald Carson, appeared in a side bar in the upper right-hand corner.

"Gotcha," Lon said.

"Got what?" Deputy Wayne dropped a bag on Lon's desk. "I made an extra sandwich. I figured you wouldn't take time to eat."

Lon reached for the bag and opened it with his left hand. "What is it?"

"It's free, that's what it is."

"Sorry. I didn't mean I doubted your sandwich skills. I'm skeptical about opening bag lunches. Remember Jane Witt's box lunches she used to sell at the resort? I made the mistake of buying one last summer. Not a good investment," Lon said. "I still don't know what was in the sandwich, but it wasn't meant for human consumption."

Deputy Wayne nodded understanding. "Remember the time Jane baked a cheesecake for the sheriff and ten minutes after he ate it bubbles popped out of his nose?"

"I remember. We didn't see him for the rest of the day." Lon took a bite of the sandwich. "Thanks. I needed this."

Lon ran his finger across the computer screen. "Take a look. Reginald Carson is the lawyer for one of the people who adopted a baby."

"You mean in addition to arranging the adoption?"

"He's the adoptive father's corporate attorney. Now we can connect one of the adoptive parents to Reginald. When you put Kimmer, Reginald, private adoptions, the abducted baby, the adoptive parents and Celeste together in a pot, what have you got?"

"A deputy with an overactive imagination?"

"No," Lon argued. He looked toward the dispatch office and lowered his voice. "You've got an old murder and a reason to suspect Kimmer in the recent abduction."

"Celeste disappeared fifteen years ago. What does her disappearance have to do with the recent abduction?"

Deputy Wayne's challenge irked Lon, but he realized his partner's challenge centered more around proof than questioning his sanity. "Okay. See if this makes sense. Reginald Carson is still in the adoption game according to a recent article. Another article listed Judge Kimmer in attendance at a banquet last month where Carson received an award. Carson is listed in the notebook Sadie found." Lon held up a fourth finger while finishing the list of possibilities. "Kimmer is rolling in dough. I'll bet it isn't because the county pays their judges huge salaries."

Static on Deputy Wayne's speaker crackled. "Sadie Witt just pulled up in the shuttle van in case you want to hide." The dispatcher's voice faded as Sadie walked through the door.

Lon shoved papers into a folder. He hurried to follow Deputy Wayne around the corner.

"Wait a sec, Lon. I've got something to tell you." Sadie held up the glass she had taken from the Avery's cabin. "You'd better run a fingerprint check on this. I think the prints belong to the person who abducted the baby."

34

"I don't like it. I don't like it one bit." Dan Avery glanced through the screen door for the fourth time.

"She owns the resort. Sadie probably checked on something," Pam said. "It's no different than the housekeeping crew dropping off clean towels every day. Maybe she had a legitimate reason." Pam propped the baby on her shoulder and rocked back and forth attempting to ease him out of his agitated state.

"Clay said she left with something in her hand."

Pam sighed deeply. "Since when do you believe a nosy neighbor? Especially Clay. He couldn't even walk straight."

"Clay told me Sadie had something in her hand. I believe him."

"Quit raising your voice. You're scaring him. I mean her." Pam shook her head in frustration. "Her. I've got to stop making that mistake."

"Would you please shut that kid up? His constant crying is getting old. It's all he's done since we brought him home. What the hell is wrong with him?"

Pam's nostrils flared as she pointed her finger. "Keep your voice down. Do you want people to hear you?" She shifted the baby to her other shoulder. "You're the one who wanted to come to Pinecone Landing. So deal with it. I don't know what's wrong with him, but we can't take him to the doctor until we get back to Minneapolis. You know we can't risk taking the baby to a clinic in Pinecone Landing. Try to remember to call the baby her, not him."

Dan pressed the palms of his hands against his forehead.

"Just get the kid to shut up so I can think." He massaged his temples with his thumbs. "I agree with Clay. I think that crazy broad is up to something."

"You're overreacting. The fact the deputies are in Clay's cabin had nothing to do with us. Clay said they found an old skeleton. He said it had been there for a long time." As the baby's sobs let up, Pam paced the floor to keep the soothing motion flowing.

"That's what has me worried. Kimmer wanted me to excavate some old stuff from under Clay's cabin. I'll bet it's the skeleton. Maybe dealing with Kimmer isn't such a good idea after all."

"Nonsense. We decided to forego the middle man and that's exactly what we're going to do. I had a chat with Kimmer and he agreed to up our abduction fee."

"You what?" Dan stared at Pam.

"You heard me. I needed to see for myself what makes Kimmer tick. When you took Clay fishing, I went to visit him. He agreed to up the ante. Now relax. Grab a beer and sit down." Pam turned toward Dan as she walked into the cabin. "Don't underestimate me again, Dan."

After feeding the baby, Pam closed the screen door behind her, easing the latch silently into place. Belly LaGossa whined with delight when Pam neared the Adirondack chair. "What's that repulsive dog doing here?" She pushed Belly aside with her foot. "You know I don't like him. He drools all over everything." Pam ran her fingers across the seat of the chair. She grimaced and held up her hand. "See what I mean. He slobbered on my chair."

"I wouldn't worry about the dog, if I were you. You've got more important things to worry about." Dan held up a tag, letting it dangle from his fingers. "Look familiar?"

Grabbing the tag, Pam said, "It's from the booties I

bought. Where'd you get it?"

"I found it under the chair." Dan pointed to the third wooden chair on the porch.

"That can't be. I put it in the wastebasket in the bathroom. I put all the tags in there."

"I'm telling you I found it under the chair." Dan's voice shook. "Now tell me Sadie wasn't up to something. I'll bet she dropped it. You were careless and now she's suspicious."

"Why would she be? Every mother buys clothes for her newborn. No big deal." Pam stared at Dan. "What's wrong with you? Ever since you talked to Kimmer this afternoon, you've been a basket case."

Dan drew a deep swig from his beer bottle. "You're probably right." He patted Pam's hand. "Sorry, Babe. Kimmer set me on edge. He asked twice when we intended to head back to Minneapolis. He acted like he had a hot poker up his butt. He got angry because I didn't do the excavation job like he had asked."

"I didn't know he had set a time limit," Pam said. "He didn't indicate it when I visited with him."

"He hadn't. In fact when he told me about the job, he led me to believe I could do it whenever I got around to it. Today he got all pissed because I hadn't taken care of it right away."

Pam sat rigid. "Do you mean to tell me Kimmer had something to do with those bones?"

"Maybe. He told me he'd make it worth my while if I didn't tell anyone about the job. He wasn't happy when I told him Clay would help. Something sure made him nervous."

Pam and Dan jerked in unison as Clay walked out of their cabin and let the door slam behind him.

He twisted the cap off a beer bottle. "I hope you don't mind, but I let myself in your back door. I'm out of beer."

"Geez, Clay. You scared the crap out of me," Dan said.

Pam winced and patted the air. She turned her ear toward the bedroom window. "Keep your voice down. I just got the baby to sleep."

Clay dropped down into the third porch chair and placed his feet on the railing. "Are you sure you don't need me to help you with the hospital job? I sure could use the work."

"What?" Dan glanced at Clay in alarm.

"The hospital job. You know the one you got the blue prints for."

Dan picked at the beer label with his thumb nail. "I decided not to do the job."

"You're lying. I bet you hired the tall skinny guy instead of me. I suppose he'll work for a buck less an hour. He's too old. He can't do heavy work." Clay tossed his empty beer bottle over the railing onto the lawn. "It figures. I knew you'd stab me in the back. Everybody else does."

One side of Dan's mouth twisted up in confusion as he stared at Pam.

Pam shook her head and shrugged.

"I don't have a clue what you're talking about. I considered doing a hospital job, but decided against it. Pam and I are heading back to Minneapolis. That's all there is to it."

"Then why was the old guy looking at the blueprints in your cabin?"

Two heads swiveled in unison toward Clay.

Dan's fingers tightened around the chair's wooden arm. "Who did you see in our cabin?"

"That tall guy. The one who's been drooling over the Witt sisters. You know. The one with the baggy face."

"Bernie Johnson?"

"Yeah. He and Sadie sat on your bed looking at the blueprints."

"Shit," Dan mumbled, as the word stuck in his throat. "Did they say anything?"

"I don't know. I peeked through the screen door, but I couldn't hear them. Sadie had some stuff in her hands when she left, though."

"Why don't you run down to the liquor store and get some more beer." Dan stood and pulled his wallet from his back pocket. He pulled out a twenty and handed it to Clay. "Join us tonight and we'll make plans for tomorrow afternoon. I hear the fish are biting."

"That's a great idea," Clay said. "I'll ask Aanders to go with us. You know the father-son thing."

Pam waited until Clay cleared the paved path. "Why did you ask him to join us? What's the matter with you?"

"Nothing's the matter with me. It's part of the plan. Sadie's on to us and we've got to get the hell out of here. Get in there and get everything packed and ready to go."

"Right now? You mean we're leaving right now?"

"Not now, Pam. Use your head. If Sadie suspects anything, she's probably watching our cabin. I'm going to the lodge and rent one of their boats for tomorrow afternoon. If she thinks we've got plans through tomorrow, she'll ease up."

"I don't get it," Pam said. "Why pack now?"

"Because we're going to leave tonight when everyone's sleeping. We'll set the alarm for 2:00 a.m. and head out before they have a chance to miss us."

35

Lon waved the telephone receiver in the air to notify the deputies the call they had been waiting for had come. "It's Sadie. The lights in the Avery's cabin just went off. She said the rest of the resort is quiet." Lon glanced at his wrist to synchronize watches. "I've got four minutes after midnight. We'll meet outside the lodge entrance. No lights. No sirens. No nothing. It's just the four of us going by vehicle and two deputies in a boat at the marina."

Lon nodded to Deputy Wayne. "Give them a call. Tell them to put the boat in the water and be ready to back us up by 12:45." He placed a sketch of the cabin on the counter.

Listening as Lon issued instructions, Deputy Wayne slipped into his Kevlar vest and buttoned his shirt over the protective gear.

The men examined their magazines and nine millimeters before securing them into position on their belts.

Lon pointed to Deputy Wayne. "You grab the baby. Nan's standing by to help once you've secured him. She's got extra blankets and will ride with you to the hospital."

"I'm ready." Deputy Wayne signaled his back-up.

After the eight-minute drive to the resort, Lon rolled his patrol car to a stop next to the Witt's End main entrance and waited for Deputy Wayne to pull up behind him. He wiped his clammy palms against his pants. Lon had been involved in take-downs before, but not one involving the recovery of an infant. Because Sadie had found a nurse's uniform in the Avery's cabin, Lon and the sheriff opted not to notify the hospital until after the take down. Pam might have an accomplice in the hospital. They couldn't run the risk of ruining the element of surprise.

Lon's main concern was the child. If the Averys slept soundly, catching them unaware would do the trick. If they suspected anything, and Dan had a chance to grab the pistol in his night stand, the child could be used as a pawn.

Lon jerked when the sheriff shook the antacid bottle and popped another handful of tablets in his mouth. The sheriff's skin tone had grown sallow as the clock approached the new hour.

"You seeing a doctor for your heartburn?" The sheriff's health had gone south since learning Judge Kimmer might be involved in Celeste's death. Seeing the sheriff shake his head, Lon said, "I don't know why you're so stubborn. There must be a prescription more effective than the stuff you're chewing."

Tension impacted everyone. Lon hadn't wanted the sheriff to participate in the recovery, but he had insisted. Lon headed up the team, but the sheriff made sure everyone knew he would have the final say.

The sheriff sat in the passenger's seat, his hands clenched against his thighs. His persistent throat clearing grated on Lon's nerves. The same scent hung heavy around the sheriff that hung on rookies when they waited in ambush. It was the same scent Lon knew he exuded when he approached a scene of chaos. The scent of fear. That meant trouble. One hesitant misstep, and everyone could be in jeopardy.

Both drivers extinguished their headlights as they entered the gate. They slowly proceeded past the lodge. The purr of motors and the crunch of gravel under tires broke the silence while the men maneuvered into position out of view of the Avery's cabin.

Deputy Wayne positioned his patrol car so the

passenger's door aligned with the pathway. Opening the car door, he lifted a box off the floor and placed it on the passenger seat. Reaching in, he ran his hand over the pillow, plumped it, unfolded a blanket and placed it over the pillow.

Distracted by Lon's frantic gestures, the three deputies turned toward the direction Lon pointed, straining to understand his angry whisper. "Get her out of here," Lon rasped, attempting to wave the approaching figure away.

With slippers slapping against the soles of her feet and her red satin robe flagging behind her, Sadie ran toward Lon's vehicle. "What took you so long? I called you over an hour ago. Is everything ready?"

The sheriff looked at Deputy Wayne. "She's not wearing anything under her robe." He unscrewed the cap on the antacid and popped two more tablets in his mouth.

Stepping in front of Sadie, Lon pulled her robe together in the middle and reached for the silk ties hanging at her sides. He looped a big knot in front of her stomach and pulled it tight. Redirecting her with a half spin, he put his arm around her shoulder and walked her back toward Cabin 14. Barely audible, he said, "We got your message. We have to wait to be sure the Averys are sleeping before we go in. Go back to your cabin and stay out of the way."

"I want to stay here." Sadie attempted to remove his hand from her shoulder.

"It's too dangerous. We don't know if he's armed or not."

"I already told you he is. I saw a gun in the night stand."

Lon put both hands on her shoulders. "I'm in charge here, Sadie. This is serious. The life of a child is at risk, and I can't be worrying about you, too."

"We want to help. Bernie and Jane will do whatever you want." Sadie looked up at Lon over the rim of her glasses. "Bernie could put in a few good words with the big guy up

239

stairs if you think it would help. He's got connections."

Lon watched Deputy Wayne tap his watch and signal toward the Avery's cabin. "I'm not going to tell you again. Go back to your cabin. I'm concerned about the baby and if I have to worry about you, I might make a mistake. It's because of you the child might go home. When it's over, I promise you'll get credit for solving the case."

Nan hurried over to Sadie and tugged on her arm. "Come on, Sadie. Do what Lon says."

"Okay, but as soon as it's over, I'm coming out to see what happened."

Lon walked over to his squad car and removed his shotgun before joining the other men who stood ready with revolvers in hand.

One of the men pointed toward the path. Belly stood in the middle of the paved walkway with his tail moving slowly back and forth, not quite sure this was something worth getting excited over. He sniffed deeply, pulling in the scent of fear. He settled down on his haunches.

Checking his watch, Lon held up his finger and gave the go ahead sign by pointing at the Avery's cabin.

Deputy Wayne and his backup partner ran from the shadows to the wall of a cabin separating the Avery's cabin from the patrol cars. With backs against the logs, the two men held their revolvers at their sides. They stood still and listened. Hearing nothing, Deputy Wayne gave a head wave, signaling Lon and the sheriff to approach. After joining the others, Lon peered around the corner toward the cabin.

A patrol boat bobbed near shore with one of the deputies slowly maneuvering an oar to keep the boat aligned with the shore. Reflections of a half-moon glistened against the calm water. The other deputy stood with his shotgun held inconspicuously at his side. Acknowledging Lon's hand sign with a nod, the deputy rowed closer to shore.

Rotating his finger in the air, Lon instructed Deputy Wayne and his partner to take position at the rear of the Avery's cabin. Lon and the sheriff waited until they reached their designated spots before approaching. They came to a standstill with their backs against the massive logs. Lon's flashlight thumped against a log when he pressed his back against the wood. Freezing in place, Lon glanced sideways at the sheriff, who stared back in panic. Neither man drew a breath.

Climbing over the porch railing, Lon settled onto the wooden decking and motioned for the sheriff to follow. After crouching low and duck-waddling below the window frame, Lon stood and crossed to the door. Satisfied the Averys were unaware of their presence, Lon gave the sheriff the go-ahead to assume stance on the other side of the door.

Both men unhooked their flashlights from their belts and placed them alongside their weapons.

Lon inhaled deeply to fill his lungs before slicing the air with three beats of his fingers.

As Lon's finger sliced the air on the third beat, both men switched on their flashlights. Lon pulled back with all his strength and kicked at the doorknob with the heel of his boot. Wood splintering, the door swung on its hinges, slammed against the wall.

The instant Deputy Wayne heard the shattered silence he raised his foot and struck the rear door. As the latch released its hold, the deputies shouted wildly to add to the pandemonium and entered through the kitchen. Passing through the rooms, Deputy Wayne shined his flashlight along the door frames and flipped light switches as he ran.

Lon and the sheriff shouted loudly as they entered the cabin and ran toward the bedroom. "Sheriff's Department.

Freeze. Don't move." Dan reached toward the pistol. Lon kicked at the stand causing it to tip over. Dan's Glock skittered across the floor and Lon kicked it out of range.

A baby's cry pierced the air as Lon grabbed Pam's arm and pulled her from the bed. "On the floor. I said on the floor," he screamed at the confused woman. When she failed to respond, he grabbed her shoulder and forced her to lay face down on the floor.

Lon aimed the shotgun at Dan. "Don't move," he shouted when Dan rose to his knees.

Deputy Wayne's partner and one of the deputies from the patrol boat wrestled Dan to the floor and pressed his face into the rug.

Pam's pleas went unheeded as a deputy pulled her wrists firmly behind her and secured a white plastic strip into place.

Deputy Wayne lifted the screaming infant from the travel crib, enveloping him in his large arms.

"Check the baby for a penis," Lon insisted, as he pulled Pam off the floor.

"Let's see if your little girl sprouted a dick tonight," the sheriff said, watching Lon push Pam toward the child.

Deputy Wayne struggled to unwrap the baby and unsnap the tiny diaper closures as the baby flailed in protest. The deputy peeled back one of the diaper tabs. "We got ourselves a baby boy. Here's the birthmark his mother talked about." The deputy pointed to a mark on the infant's hip.

A keening cry of realization escaped from Pam and she turned toward Dan. "I told you I wanted to quit. I told you something like this would happen."

"Shut up, you stupid bitch. Keep your mouth shut." Spittle sprayed from Dan's lips.

Deputy Wayne bolted through the door and headed for the patrol car before Dan ended his barrage of threats. Placing the baby in the box and covering him with the blanket, he waited until Nan belted the seatbelt before he started the motor. "Are you ready?"

Nan put her arms around the box as the child screamed. "Is he okay? Was he injured?"

"I don't think so. I think he's mad because they made him wear pink diapers." Deputy Wayne grinned and patted Nan's hand. "Everything's going to be okay. Relax. You're trembling so hard you're shaking the baby."

"I'm trying." Nan clung to the box.

Deputy Wayne waited until he passed through the resort gates before turning on his flashing lights and siren.

Pressing the tab on the speaker attached to his shoulder, he said, "Dispatch. This is Deputy Wayne. Notify the hospital I'll be arriving in about ten minutes. Tell them we've located the infant abducted from the hospital and to prepare for our arrival." Grasping the infant's tiny hand between his thumb and forefinger, he wiggled it back and forth as he accelerated toward the glow of the city's lights.

The driver of the patrol boat joined Lon after docking the boat. He stepped out of the way as they led Dan and Pam from the cabin. After situating Pam in the back seat of the second vehicle, Lon placed a call to dispatch requesting a crime scene investigation team. He finished by giving directions to the location.

Lon removed the magazine from Dan's Glock and pulled the slide to the rear, extracting the round from the chamber. He tucked the round into his pocket. Lon waded through a cluster of onlookers who had gathered around the sheriff.

Once the deputies strung crime scene tape around the Avery's cabin, the sheriff said, "Everything's going to be fine. Nothing to be upset about." He smiled at the many apprehensive faces staring back at him. "I want you to return to your cabins and go back to bed. Sorry to disturb you."

The crowd moved to the right as a squad car pulled away. "If everything's okay, why is a deputy guarding the door?" Conjecture buzzed through the pajama-clad crowd as they mulled the prospects.

"The sheriff's right," Sadie shouted above their questions. "Let's go back to bed. We might have good news for you in the morning."

Another wave of theories floated among the guests as they dispersed in all directions.

Turning toward her cabin, Sadie noticed Jane walking toward her. Silhouetted against the half-moon, Jane's robed figure appeared as an apparition floating along the pathway. Sadie gasped. She reached out for her sister.

"What's wrong," Jane said. "Did something happen to the baby?"

"No. The baby's fine. It's just when you walked toward me, you looked like one of the crossers crossing over to the other side. It scared me. I thought maybe you had collapsed under the excitement." Sadie threw her arms around her sister. "I don't know what I'd do if I lost you. Promise me you'll never leave."

Jane squeezed back before setting Sadie at arm's length. "I'm not going anywhere."

Sadie squeezed her eyes shut and tilted her head upward. "I'm overwhelmed with all that happened, but there's something I need to tell you. It's going to shock you."

"After what happened here tonight, nothing can shock me. Can it wait till morning? You helped save a child's life. That's enough for one night." Jane took Sadie's hand and led her toward the cabin. "You'll feel better in the morning. All we need is a good night's sleep. Then you can tell me all about it."

36

The rumble from the hospital garage door opener reverberated off the concrete block walls as the emergency bay door glided along the iron tracks. An orderly watched the outside security monitor. He had taken position to wait for the squad car three minutes after the dispatcher's call had come in.

Dr. Nordin had just finished admitting his sixteenth patient when the charge emergency nurse pulled him aside. "You're not going to believe this. The sheriff's dispatcher just called. One of the deputies is on his way in with the abducted baby."

Staring in disbelief, Dr. Nordin said, "Do we know the infant's condition?"

"I asked the same question," the nurse responded. "The dispatcher didn't know. All the deputy told her was to notify the hospital to be ready to take care of the baby. She said she heard a lot of crying in the background. She also said the dispatcher requested additional back up to escort the rescue car into town because she wasn't sure of the situation."

Barking orders, Dr. Nordin listed items he anticipated his staff would need as they scrambled in various directions. "I want you to notify security to go into full alert of possible lock-down. We don't know how the baby was found so we need to take precautions. There could be retaliation. For all I know there might be others injured coming in."

The charge nurse drew a privacy curtain open in one of the treatment bays and placed the appropriate equipment on a cart to prepare for the infant's arrival. She joined the orderly and matched him stride for stride as they paced and kept an eye on the receiving bay monitor screen.

After receiving a call from the charge nurse, the house supervisor notified security before placing the appropriate phone call to the hospital's CEO.

Awakened from a sound sleep, the CEO hesitated, trying to comprehend what he heard. "Is the infant all right? Do they know for sure it's the abducted baby?" Listening to the answers, he said, "Make sure you set up a media center. If this actually is the abducted infant, we're going to be bombarded with press from all over the state. Hell, from all over the country."

The CEO reached for his trousers. "I want security to control access in and out of the facility. I don't want mass chaos. Don't notify the parents until we know the condition of the infant. We can't get their hopes up if it's not their child."

He grabbed his billfold and keys off the bedroom bureau. "Who's the ER doc in charge tonight?" He waited while the charge nurse responded. "That's good. If anybody can handle it, he can."

The orderly spotted flashing red lights approach the driveway access and hit the door to the garage bay with his shoulder as he burst through the opening. He broke into a run. Two squad cars raced toward the emergency entrance as the orderly guided the rolling gurney across the paved apron. He bent his head to peer into the window of the first squad car as the sirens grew silent. A deputy jumped out of the first car and pointed to the second car.

Deputy Wayne pulled to a stop and pointed to the passenger side. He flung open the door and shouted to the orderly, "He's in the box." He quickly skirted the front of the car.

A third patrol car entered the hospital property and

parked across the driveway approach to block access.

The deputy who had met Deputy's Wayne's car at the edge of town and escorted him in pressed the button on her shoulder speaker and radioed the dispatcher. "We've arrived at our destination."

Dr. Nordin and the charge nurse joined the men at the car door as the orderly lifted the box from the front seat and placed it on the gurney. The nurse placed a warmed blanket over the infant. The trio pushed the gurney back into the emergency bay followed by Deputy Wayne and Nan who scurried to keep pace.

Dr. Nordin lifted the child from the box, shouting questions at Deputy Wayne. "Was the baby in distress? Was he exposed to the elements? Where did you find him?" Listening to the deputy's reply as he waited for the nurse to remove the clothing, the doctor placed his hands on the baby and began his examination. "Was he harmed during recovery?"

Turning the infant to examine his body, Dr. Nordin said, "Check the abducted baby's chart to see if this mark was indicated at birth. I need to know if it's a bruise or a birthmark." The doctor ran his hand over the mark on the baby's hip. "It will identify him if this is our abducted baby."

Repositioning the child, he placed the blanket over the screaming infant. "Find out who assisted in OB the night he was born. See if we can get a visual ID before the footprint results come back. Have the lab type the cord section we took when so we can compare it."

Deputy Wayne and Nan stood behind the door and watched through the glass window. The deputy placed his hand on Nan's shoulder. "He'll be okay. Lon did everything right and the baby wasn't harmed."

"I know." Nan hugged her arms into her chest. "If

something would have happened, he'd never forgive himself."

"Nothing happened. We caught them and they'll pay for this for the rest of their lives."

"Good healthy lungs," one of the nurses commented, attempting to soothe the baby with repeated thumb strokes over his tiny head. She inserted a rectal thermometer which added to the infant's protest. The doctor placed a hand-warmed stethoscope on the baby's chest. A nurse pressed an ink pad against his foot and imprinted the footprint onto a piece of paper.

Dr. Nordin completed the visual exam before instructing the nurse to diaper and wrap him in another warmed blanket. A second orderly wheeled a portable incubator into the exam area and readied it to accept the child if the doctor ordered it.

Nan looked up at Deputy Wayne. "He's a good man."

"The Doc?"

Nan glanced sideways, giving the deputy an impatient huff. "You know who I mean."

"I know who you mean, but I wanted to make sure you know. Lon's a good man and it's about time you realized it." Deputy Wayne's voice dripped with an intended challenge.

"I've always known it," Nan said. She ran a finger under her eyelid to wipe away a tear.

"I think we can resume normal crib procedures," Dr. Nordin advised. "His vitals appear normal. Let's admit him to the pediatric ward and monitor him throughout the night. You can notify his pediatrician and see if there's anything else he wants done."

A nurse from the OB wing delivered a warmed bottle of formula and waited until the doctor nodded in her direction. Dabbing the nipple against the baby's lips, a drop of warmth trickled from the opening. The infant's sobs lessened as he drew firmly on the nipple.

Commotion from the lobby filtered into the emergency room while the ER staff finalized documentation of the baby's examination. The CEO slipped through the badge-accessed doors. He headed toward Dr. Nordin. "Good Lord. The parking lot is filled with cars already. It appears everyone in the county had their scanners on. It's the middle of the night. What's wrong with those people?" He looked down at the infant. "How is he? Is he our abducted baby?"

"We just sent the footprints to the lab for processing," the charge nurse said. "They'll notify us as soon as the results are back. The OB nurse on duty the day of the abduction gave us a visual ID on the birthmark."

The CEO joined Nan and Deputy Wayne. "Good to see you again, Deputy. I'm glad it's under happier circumstances. As soon as we get a positive ID, you can contact the family." Shaking his head in sympathy, he added, "I'd bet dollars to doughnuts one of our nosy community members already notified the parents. I wish they'd ban those scanners."

"From what Deputy Wayne told us, they caught the people who did this." Dr. Nordin removed his Latex gloves and tossed them into a waste container. He pulled a fresh pair from a box hanging on the wall and tugged the first glove over his hand. "Do you think this abduction is connected to the one last summer?"

"We're not sure, yet," Deputy Wayne said. "We hope it is. That will put a lot of minds to rest."

"Now if only you can figure out who killed Celeste Perry." Dr. Nordin slid the privacy curtain along the track and stepped up to his next patient.

"I think we're almost there," Deputy Wayne murmured. He placed his hand behind Nan's back and ushered her toward the patrol car.

37

"Can you believe it?" Sadie placed the phone back in the base. "The hospital CEO wants me to stop by for an interview. Apparently he's setting up a press conference."

"I'm proud of you," Jane gushed. "You helped recover the baby. So did Bernie. What a wonderful ending to what could have been a tragedy. Just think of the publicity this will bring to the resort." Leaning down to scratch Belly's ear as he joined them, Jane cooed, "My little lamb. You didn't seem impressed with all the commotion last night. You just sat on the path and watched the whole thing, didn't you?"

Grunting as he plopped down between the sisters, Belly snorted his lack of interest into his zebra sequined neckerchief.

"By the way, Jane, quit leaving your scissors lying around. When Belly dozed on the rug yesterday, Sally became fascinated with his testicle."

"Is that what she wanted scissors for? Oh, dear," Jane said. "Aanders told me she wanted to cut something out. I thought he meant out of one of your fashion magazines."

"I don't think that's what she had in mind. It looked like she intended to play doctor lady." Sadie ran her hand down her hip. "Do you think I should wear this for the interview?"

"Why do you even ask? You're going to wear what you want anyway." Jane studied the chair under the clock. "Is Jed with us now?"

"Jed and Sally are both here. Jed's going with me to the hospital when I meet with the CEO."

"Why? The CEO can't see him."

Sadie took a deep breath. "Your brain would make a good doorstop."

"That's not nice. Especially after I complimented the pants off you?" Jane withdrew into a pout.

"I'm sorry. I appreciate you. Really I do. Jed's going to the hospital with me because there's a woman in critical condition in the ICU. Nan told me about her. They transferred her from the Emergency Room to Intensive Care when Nan and Deputy Wayne were at the hospital with the baby. They don't expect the woman to survive."

Jane looked toward the chair under the clock and then back at Sadie. "I'm glad Jed found out what happened to Celeste. I know how much he loved her."

"Tell her I'm glad, too," Jed said. "Tell Jane I'm going to miss her cooking."

A corner of Sadie's lip twitched. "Jed's glad, too." She jerked as a bare foot tapped her leg. Sadie glared at Jed before adding, "Jed said he's going to miss your cooking."

"Isn't that nice." Jane bowed her head coyly. "He was one of my favorite customers when I used to cook at the lodge."

"To think that's not what killed him."

"Killed who?" Bernie peered through the screen door. "Got any extra coffee?"

Sadie stiffened. "I thought you said you were heading back to Minneapolis this morning."

"I am, but first I need to talk to Jane."

Sadie's stomach flipped a sour summersault erasing the joy she had experienced over the infant's rescue. How dare Bernie ruin her moment. Jane would throw a conniption and give her the silent treatment for a week when she found out about Bernie.

Bernie pushed past her. "I need to talk to Jane."

"About what?"

As Bernie pulled out a chair and sat at the table, footsteps clopped across the porch floor.

"Sadie? Are you in there?"

Jane held the door open for the resort manager. "Can you help out at the registration desk? One of the girls got sick and had to go home. I'm swamped. I have to replace an O-ring in one of the cabin's faucets. I've got another receptionist coming to help at the desk, but she won't be here for an hour."

"I'll do it," Jane said. "Sadie's got a meeting at the hospital. She's going to do a press conference."

The resort manager looked at Sadie. "You're not going to wear that, are you?"

"What's wrong with this?" Sadie ran her hands over her silver and black zebra sequined top. "I paid good money for this."

The manager squinted. "You can't go on TV wearing that."

"Yes I can. It makes a statement."

"You want to make a decent statement, don't you? I mean about the resort. If they see you in zebra and sequins, they'll think we're a no-tell motel." The manager tapped his finger tips together in front of his chest. "Think about who'll be there. They're professionals. Think about how many will see you on television."

"I know. I watch TV. The sexy guy on the *Today Show* is going to ask me questions."

Bernie crossed the room and stood next to the manager. "It's important you make a good impression, Sadie. Your marketing image can make or break the resort's future. You want people to feel they can trust you."

"Oh really," Sadie droned. "Coming from you I feel so much better."

"Sadie's not going to listen. You're wasting your words." Jane hung her apron on the oven door. "I'd better hurry over to the lodge. I just saw another television crew pull up."

"That's the third one this morning. They want to see where they rescued the baby. They can't get close because it's still a crime scene," the manager said, "but those sneaky devils won't give up. I did what Sadie suggested and hired an off-duty deputy to keep them away."

Bernie watched Jane follow the manager down the path toward the lodge. "I'm going to tell her, Sadie. She needs to know."

"Know what?" Jed lifted Sally onto his lap.

Sally leaned back against Jed's chest and cradled the still unopened box with the surprise.

The cabin door slammed, bouncing twice against the frame as Aanders rushed through the door. "Did you see the big TV truck? There's a television reporter here and the deputy is hollering at her. So is Jane. She's giving orders like she's the president."

"She'll be fine. It gives her a reason to feel important. It keeps her out of my hair."

Bernie sat at the table.

Sadie drew in a deep breath and held it. "Bernie lied to me."

Bernie looked around the room. "Who's here besides Aanders?"

"Jed and Sally."

"I didn't lie. I just withheld the truth."

"About what?" Aanders plopped into Jane's recliner.

"I'm a priest."

"What?" Jed rotated his gaze toward Bernie. "A priest?"

Aanders frowned. "You mean like a God type guy?"

"What other kind is there?" Bernie looked at the chair

under the clock and then back at Aanders. "Sadie's blowing this out of proportion. I can explain."

"Wait a minute," Jed said. "That's what Sally meant when she told us Bernie had kids. They called Bernie by his title, Father Johnson, but Sally confused the word dad with father." Jed stared at Bernie. His mouth hung open. "Do you mean to tell me Jed's a priest and he's pursuing Jane?"

Aanders looked at Sadie. "I thought priests couldn't think about women. I thought they had to sign a paper saying they wouldn't think about you-know-what when they joined up." Aanders thought a bit before adding, "Aren't you worried about going to hell?"

"Ask Bernie if he's been thinking about you-know-what since he's been visiting Jane. I can't think of any other reason a priest would join a dating site, can you?"

"Bernie's got a lot more explaining to do than that," Sadie said. "He duped both of us and I want to know how he could do something so despicable to Jane. This will devastate her."

"You mean she doesn't know yet?" Aanders lips contorted into a scowl. "Oh, oh. She's going to have one of her hissy fits, again. Boy, is she going to be mad at you."

"It's me she should be angry at. I'm the one who didn't divulge the truth."

"I wondered why Bernie used the term 'blessed' so often." Jed rested his chin on Sally's head. "If I'd have been thinking, I'd have caught on."

"I knew it," Sally said. "Cuz he prayed on his knees and sang pretty songs to Jesus. He asked Jesus to help him do the right thing. I thought he meant about the big fish. You know the one you told him to release because it was too big. He kept it."

"Sally just told me you kept a walleye over the allowed

limit. That's against the law. You're going to get us in trouble. If you're caught keeping illegal fish in our bay, you'll have game wardens swarming all over the place. It'll drive our customers away."

Jed ran his hand through Sally's hair. "Lots of people pray on their knees. That doesn't mean they're priests."

"I know. My dad prayed on his knees when we said our prayers and he wasn't a priest. I wish he'd hurry up and come back. I sure miss him."

Jed brushed his lips against Sally's hair.

Sally jumped off Jed's lap and ran into the inner room with the box clutched in the crook of her elbow. Belly's nails clacked across the floor as he waddled after her.

Jed's frustration with his inability to connect Sally with her father tugged at Sadie's heart. Sally would never reconnect with her father. She was deceased. He wasn't. Even though Sadie didn't own a death coach manual, one thing she knew from experience was to remain emotionally detached from her crossers. Usually it wasn't a problem. She rarely knew the crossers who landed on her porch. This time she not only knew both of them, she knew their histories and their families. Maintaining arm's length became impossible.

Sally's funeral had taken place in Minneapolis where Sally's mother had purchased a burial plot. Sadie knew Sally's longing for her father would forever go unanswered, because what she didn't realize was her father had already bid farewell at graveside.

"I'm still worried about how Sally will handle the parallel world," Jed said. "She still thinks she's going to see her parents again."

"I'm worried too. You need to do what you feel is right. You've made a sound decision. I'm proud of you. Sally doesn't realize it, but she'll have a good life with you."

"I'll do my best. I hope to make up for the father she'll miss."

"You're right Sadie. Jed made a good decision. Sally's lucky to have him." Bernie placed his hand on the back of Sadie's chair. "Now you need to listen to me. I signed up on the dating website to see if I actually had the nerve to do it. I figured if I could do it, I could do the rest. I got several replies, but Jane's bio was the most interesting. When I saw her photo, I had to meet her."

"You made the decision from her photo?" Sadie squinted in disbelief. "You've got to be kidding."

"From her photo and because she wasn't in the metro area. Someone located four hours north of Minneapolis seemed safe. The others who replied lived within forty miles of the rectory. It would have been too risky."

"You're loathsome," Sadie said. "Jane doesn't deserve this. I entered her into this with good intentions."

"I'm at a crossroads with my life. Please try to understand."

"So you decided to sneak around and ruin someone's life? I can just picture you at o-dark-thirty sneaking into another woman's cabin. How many did you line up before you came up north?"

"That's not fair. Jane's the only one. I've agonized over this for years. I'd lost the commitment I needed to continue my calling. I'm a coward. I didn't want to give up my vocation before I was sure."

"Ask him if life outside the church is really what he wants," Jed said.

"What do you want, Bernie? I need to know. Jed wants to know, too. We worry about Jane more than you realize."

"I feel whole again. I feel alive. I've got to make the change before I can pursue her further. I've got to resign my position and finalize everything. It's going to be difficult, but I know it's what I need to do."

"If it's really what you want, then come back when it's final. She won't be so upset after the fact. If you reverse your decision and approach her again, my threat to expose you still stands."

"She'll be upset," Aanders said. "She'll still be mad because you stuck your nose in her business. I told you not to do this."

A loud squeal echoed from the inner room. "Oh, it's beautiful. My own princess dolly. You got my princess dolly back from the pawn shop." Sally ran from the inner room clutching the princess doll in her arms. "Look. It's the doll my daddy gave me. You got my doll back."

Jed held his arms out as Sally ran into them. "I thought I told you to wait to open it."

"I tried, but I couldn't. Belly made me do it. He chewed the box and it fell on the floor. I scolded him, but then I saw her hair sticking out and I had to look." Sally tipped her head up and beamed into Jed's face. "She's beautiful. I'm never going to put her down. Ever."

"You've got Sadie to thank for finding your doll," Jed said.

"Thank you, Sadie," Sally gushed.

"You're most welcome. Jed suggested I find her for you. Does your dolly have a name?"

Sally slipped out of Jed's embrace. She held her doll toward Jed and turned the white-gowned beauty to face Sadie. "She still has the same name I gave her before. Her name is Celeste."

38

Sadie parked the hearse shuttle in the no-parking zone under the hospital portico. "You shouldn't have trouble finding someone on the brink. From what Nan said, it's only a matter of time." She patted Jed's leg.

Jed climbed out of the shuttle and held his hand out to Sally. When she didn't follow, he bent down and peered into the vehicle. Sally sat behind the driver's seat cheerfully marching her Celeste dolly across the seat on her way to a tea party.

"Come on, young lady. We need to take care of business."

"I don't want to. I want to play with Celeste."

"Bring her along." Jed lifted Sally out of the back seat and followed Sadie through the sliding glass doors into the hospital lobby.

A physician exiting the hospital shot a puzzled glance at a co-worker, "Why is a hearse parked in front of the hospital? I thought they used the morgue bay to pick up bodies."

"They do. That's not a hearse. That's the Witt's End shuttle. I've seen it hauling guests around town."

"You're kidding. A hearse? Who'd ride in a hearse if they didn't need to?"

The co-worker said, "It's one of their gimmicks. There was an article in the paper a month ago about it. Didn't you see it?"

Two television vans, sporting satellite dishes, sat at the far end of the parking lot. Cables stretched across the lot, ending beneath two tents containing video crews and on-air reporters.

"Are you nervous?" Jed looked Sadie up and down.

"Not yet. How do I look?" Sadie tugged at her gelled spikes and turned her head both ways for Jed to see.

"You look like the Sadie I never knew before. The real Sadie."

"Is that good?"

Jed grinned. "Let's put it this way. America is about to meet the one and only Sadie Witt. You're going to rattle their perception of the senior citizen."

"Then that's good." Sadie glowed with determination. "It's about time we shed this fuddy-duddy label."

"Atta girl. I'm going to miss you. Any chance I'll run into you in the parallel world?"

"I hope so. But with my luck, I'll go through to the other side on my first attempt and end up eating Jane's cooking for all eternity."

"So hell it is, then?"

Sadie had to admit she'd miss Jed's wry humor. He had a knack of balancing the entire context of a conversation on the head of a pin.

"You just walked by the CEO's office." Jed pointed toward a massive oak door. "I thought he's the one you came to see."

"I did. I thought I'd go with you to Intensive Care. The CEO can wait." Sadie held her hand out to Sally. "I'd like to spend time with the two of you before you go."

The elevator doors slid open and Sadie followed Jed and Sally down the hall to the nurses' station.

"Congratulations, Sadie." One of the nurses gave her a hug. "We heard about the excitement at Witt's End. It was on every news channel this morning." Two other nurses joined them, bubbling with excitement.

"Were you in jeopardy? Who rescued the baby? Were any shots fired? Was the baby in danger?"

The charge nurse held a finger to her lips as she joined them. "Keep it down folks." She led the group to a corner near the desk. "Good job, Sadie. I can't believe it happened in our own back yard." She dug in her pocket for her pager and read a message as it scrolled across the read-out bar. Tucking it back in her pocket she said, "Two big incidents in one week. First they found Celeste's remains and then the baby. You're going to be famous."

Sally shoved her doll under a nurse's nose. "I got my Celeste back, too."

Jed tugged on the neck of Sally's shirt. "Let's go for a walk while Sadie's visiting."

Jed led Sally past three rooms before he noticed sobbing and sniffling coming from a woman standing at the foot of a bed. He paused at the door. Sally wandered into the room and inched her way closer to the bed.

The mother of the dying woman held her daughter's hand to her cheek and sobbed. "We're here now, Ali. We love you." The others in the room brushed at tears and held fast to one another. "You need to let go."

Jed listened as they told the woman she had suffered long enough and they wanted her to be free. Jed moved closer and peeked around one of the men leaning on the bed.

A nurse entered the room and took the woman's vitals. She jotted the information on the chart. She motioned for the woman's mother to join her at the rear of the room and whispered to her. The woman moved back toward her daughter and embraced her as she burst into tears.

Sally tiptoed up to the bed. She leaned against the blanket and placed her head on the edge of Ali's pillow and ran her finger under the lip of the pillowcase.

The woman's mother reached down and smoothed her daughter's hair before placing a kiss on her cheek. She straightened her hospital gown and gently pulled the covers up to her chin. Each family member took turns planting a kiss on her forehead as they bid their final farewell.

Sally walked Celeste along the bed sheet until the doll came within inches of the deceased woman's hand. She casually looked up at the woman's mother. "Why are you crying?"

"She's crying because her daughter died. She's very sad." Jed reached his hand out to Sally. "I want you to come and stand by me. It's time for us to go. First you need to say good-bye to Sadie."

The nurse placed her arms around Ali's mother and embraced her. One of the other family members pulled a cell phone from her purse and with fingers trembling, dialed the first of many relatives she needed to contact.

Sally pulled away from Jed's grasp. "She's not dead yet. See." She pointed at Ali as the girl opened her eyes, smiled at Sally, and effortlessly moved her legs to the edge of the bed.

"I knew you were coming. I saw you in the hall yesterday with him." She pointed at Jed. "I hoped you'd come back. I heard Mom tell my aunt they found your body behind the Fertile Turtle. She said you were at rest. I knew you weren't."

"I'm not resting. I'm here," Sally said. "See. I'm right here."

As Ali slid from the bed and her feet touched the floor, she reached for Sally's hand.

She looked up at Jed. "Are you ready?" The light around Ali began to intensify.

Sally looked toward the door. "We need to get Sadie. She might want to come, too."

Jed felt a cool breeze spread through the room. A rumbling in the distance deepened as Ali's hospital gown moved with the air currents. Sally ran to the door. "Sadie. It's time to go. Ali wants us to go with her. Hurry up."

Sadie stepped through the doorway as Ali's body wavered and rose off the floor. Spears of light penetrated her translucent image. The rumbling drew closer.

Sally looked back at Ali who held both arms out to her. Ali shouted, "Hurry, Sally. I can't wait much longer. It's time to go."

Sally motioned toward Sadie. "Hurry. It's time to go." She ran toward Sadie and reached out as the wind from the tunnel drew her back toward Jed and Ali.

Tears flowed freely as Ali's family gathered around her bed one more time. A few family members stepped into the hall to escape the sorrow of the moment. It was more than they could bear. Ali's mother embraced her daughter's lifeless body. "I love you," she sobbed.

The nurse gently guided the mother to a chair. "You don't have to leave yet. Take all the time you want. We'll notify the mortuary when you're ready." She placed a mortuary brochure in the woman's hand. She circled the phone number. "Nan Harren will contact you if she doesn't hear from you by tomorrow morning."

Sally shouted, her eyes darting frantically from Sadie and back to Jed and Ali. Hearing her name called, she shouted, "Wait. We need to make Sadie come with us."

"Go Sally," Sadie shouted, shielding her face from the spiraling breeze. "Go with Jed."

"If you're coming, you've got to come now, Sally," Ali warned. The strength of the breeze escalating through the tunnel pulled her further into the light. "I can't wait any longer."

Sally ran toward the light shielding her eyes from the wind. "Wait. Wait for me," she yelled over the roar and reached toward Jed.

"Step forward, Sally. Step into the light." Jed continued to shout encouragement as he slipped further into the vortex. Sally's hair lashed like a streamer. He strained to reach for her outstretched hand.

Sadie saw the shadow at the same moment Sally did. Pete Tyler, Sally's father, stood at the base of the vortex with outstretched arms.

"Daddy," Sally shouted, running past Jed and into Pete's open arms. "Daddy. Where have you been? I've been looking all over for you."

As Jed's hospital gown whipped in frenzy, he shouted, "No. Sally." He reached for her before turning back toward Sadie.

Sally and Pete rose higher into the vortex. Sally shouted against the wind, "Hurry Jed."

Jed tried to step back toward Sadie. The momentum of the wind's force pulled him deeper.

"Go, Jed. You've got to go to the parallel world," Sadie shouted. "I had no idea Sally's father had died. Nobody told me."

Pete shouted, "Once I lost Sally, I had no reason to live. My wife made sure of that. Now we'll have a good life together. I've been to the parallel world and came back for Sally. I was given a grace period to see if I could find her."

Jed strained against the growing wind. "Then I'm going back through the tunnel to find Celeste. If I can't be with Sally, I don't want to go."

"You don't have a choice. Whoever goes through the tunnel first determines where you go. Pete chose to come back from the parallel world to get Sally."

Jed struggled back toward Sadie. His fingertips brushed against the back of her hand.

"You're a good man, Jed." Sadie held her voice steady against the thunderous roar. "Think of the children who end up in the parallel world without parents. Sally could have been one of them. I'm sorry I didn't know about Sally's father, but maybe it's for the best." Sadie squeezed Jed's hand. As she let go, a tear trickled from her eye. "There are no accidents. Things happen for a reason. We don't always know what they are, but this time I do. And so do you."

Jed's hand dropped to his side and he let the momentum of the wind draw him back. His chest heaving with sobs, he turned away from Sadie. He reached for Pete's hand. "I'm ready."

Jed turned back toward Sadie as he faded into the distance. "Thank you," he shouted. With a final wave he added, "Please see that my folks are taken care of."

39

"You looked wider."

"Wider?" Sadie put her fists on her hips and glared at her sister. "What do you mean wider?"

"You know. They always say you look fatter on television."

"Well thank you very much. I didn't ask if I looked fat. I asked how I looked."

"Wider."

"Oh for Pete's sake," Sadie groaned. "Did I sound good? Did I make a good impression?"

"Kind of." Jane's voice trailed off.

"Kind of? Either I did, or I didn't." Before Sadie had left for the press conference, Jane had been giddy with anticipation. Now her sister's tendency to drift toward melancholy had resurfaced like it had after Mr. Bakke's death. The abrupt change concerned Sadie.

The screen door banged against the frame and Aanders hurried into the cabin. "Boy did you look cool on TV. The guys I go to school with want to see the cabin where you found the baby. Then they want to see where you found the bones."

Nan and Lon followed Aanders through the door and joined Sadie at the table. "What happened to your manners, Aanders?" Nan placed her hand on her son's shoulder. "You're supposed to knock first."

"That's okay," Sadie said. "We're all a bit excited."

"Where's Bernie?" Nan looked out the window.

"He must have been in a hurry to get back to

Minneapolis. He didn't even have the decency to say good-bye." Jane shot Sadie a frigid look. "You sure know how to pick them. It just proves your taste in men stinks." She slammed a cabinet door before opening a drawer and rummaging for a spatula.

Sadie glanced at Aanders. "That's not true. I have good taste in men. Besides, Bernie stopped to see you before he left, but you were assisting at the lodge. Remember?"

"Of course I remember. I still don't understand why he had to leave in such a hurry." Jane placed the spatula next to a steaming pan of rhubarb crisp. "Did he really stop to see me?"

"Would I lie? Of course he did." Sadie shot a fleeting warning at Aanders as the young man slouched in his chair. "Bernie was disappointed you weren't here. He had things to do back in Minneapolis and said he'd call later. I'm sure he will. You made quite an impression. You need to give him time. I don't think Bernie was prepared to fall in love so fast."

Jane grinned as she slid the spatula into the pan. "I suppose I can give him space if you think it would be wise. I tend to have that affect on men."

"Sadie, are you ready to go down to the station?" Lon pushed through the screen door and waited for Sadie to follow.

"Ready? I can't wait." Sadie clapped her hands together.

"You've earned the right to be there. Because you were instrumental in the take-down, you might as well see it through to the end."

Lon leaned his left shoulder on the wall and rapped his knuckles against the folder before tossing it onto the interrogation table.

"What's that?" Dan pressed his back firmly against the metal chair.

266

"A tape recorder. I'm recording this interrogation. I already informed you."

"Not that. I mean what's in the folder?"

"This? This is evidence." Lon opened the folder and paged through the sheets. "It's what we need to prove you abducted the infant." He closed the folder as Dan leaned forward to look at it.

"Bullshit. I didn't abduct no infant. You don't know what you're talking about."

Lon scratched his head. "Well you got me there, Dan. You didn't actually take the baby, your wife did." Lon lifted a box off a chair and set it on the table. He pulled a nurse's uniform from the box and placed it in front of Dan.

Sadie squeezed Jane's hand and whispered, "It's just like on TV. Look at the sweat on Dan's forehead."

Jane leaned closer to the one-way window. "Are you sure Dan can't see us? I don't want him coming after us. He's a dangerous character. He was packing heat."

The sheriff grinned. He leaned close to Jane. "You're safe in here. They can't see or hear us."

Sadie and Jane sat at a table in front of the viewing window. A deputy and two technicians monitored the recording equipment while Lon and Deputy Wayne questioned Dan. The sheriff said, "The main reason Lon wanted you here is to verify information. You know the history of Cabin 12 better than anyone."

The sheriff instructed the technician to adjust the volume and test the headphones. Jane whispered to Sadie, "Cabin 12? Why Cabin 12? Who else are they interviewing?"

"Probably Clay," Sadie said. "Dan might have told him something."

"Recognize this?" Lon held up the uniform.

"No."

"You don't? That's odd. Isn't this a photo of your wife?" Lon dangled the ID badge in front of Dan. He placed it on the table and tapped Pam's photo. "That is Pam. That's the woman who abducted the baby from the hospital."

"The hell it is," Dan shouted. He stood and knocked the chair backward.

Deputy Wayne righted the chair. He pointed at it. "Sit."

"You better do what he says, Dan. We're going to be here a long time. You might as well get comfortable." Lon pulled out a chair and sat across from Dan. "Are you sure you don't want an attorney?"

"I already told you. I didn't do nothing. Why do I need an attorney?"

Deputy Wayne grinned at Lon. "He doesn't look that dumb, does he?"

"Not really." Lon contemplated Dan's features.

Squirming under their scrutiny, Dan glared back at the deputies. "What?"

"What puzzles me most is what a beautiful woman like Pam sees in a loser like you." Deputy Wayne shrugged and removed his cap. He tossed it on the table. "I just can't figure it out."

Dan's back stiffened as he leaned into the table. "You leave her out of this."

Lon laughed. "I don't think we can. She's your partner, isn't she?"

"She didn't do anything," Dan said. "That's our baby."

The smile vanished from Lon's face as his eyes flashed a warning. "Now I know you're stupid. The baby we found in your cabin is the same one abducted from the hospital. The cord blood, the birthmark, and the foot prints are a match. Just because we're not a fancy metropolitan sheriff's department doesn't mean we can't solve a case."

"Yeah, right." Dan snickered before adding, "That will be the day."

"Thank goodness Pam's mother didn't drop her on her head like your mother did." Deputy Wayne strolled slowly around the table and stood behind Dan. "At least Pam's not stupid. She told the truth."

Dan looked back over his shoulder.

Silence hung in the air as the deputies stared at Dan.

"Did something happen to the sound?" Jane looked toward the technician.

"It's a tactic. The longer they keep him guessing, the more likely he is to cave in."

"Then he is dumb," Sadie said. "It's obvious they're trying to make him think Pam spilled the beans."

"I know that and you know that. When you're facing 30 years in prison, you're willing to take the chance they're bluffing." The sheriff stood when the dispatcher handed him a note. "Put him in a holding room for a few minutes."

When the sheriff sat next to Sadie, she leaned in close to his ear. "He needs an attorney."

"My guess is he's trying to look innocent. Most people think when they request an attorney it's obvious they've got something to hide." The sheriff's eyes narrowed as he stared at Dan. "I have a sneaking suspicion Dan's got a trump card. He'll play it when the time is right."

Lon opened the folder and turned the writing so Dan could recognize it. He flipped the top sheet over, but slid it strategically so Pam's signature was exposed on the sheet below. "Do you want to know what Pam said?"

Dan stared at the signature. He reached for the folder.

Lon pulled it from Dan's reach. "Your wife told us everything. She's willing to give us evidence in exchange for a lighter sentence."

"That bitch. She wouldn't do that." Dan slammed his fist against the table. "You're lying."

Lon paged through the folder and pulled out a sheet. "Does the name Reginald Carson ring a bell?"

An agonizing scream burst from Dan's lips as he swept the folder off the table. "I'll kill her. I knew it. I knew she'd do this to me."

A deputy burst through the interrogation door to help the men subdue Dan. While Deputy Wayne handcuffed Dan's hand to the table, Lon gathered the papers and picked the recorder up off the floor. He tested the recorder before placing it back on the table.

"You could learn a thing or two from your wife. Maybe making a deal isn't all that bad." Lon opened the folder again.

"You already got everything you need," Dan spat. "You're crazy if you think I'm going to help you."

"From what Pam said, you're sitting on evidence that's more important than you realize. If you're willing to share, I'm willing to talk to the DA about reducing the charge."

"What are you talking about?"

"I'm talking about two people," Lon said. "Who else is involved?"

"I already told you. Nobody."

"What about Clay Harren?"

"That idiot?" Dan laughed. "You can't be serious. Most of the time he doesn't know his pecker from a banana. He didn't have anything to do with the abduction."

"Then who did?"

"You tell me if you're so damn smart."

"How about the honorable Judge Kimmer?" Deputy Wayne raised his brows in anticipation. "That name ring a bell?"

"That bitch really stuck the knife in deep, didn't she?"

Dan rolled his head back toward his shoulders and ran his free hand across the nape of his neck.

"Actually, it started coming together when Sadie found the bones under Clay's cabin. We already figured out something was going on between Kimmer and Reginald Carson, but when Pam told us you worked for Carson, we realized we'd hit pay dirt."

"I'm still upset with Bernie," Jane said. "He gave me his cell phone number, but when I call, he says leave a message."

"I told you he had business to tend to. He'll call when he has time." Sadie folded the newspaper in half. "Look at this. Here's a picture of Judge Kimmer being taken out of the station on a stretcher."

Jane stood next to Sadie and peered over her shoulder. "Did Lon say if he's still on the critical list?"

"I think he's going to make it. It was a heart attack. Wouldn't that have been a kicker if he'd have croaked in the interrogation room?"

"When Kimmer collapsed, I thought the sheriff was going to have a stroke. Thank goodness they got him to admit everything first."

Sadie ran her finger along the print. "The paper says Kimmer confessed because he couldn't bear the burden any more. That's a bunch of baloney. He confessed because Dan named him and because the notebook we found with Celeste's body was his."

"How did you finally realize it was Oinketta's writing?"

"It came to me when I listened to Lon accuse Kimmer of killing Celeste," Sadie said.

"Kimmer didn't kill Celeste. He said Oinketta's husband killed her."

"When Celeste realized Kimmer was involved in an

271

abduction ring and threatened to expose him, Kimmer got Oinketta's husband to try to reason with her. Kimmer told him he'd take Oinketta down, too, if he ever was arrested or went to trial. His own sister. Can you believe it? When Oinketta's husband tried to get the notebook back, they scuffled and Celeste fell and hit her head. She died in the fall."

"I still don't know how they managed to bury her under the cabin," Jane said.

"Kimmer knew his folks never used the cabin. He thought it would be safe to bury her there and move the body later. Kimmer had no way of knowing his folks had signed over the deed and we were the new owners. He never had the opportunity to move the body."

"What does that have to do with Oinketta's handwriting?"

"Lon suspected the killer and the person with the handwriting were one and the same. When I remembered Oinketta had been Kimmer's secretary before Celeste took the job, I mentioned it to Lon. He pulled a few old court documents and sure enough, the writing matched. Oinketta used to keep Kimmer's books. Lon used the same ploy Kimmer had used on Oinketta's husband and threatened to have Oinketta indicted as an accomplice. When Kimmer heard that, he admitted everything. Apparently he no longer felt the need to involve his sister."

"Do you think Oinketta was involved?" Jane stared at the photo of Kimmer's rotund belly protruding high above the stretcher.

"Lon doesn't think so. He thinks she documented names and numbers according to what Kimmer gave her. Strictly bookkeeping. He doesn't think she was smart enough to figure it out. At least that's the impression Lon got when he questioned her."

"I wouldn't be so sure," Jane said.

"Lon checked Oinketta's financial records. There's no evidence of suspicious income, so Lon doesn't think she ever pocketed any money from the abductions. Lon figures Oinketta's husband took Celeste's murder to the grave. Only he and Kimmer knew about it."

Jane walked to the screen door. "Come on in, Aanders. It's been quite a week, hasn't it?"

Aanders plopped into Jane's recliner and grabbed the remote control. "I'm glad Sally's gone. What a pest. She followed me everywhere. It was spooky waking up at night and finding her staring at me."

"I have to agree, but I'm afraid you're going to have to get used to it," Sadie said.

"Why can't they all be grownups like Jed? I really liked him."

"Me, too. We'll have to wait and see who our next guests will be." Sadie pulled the remote from Aanders hand. "How about going fishing?"

"Really?" Aanders jumped up and ran to the door. "Can I drive the boat?"

"Let's take the pontoon. That way we can roast hot dogs on the grill and take our sweet time. I want to try the new fishing rod I bought last week."

"Cool." Aanders threw open the screen door. He stopped in his tracks. "Oh, oh."

"What?" Sadie's nose brushed against Aanders' right arm as she bumped into him.

"I don't think we're going anywhere. There's a man sitting on your porch swing. He's got a gun." Aanders turned back toward Sadie. "I think he's a crosser."

Robin Trelz
is the winner of the
Dog Treat Recipe Contest
featured at
www.bsolheim.com

MYSTERIOUS MEATBALLS

- 1 pound ground chuck
- 1/2 cup uncooked minute rice
- 1/4 cup plain dried bread crumbs
- 1 egg
- 2 tablespoons ketchup
- Parmesan cheese

Mix all ingredients except cheese. Form into small meatballs with a melon scooper. Sprinkle with Parmesan cheese. Place in a 9" by 12" glass baking dish sprayed with cooking spray. Bake in a 350 degree oven for 35-45 minutes until cooked through. Let cool.

I keep enough in the refrigerator to use within three days and freeze the rest. They make excellent bit-sized treats to give throughout the day. My dogs love them!

Robin Trelz
Decatur, Illinois

Like the main character in her Sadie Witt mystery series, Beth Solheim was born with a healthy dose of imagination and a hankering to solve a puzzle. She learned her reverence for reading from her mother, who was never without a book in her hand.

By day, Beth works in Human Resources. By night she morphs into a writer who frequents lake resorts and mortuaries and hosts a ghost or two in her humorous paranormal mysteries.

Raised and still living in Northern Minnesota, she resides in lake country with a menagerie of wildlife critters.